HARD HITTER

WILD CARD - BOOK THREE

NIKKI HALL

Thanks for picking up this copy of Hard Hitter! If you'd like to go back to where the series begins, grab your FREE copy of Game Changer, the prequel novella for the Wild Card series.

For a FREE copy of Game Changer, go to www.nikkihallbooks.com/signup.

For everyone who refuses to let life hold them down. Fly.

1

Noah

Chloe Asher would be the death of me. I was tired, bleary eyed, and awake way too fucking early in the morning to deal with her. The sun hadn't even come up yet.

I'd only been asleep an hour or two when a crash had me bolting into the hallway of our apartment, where I found the subject of most of my fantasies standing outside my door. If she hadn't been D's sister, I'd have gone back to bed, preferably with her next to me.

Instead, Chloe's wide green eyes darted between me, my roommate, Mac, and the llama picture she'd knocked off the wall. Her dark hair tumbled over her shoulder in soft curls, and in the dim light from the living room, her tiny dress shimmered blue green like the mermaid she'd been in my dream.

Not that I'd ever admit to dreaming about her.

At some point after I'd left the party at her place last night, she'd ditched her pointy-heeled shoes, and I forced myself not to immediately scoop her up in my arms to protect her bare feet from the broken glass littering our floor.

"Don't move," I grumbled when she looked like she'd take a step toward me.

She scowled at the gym bag in the middle of the hallway. "Do you guys have to be pigs all the time?"

Mac, owner of the offending gym bag, shrugged. "I live here, and no one else complains. Besides, you're the one who made the mess."

He ran a hand through his tousled hair and glanced back at his door, a sure sign he wasn't alone in his room. We couldn't leave Chloe standing in the middle of the glass, but Mac only wore a towel wrapped around his waist.

I could reach her from where I stood, and I wouldn't end up naked in the process. With an internal groan, I beckoned her to lean toward me. Chloe's eyes narrowed, but she shifted her weight in my direction.

Keeping my hands at her waist, I lifted Chloe out of the danger zone—she weighed next to nothing. I deposited her on glass-free carpet then backed away nearly to the living room, crossing my arms over my chest to keep from reaching for her again.

RJ and Parker, the last of my roommates, shuffled out of their room and stopped short. At least they'd taken the time to put on clothes. I didn't need another reminder that everyone was getting laid except me.

"What the hell is going on out here?" Parker asked.

I watched Chloe, surprised to see the slight wince. She wasn't the timid type, and honestly, breaking shit in someone else's apartment in the middle of the night was entirely on brand for her.

When she didn't answer, I gave him the only information I had, hoping she'd fill in the rest. "Chloe tripped over Mac's gym bag and knocked the llama off the wall."

Parker's brows drew together as he took stock of the floor, Mac's lack of clothing, and Chloe's outfit from last night. I clenched my jaw against the unbidden urge to defend her. She was perfectly capable of defending herself if she chose.

Except she didn't.

Parker glared at Mac, I glared at Parker, and Mac edged closer to his door. None of us were in top form, especially since I was probably the only one who'd slept.

RJ broke the standoff. "Chloe, what are you doing in the hallway?"

Chloe's eyes flicked to RJ, then back to me. "I needed some help, so I came over here to ask. I'm sorry I bothered everyone."

There it was. The only reason Chloe paid any attention to me now—when she needed help. After spending hours watching her flirt with every guy at Eva's birthday party, I wasn't in the mood.

I nodded at Mac. "Looks like you're taken care of. I'm going back to bed."

Mac sputtered. "What? No, man. I'm half-assed naked."

I narrowed my eyes at him, willing him to take this one for the team, but Mac didn't get my telepathic message.

He rolled his eyes as if we were confused about his state of undress. "Like butt-assed naked but still got a towel on? Noah can help her."

In an act of friendship aggression, he went back into his room and shut the door without another word. The one time I *wanted* him to be loud and annoying. I chanced another look at Chloe. Her face seemed more expressive than usual minus her glasses, pleading with me to help without making a fuss.

Or maybe I was still suffering from the weird-ass dream where I'd had her naked in the pool with gleaming scales hugging the curves of her hips.

I clenched my jaw, unwilling to give in this time. "Parker or RJ then."

Chloe winced. "They can't help."

The couple shared a look I couldn't read, and RJ took a tentative step forward.

"Are you sure I can't help?" she asked.

I knew I liked RJ, and her soft question put her firmly in favorite roommate territory. Unfortunately, Chloe shook her head. Why was she so determined to make me suffer?

Chloe caught her full lower lip between her teeth, and a bolt of heat shot down my spine. As if she could sense my reaction, her gaze skipped back to me. The last time I'd showed up to help her, when the hockey fuckboy had abandoned her drunk at a party, she'd spent the entire drive home explaining in vivid detail how I'd missed out on the best blowjob of my life.

Sweat gathered between my shoulder blades just thinking about it.

I wasn't sure she remembered—we'd never discussed it —but I'd swear on Mac's signed Wonder Woman poster she hadn't been blackout drunk. Our gazes clashed and held, a battle of wills I was already losing.

Her fingers tangled together in front of her, and the image of drunk Chloe from months ago gleefully tossing her shirt at a hooting frat boy tightened the muscles in my back. How much worse could this situation possibly be if she was standing in front of me, barefoot and sober?

In the back of my mind, I knew it didn't matter. I'd

promised D I'd take care of her. Even without the promise, Chloe had always been a special case. If she needed me, I'd be there.

I sighed and ran a hand through my hair. Fuck. I was going to regret this. "Fine."

A relieved smile flashed across Chloe's face, there and gone so fast I might have imagined it. I shifted to give her space to pass me, and she didn't spare the others another glance.

Parker's door closed softly behind us, and I found myself alone in the dark with her once again. Better get this over with. Chloe waited while I grabbed my shoes and keys from the living room. Hopefully, sweats and a TU football shirt would be appropriate attire for whatever she needed me to do.

I dragged my gaze away from Chloe's perfect ass as she led me out into the cold night. "Where are we going?"

She nodded at the apartment she shared with Eva. "I have a small problem in my bedroom."

I frowned at her. "Chloe..."

She rolled her eyes. "This isn't a come on. Eva's staying the night elsewhere, and I can't handle this on my own. I'd hoped the problem would be resolved by the time I finished cleaning, but..." She trailed off with a shrug.

Guilt pricked at the thought of her picking up the huge mess we'd left in their apartment. I'd assumed Eva would hire a cleaning crew like she usually did.

I couldn't imagine Chloe picking up trash in the tiny dress she was still wearing. Why wouldn't she change? Her massive wardrobe had to include something more comfortable than sequins. I didn't understand Chloe on the best of days, so I had no hope of keeping up while sleep-deprived and horny.

Goosebumps raised on my arms as the cold night air hit my skin. I was a furnace most of the time, so if I was cold, Chloe had to be freezing. Despite the frigid January temps, she hesitated outside her door.

"What's going on, Chloe?"

She huffed out a breath. "I don't want you to get the wrong idea."

The guilt solidified into a hard knot in my stomach. My life would be a lot easier if I could write her off as a silly party girl, but I'd seen the parts of her she only let out when she thought no one was looking. When it came to Chloe, I was always looking.

"You came to me for help," I reminded her.

The edge of her lips quirked up, and she tilted her head in assent.

She led me through the dark apartment to her room. I expected a spider or broken furniture, but when she flipped on the light, my brows rose. Fury ignited, hot and fast.

A lanky guy with an unfortunate target tattoo on his back lay face down in Chloe's bed. Naked.

I almost turned around and went right back home. "You want me to get rid of your hookup?"

She groaned. "He's not my hookup."

I didn't want the details. The football season may be over, but I was pretty sure Coach would still make me run until I puked if I beat the shit out of a random dude in Eva's apartment. Don't ask me how, but Coach had a soft spot for Eva. Her influence was everywhere.

Despite my irrational rage at the guy, I tempered my voice for Chloe. "Need me to move him over so you have space?"

"Dammit, Noah. It's not like that. I don't know this guy, and I definitely didn't invite him into my bed. All I want to do is sleep, but I'm not about to lock myself in the apartment with a random drunk dude who may or may not murder me before morning."

It was on the tip of my tongue to offer her my bed for the rest of the night. Talk about bad decisions. Her eyes sharpened like she'd read my mind, or maybe my face, but even I wasn't that stupid.

I rubbed the back of my neck, markedly calmer knowing she didn't *want* the guy in her room. "Eva's not here?"

She sagged in relief. "No. Mysterious booty call. Can you please use your giant muscles to get rid of this guy?"

My jaw clenched, really unhappy with my role, but I moved toward the bed anyway.

What was I supposed to do with him? We couldn't leave him outside to freeze his balls off, and I definitely wasn't bringing him into our apartment with Mac's mystery girl and RJ there.

With some effort, I hauled the guy up by his armpits, trying my best to ignore the full frontal on display. He grumbled something about trolls, and his breath knocked me back a step. Once I blinked away the acrid tears, I got a good look at his face.

Thank fuck, I recognized him. Miller something. Second string kicker. Not really a surprise he was a football player considering Eva's social circle. He was a freshman, so he'd be living in the athlete dorm. I could drop him off in the lobby with a spare blanket.

Chloe held the doors for me as I muscled him out of her apartment and across the parking lot to my car. He didn't stir as I heaved him into my passenger seat, and I made a mental note to scrub down the leather tomorrow.

As soon as the door closed, he slumped against it, snoring lightly. Chloe followed me around to the driver's side, pulling me to a stop before I could climb inside. She searched my face, and my stupid heart took off at her close proximity.

"What are you going to do with him?"

I raised a brow. "Worried about *him* now?"

"D would never forgive me if you murdered someone on my behalf."

"Bold of you to assume they'd find the body."

She scowled at me, and I relented.

"He's a freshman football player. I'm going to return him to the athlete dorm where he can sleep off his bad decisions in public."

The breeze picked up, and she shivered. "Do you want me to come with you?"

"No. Go back inside, put on something warm, change your sheets, and get some sleep."

Chloe wrapped her arms around herself, shifting her weight from foot to foot, finally gracing me with the wicked smile I expected. "Always a pleasure watching you manhandle another guy."

"Chloe," I growled, now completely sure she remembered the night with the hockey asshole.

She patted my chest. "If you ever need help in the bedroom department, give me a call."

My dick went from half-hard to rock solid in the span of a breath. Thank god the dark parking lot didn't reveal many details.

"Not interested," I lied.

"You made that very clear when you turned me down the first time. In this case, I meant if you ever need help removing a lady from your bed, I'm your girl."

I grunted, forcing myself to climb into my car instead of

leaving her unwanted visitor here and taking his place. "Get inside before you freeze."

She gave me a finger wave and hurried back to her apartment. Alone. I'd give my left nut to be the one keeping her warm, but a relationship between me and Chloe would never work. She wanted a temporary fun time, and I wouldn't disrespect D's sister by treating her like a disposable party favor.

I wouldn't treat any woman that way, but especially not Chloe. D was my first and closest friend here at TU, and without him, I'd be alone in the athletic dorms counting the days until graduation. D was closer to me than my family, and he'd trusted me with his sister.

Chloe was off limits, and I'd kick the ass of anyone who touched her.

2

Chloe

How did this keep happening to me? I was supposed to be in a nice, normal math class, but as I scanned the lecture hall, the sheer amount of Teagan University athletic gear made me break out in a sweat. Jocks everywhere.

I assumed my mistake was taking the lowest level of math I could—don't judge, my last school didn't require extra math classes for a communications major—but I immediately felt guilty for the assumption. Athletes weren't stupid. My brother with his psychology degree was a shining example of that, and I handily proved non-athletes weren't exactly geniuses.

Life wasn't a competition, but if it was, I'd be losing.

"Ms. Asher?" The professor—I couldn't remember his name for the life of me—raised an eyebrow, and I wasn't sure if he'd asked me something or if he was just confirming my identity.

I took a wild guess since he hadn't started class yet. "Yes. Present. Sorry. Please continue."

A couple of girls down the row tittered with laughter. I

hoped I hadn't just doomed myself in this class. Old me might have considered the moment worth it if I garnered attention from the hot guy in the row behind me or the party girls sleeping in the back, but new me wasn't about that life.

Luckily, the professor didn't seem to give a crap. He shook his head and called another name, prompting a girl in the front row to shoot her hand in the air. Seriously? Who still raised their hand in college?

The guy sitting next to me wearing way too much body spray slid his phone in front of me. I glanced down at a picture of me hugging my brother during the draft last year. The camera guy had gotten a close up of my face, and I winced at my goofy smile.

Body spray guy leaned in to whisper, loudly, "That you?"

I nodded and shoved the phone back at him, hoping my resting bitch face and lack of eye contact would discourage him from invading my breathing space again. No such luck.

He let out a low whistle. "Nice. D's a legend, and he's killing it in New York."

Before I could respond, he shifted the other way to talk, loudly, to the guy on the other side of him. "Told you, man. She's D's sister."

The other guy eyed me up and down. "Hot."

I resisted the urge to roll my eyes. The gesture would be wasted since neither of them was looking at my face. Nothing like objectification to start my Monday right.

Body spray guy leaned closer again. "Why don't you come party with us—"

"Gentlemen, you're disrupting the class." Professor something-or-other interrupted the worst pick up line I'd heard in a while.

The douchey friend crossed his arms, completely

unconcerned. "Sorry, teach, but we got football royalty in here."

This time I did roll my eyes. I knew the basic rules of the game, and I knew my brother was incredibly talented, but thus ended my interest in sports. Unfortunately, the sports world was interested in me.

Body spray guy nodded my direction. "Courtney here is D's sister."

"Chloe," I muttered, though I probably should have saved my breath. The professor frowned and launched into a clearly prepared speech about expectations in the class, including paying attention during the lectures.

I'd been dreading the association with my all-around perfect brother, and the student body did not disappoint. Whispers and furtive looks surrounded me as the class realized I was related to Derrick Asher, football god and quarterback extraordinaire.

For a largeish university, the gossip was intense. I loved my brother—if anyone dared to talk shit about him, I'd be the first to throw down—but I'd chosen a small private college without a football team for this exact reason.

Too bad I screwed up enough for my parents to intervene and send me here where I'd have a "support system" to help. Parent speak for D's friends watching every move I made to be sure I didn't set anything else on fire. Literally or figuratively.

They never understood why I needed my own space where I wasn't "D's little sister", and they sure as hell didn't know the truth about why I'd suddenly applied to all new colleges at the end of my senior year of high school. My asshole ex, Vince. Come to think of it, body spray guy looked vaguely similar.

D knew about my ex because he'd cleaned up the mess,

as usual, and I'd been happy to push my boundaries at every instance since in an effort to forget the way Vince fucked with my head. I winced. Probably not the healthiest coping mechanism considering I ended up exactly where I'd tried to avoid in the beginning.

A guy two seats down actually pulled out his phone to take a picture of me. I fluffed my hair and gave the asshole invading my privacy a sharp grin. Might as well make sure the pictures looked good.

I spent the rest of the class pointedly ignoring the people around me, especially body spray guy, until he mumbled *bitch* under his breath. His friend laughed and so did the girls in front of him.

Awesome. I told myself I didn't care what these people thought of me, but the squishy part in my chest suddenly ached for my stolen anonymity. At my last school, I'd gone too far in the opposite direction trying to make a name for myself. This time, I planned to figure out what *I* wanted, not what would provide me the most separation from D's brand of easy perfection.

The professor ended class early by assigning homework and encouraging us to enjoy the nice day. I snorted as I put away my unused laptop along with the syllabus he'd handed out. He seemed nice enough, smiling like he meant it, but I doubted I'd be enjoying the day.

The picture taken of me in class was already making the rounds on TU's social media. I'd surreptitiously checked three-quarters of the way through class, and despite my brother no longer being a student here, speculation ran rampant about my reasons for transferring. My personal favorite was an accidental pregnancy from an affair with one of my professors.

I hoped I'd look this good pregnant one day.

None of D's friends—my friends now, I guessed—chimed in. The guys and Riley were all at practice, and Eva was meeting with a professor. Probably for the best, since having D's crew defend me would only feed the frenzy.

After two weeks of living with Eva, and basically living with the rest of them, I could honestly say I only felt completely comfortable around Noah. I'd known them all for years, except Riley, who was new to the team after D left, but old me would have died before letting any of them see past the confident exterior.

New me didn't know how to let go of the armor. Noah was the exception only because he'd already seen me at my worst when I propositioned him shortly after my breakup—and he'd rejected me soundly. Couldn't really get any lower than that despite years of trying.

My bad mood followed me as I blindly trailed the crowd down the halls toward the building's entrance. Sunlight streamed through the tall windows in the lobby, mocking my foul mood. Today felt like spring, despite the late January chill, but I might as well have been stuck in the frozen tundra.

I barreled out the double doors with my attention on the contents of my tote bag. Why couldn't they add usable pockets? My sunglasses disappeared into the depths every time I needed them.

Four steps from the exit, I slammed into a warm human wall. Strong hands steadied me as I bounced off a broad chest made entirely of muscle. Fire licked up my neck at the touch, and I knew without looking whose fingers were wrapped around my arms.

Noah frowned down at me, his usual expression where I was concerned. "Are you okay?"

I stepped back and slid on my sunglasses to cover the

shock of heat I wasn't sure I could hide. "Fine. What are you doing here? I promise I don't need a babysitter to follow me to class."

He jerked his chin at the building next door. "I'm not here for you. I'm getting coffee then meeting Mac to watch film."

I glanced over and raised my brows at the giant sign with claw marks slashing through the words Wildcat Coffee. "Don't you have coffee in your fancy football facility?"

Noah aimed his glare at the people coming out the doors behind me. "Our coffee sucks. Why don't you come with me?"

The stream of students passing us slowed to a trickle, giving us plenty of space thanks to Noah's glower.

"How could I refuse such a kind offer?" I smiled sweetly at him, but he shook his head without looking at me. Another wasted expression. "You're buying."

A smile flitted across his face, and I was glad I'd donned the sunglasses. My heart picked up at the curl of his lips, not that I'd ever let him see how he affected me after the last disastrous time we'd been alone. "I'll get you whatever you want if you answer a question for me."

In general, I didn't like the 20 Questions game—too much chance to reveal things I didn't want—but a single question I could do if it came with a hit of caffeine. "You're on."

I linked my arm through his, letting him lead me away from the building as body spray guy and his buddy came out the door. I could imagine the harassment I'd receive if they saw me hanging on a football player, so I shifted to hide behind Noah's giant body.

He didn't seem to notice, simply accepting my new position slightly in front of him and reaching over my head to open the door for me. The inside of the little coffee shop was just as aggressive as the sign. The walls were painted red, white, and black with paw prints and fake claw marks everywhere.

Most of the tables were filled with people, but I spotted an empty two top as we got in line to order. Despite the garish décor, the place seemed popular, and it smelled fantastic, like good coffee and cinnamon rolls.

Damn. Now I wanted a cinnamon roll.

We made it to the front of the line, and I had to swallow a laugh. The guy taking orders looked like a pissed off professional athlete. He moved with the same grace as my brother and another big guy I strived not to notice on a daily basis—tall, with broad shoulders under a Henley that showed off every muscle in his very nice arms.

His scowl rivaled Noah's the time last year he'd found me with a guy in D's room at the apartment, but the best part was someone had plopped a set of fuzzy black cat ears on coffee guy's head. Crooked. I couldn't stop staring at them until he cleared his throat.

"What do you want?" His gravelly voice should have been hot—the rest of him certainly was—but with Noah standing next to me like my own personal fantasy, I couldn't get into it.

"Double shot mocha latte, medium, and a cinnamon roll." I pointed to the giant roll in the display, just in case.

The guy punched in a couple of buttons and grabbed a cup. "Name?"

"Chloe."

Noah moved forward to place his order, and I accepted a paper bag with my cinnamon roll from a perky redhead working behind the grumpy hottie. She wore cat ears too, but they didn't have the same effect on her.

I stuck my face in the bag and inhaled deeply, letting out a happy little moan. Noah stiffened next to me.

"Go find a table," he growled, shifting away from me to smile at the redhead.

A tiny pang of hurt took away some of the joy I'd gained from the cinnamon roll. I pretended not to hear him tell her how nice her cat ears looked as I strode away with my chin high. If I'd had my coffee, I might have walked right out of the shop.

I'd been dismissed plenty in my life, but it never got any easier. This was why I had a "no dating, no second chances" rule. If I didn't get too involved, guys couldn't decide I wasn't worth the effort and crush me with casual rejections.

Instead of leaving, I grabbed a fork and carried my consolation cinnamon roll to the small empty table in the corner. The seats were a tight fit, and I was curvy enough to be uncomfortable. I couldn't wait to see Noah try to squeeze himself into the space.

He grabbed our coffees, and I tried not to watch him swivel his hips to get around the students spilling into the narrow path between the tables. I failed. I wasn't the only one.

Noah attracted attention. On top of his huge stature, he was fucking hot. His dark auburn hair, just starting to curl at the ends, begged a woman to shove her hands through it, and when he focused his eyes on you—hazel today, instead of the usual green—it was like you were the only woman in the world.

I quickly shoveled cinnamon roll into my mouth to mop up the drool while glaring at the skinny blonde with the cute little nose stud at the next table. She didn't notice, and luckily for me, neither did Noah as he approached our cramped corner.

He pulled his chair out as far as it would go with his foot and eased down. With one shoulder pressed against the wall, he stretched his legs out, bracketing mine under the table. Noah met my gaze with a tiny smirk, making me question the sanity of my table choice. Tingles raced up my arms and across my back as I realized I couldn't get up without basically climbing over him.

We weren't touching, but I swore I could feel the heat of his legs just below my knees. I felt a different heat pulse much higher and squirmed to relieve some of the ache caused by all the direct eye contact.

Noah set both cups in front of him on the table. "I get two questions now."

"That wasn't the agreement." I snatched my coffee, setting it as far away from him as possible in case he got handsy.

Noah rested his arms on the table, leaning forward to eye my late lunch. "Neither was that monstrosity, yet you're already halfway through it."

I licked icing off my lip, and a petty part of me enjoyed the way his gaze followed the movement. See? I didn't need nice smiles from him when I could get his attention other ways. He might not want to pursue the attraction between us, but that didn't mean it wasn't there.

Not that it mattered in the least. I didn't chase guys who weren't interested. Hell, I didn't chase guys who *were* interested. I wasn't the relationship type, too much opportunity to fuck things up, but I liked to know they wanted me enough to put in some effort.

If they couldn't see my worth, they weren't worth my time.

I took a quick sip of my drink, wincing when the hot

liquid scalded my tongue. "Ask your questions, and we'll see if I answer the second one."

Noah lowered his voice, forcing me to mimic his position to hear him. "Why did you really transfer here?"

Only my parents and D knew about the fire and the dean's subsequent strong suggestion I pick a new school. I wasn't in any hurry for that reputation to follow me to TU, but I didn't like the idea of lying to Noah.

D trusted him, and so did I, or I wouldn't keep running to him for help. Still, I could answer his question with most of the truth without making myself look like a criminal.

"My last school wasn't a good fit for me. They were pretty strict about their graduation requirements, and I wanted to be able to explore a little more in my educational choices." I patted myself on the back for a solid five seconds, proud of the truth-adjacent answer.

Noah didn't take his eyes off me as he took a slow pull from his drink, and a heavy feeling of foreboding twisted in my gut.

"Did you decide that before or after you set your dorm on fire?" he asked innocently.

Fuck. I was going to kill D and his big mouth.

3

Noah

Panic flashed across Chloe's expression at my comment, and I nearly ruined the moment by smiling. The effort to maintain a straight face paid off when Chloe launched into a quiet series of very inventive curses. Her jaw locked for a long second, and I thought maybe I'd finally crossed the line that would push her away from me.

The moment tore me in two. On one hand, I wanted to spread her across the ridiculously small table and live out one of my dirtier fantasies which suddenly involved cinnamon roll icing instead of peanut butter.

On the other hand, if she decided to give up on tormenting me, I could finish out school without betraying one of my closest friends. I was already in deep.

True, the coffee at the facility was surprisingly bad, but I could have hit up any of the coffee shops on our side of campus. Eva loved this place, and she'd talked about how lucky Chloe was to have a class right next door.

The timing had worked out in my favor.

Chloe slumped back in her seat, apparently done raging

at her brother, and slurped her coffee. "How long have you known?"

"Since a couple of days before you moved in. D wasn't sure you'd follow through until then, and he wanted us forewarned in case your pyromaniac habits continued at TU."

"It was one *small* fire, and it was an accident." Her dark eyes caught mine, the usual confidence replaced with trepidation. "Please don't say anything. There's..."

She trailed off and flailed her hand around as if waving away smoke. I got what she meant. A fire in her dorm, no matter how small, had to come with serious complications and a hell of a blow to her reputation.

"I don't spread gossip." She nodded with relief, but I wasn't done. "You haven't answered my question yet. Why did you transfer *here*?"

Chloe sighed and glanced around the room again. "It wasn't my first choice, or any of my choices. My parents pay my expenses, so they gave me the option of TU or taking a break from school to work. Since I'm not ready to move back home permanently, I picked the lesser of two evils." Her eyes flashed to me, and she continued softly. "I love D, but I hate living in his shadow."

She'd told me the unvarnished truth, more than I'd expected, and it warmed a part of me I didn't want to focus on too closely.

I reached across the couple of inches that separated us and took her hand. "When I look at you, I don't think about D."

Chloe held my stare, and the air between us thickened with unspoken words. A crash in the depths of the shop made her jump, breaking the moment. She pulled her hand away to wrap her fingers around her paper cup.

Her lips quirked. "Weird. When I look at you, D is all I can think about."

My dick perked right up, but I managed not to react. Chloe flirted the same way she drew breath—instinctively. She wouldn't follow through on the offer. Hitting on me was her way of creating distance. If she treated me like everyone else, she didn't run the risk of another rejection.

But damned if I didn't want to give in to the temptation and call her bluff.

I looked away and gulped down my lukewarm coffee in a desperate attempt to think about anything else. From the corner of my eye, a familiar blonde head caught my attention at the counter. I glanced over to see Eva glaring daggers at the guy taking her order. If looks could kill, he'd be bleeding out on the floor.

Unlike when he'd interacted with me or Chloe, his eyes were trained on Eva. He looked vaguely amused, and I assessed him as someone who could handle her rule the universe vibe. She offered him a tight smile and spun on her heel, causing her hair to flare out around her.

Eva was nothing if not committed. She made it one whole step into her dramatic exit before she spotted us and dropped the attitude.

"Noah," she squealed, making a beeline for our table. "Chloe!"

The other students who hadn't given me the time of day moved out of her way as if she were parting a body of water. Eva had that effect.

She plopped down in my lap, and I thanked the coffee gods my dick had calmed down after Chloe's comment— and the noise she'd made over the cinnamon roll. With the reminder echoing in my mind, I shifted Eva to one leg just in case.

She looped an arm around my neck and waggled her eyebrows at us. "What's going on here? A secret rendezvous?"

Chloe laughed, back to her usual carefree vibe. "Not quite. I ran into Noah after class, literally, and forced him to buy me coffee."

Eva nodded as if the story made perfect sense. "Good choice. This place has the best coffee in town." The guy she'd been trying to murder with her mind called her name, and she scowled over her shoulder at him. "Unfortunately, it has the worst employee."

Chloe's lips curved into a slow smile as she eyed the people behind the counter. "I don't know, the cashier is hot in an angry fuck kind of way."

Bitter jealousy rose in my throat, and I had to swallow hard to keep from setting Eva aside to take a shot at a guy wearing cat ears. If I hadn't been staring intently at Chloe's face, I might have missed the heated glance she cast my way.

Eva jumped up with a scoff. "Too bad his personality ruins it."

Chloe waited until Eva returned with her coffee to pounce. "So you admit he's attractive."

"I'm not blind—I'm picky. That's why I'm taking Mac to the athlete alumni dinner." Her sly expression should have warned me, but I was too busy trying not to add "angry fuck with Chloe" to my extensive list of fantasies. "Who are you taking, Noah?"

I blinked up at her, but I wasn't fast enough.

She tapped her chin with a finger and smiled wide at Chloe. "I have an idea. Since Noah doesn't have a date yet, you two should go together. D and Nadia are coming back for the evening, so it's perfect. You can see your family, and I get another lady friend to help me coerce RJ into going dress shopping."

I frowned at her, trying to regain some control in the conversation. "Who says I don't have a date already?"

Eva sent me a pitying look. "You put off getting a date every year until the last minute then pick some horrendous airhead who I'm forced to endure while you ignore her in favor of talking football with the guys. Sound familiar?"

She wasn't wrong, but I had the distinct feeling I'd been set up. Chloe pursed her lips, and I couldn't tell if she was considering the idea or trying to come up with a way to refocus Eva.

"It's not my fault they require my attendance *and* a date," I muttered.

I avoided as many public appearances as possible. TU liked to prance their championship athletes in front of the donors and the press, claiming they were preparing us for our futures in the sports world. I hated it.

Unlike some of my roommates, football wasn't my life. I loved playing, but in the end, the game offered me access to the future I really wanted—and an escape from a past I wanted to avoid.

Chloe and I had that much in common, though her past clung to her like colorful wings and mine stayed mostly hidden in the dark.

Eva tapped her fingers against my shoulder. "I'm simply saving you the trouble of auditions. Clearly two get along or you wouldn't be having coffee together in a secluded corner while Mac waits at the facility for you to bring him coffee."

I gave her the side eye. "How do you know Mac is waiting for me?"

She patted the pocket on the side of her leggings. "He's

texted me four times since I told him where I was going for coffee asking me to remind you he wants hazelnut, not vanilla." On cue, her leg vibrated again. "Five times."

"Mac doesn't need any more caffeine," I said.

"True, but it makes him happy." She shrugged. "This one's on you. I have class in a minute."

I huffed, fully prepared to abandon film time in favor of finishing my conversation with Chloe, but my own phone chimed an incoming message. Mac could be a menace.

Eva raised a brow at me. "You know he won't stop until you answer him."

"Or until I smother him in his sleep."

Chloe let out a quiet laugh that tripped over my nerve endings. As much as I didn't like feeling manipulated, Eva's idea wasn't bad. Chloe would be a better choice than anyone I picked. I couldn't seem to stop searching her out, so I might as well lean into this new circle of hell.

If nothing else, I'd give Chloe a chance to see her brother and Nadia.

D was insanely busy with his team, and he'd told the group chat he wouldn't have time to hang out this trip except for during the dinner. Purely business, which I'd guess didn't include Chloe.

My phone made another noise, and Eva stood so I could wrestle it out of my pocket. She offered me a sad smile as I sent Mac a text telling him I was on my way.

"You're so whipped."

"I think what you mean to say is I'm a good friend. He'll get his hazelnut coffee, and you'll get your preferred tablemate."

She perked up, turning to Chloe. "Dress shopping this weekend. RJ is free on Sunday."

Chloe met my gaze with raised brows. "I don't believe I was asked."

My lips twitched. "Need me to get down on my knees?"

Color flushed her cheeks, further proof that she remembered the night with the hockey asshole. She'd nearly smacked me in the face while declaring herself off limits for all time unless I got on my knees and begged. Drunk Chloe was a full-body experience.

She tossed her hair over her shoulder, a dare in her eyes. "Now that you mention it, yes."

Eva let out a low whistle and took several steps back while digging out her phone. "Hold on, I want to film this. For posterity. And blackmail."

My skin itched as several people at the closest table turned to see what drama Eva was stirring up. The whole situation was getting out of control, but Chloe propped her chin on her hand, waiting for me to give up and walk away.

Fuck that. She wanted a show? I'd give her one.

I extricated my legs from the table and turned her chair to face the tiny bit of space in the walkway before dropping to my knees in front of her. Cold from the concrete floor seeped into my jeans, a stark reminder of our very public location, but when I focused on Chloe's face—on the sharp need she quickly hid behind a smirk—the rest of the room faded away.

Her lips parted as I palmed her knees and eased them open, wide enough to fit my hips between them. My thumbs stroked the inside of her thighs as I slid my hands higher, wishing it was summer and she'd worn a skirt instead of leggings.

Chloe's breath caught, an almost inaudible hitch. The lizard part of my brain insisted we stake a claim. Now. While we had the chance. My fingers tightened on her legs, holding on for dear life instead of plunging into all that glorious hair and taking what was mine.

Her eyes widened as she leaned forward, just a little. The moment stretched, and she sighed my name. A question and a plea. I knew she'd go along with whatever I did to her, but I didn't want to be another regret in her life.

With some effort, I clawed back control, though I couldn't make myself move away. "Come with me to the alumni dinner," I murmured.

She pressed her lips together and nodded.

Someone to the side of us hooted, and I winced. Chloe blinked a couple of times, clearing the daze from her eyes. I hadn't meant to take the challenge this far, but it was too late to go back. With the spell broken, I stood and backed away.

Chloe's chest rose and fell with uneven breaths, but she crossed her legs and tilted her head in concession. "That'll do."

I took my seat, and the chaos of the coffee shop came rushing back. A surreptitious glance around showed me none of the other patrons were giving us much attention. Even the girls at the next table over had gone back to their conversation.

Eva fanned herself. "Well, that vid's not going to D anytime soon."

I crossed my arms. "You mean never. Don't cause problems where there aren't any."

She patted my bicep. "Don't worry. I'll save it for my speech at your wedding."

Chloe pointedly checked her watch. "You're going to be late to your class."

Eva looked at her screen, then frowned. "Crap, you're right." She shoved her phone back in her leggings pocket and grabbed her coffee from the table. "Luckily, the TA loves me. He's fine if I show up late every once in a while."

I shook my head. It was the first week of classes, and Eva already had a fan club. She was going to rule the world one day. I only hoped I'd stay on her good side.

"Dress shopping on Sunday," she sang as she grabbed the tote bag I hadn't even noticed behind my chair.

Just like that, Eva managed to arrange things exactly to her liking. As usual. She toasted us with her coffee and sauntered out of the shop, flipping off her nemesis behind the counter without breaking stride.

The alumni dinner would probably be a disaster, but I didn't regret giving in. D would be there to act as a buffer—hopefully one strong enough to counter the increasing draw I felt every time Chloe looked at me with need in those big green eyes.

4

Chloe

I F D sent me another text message, I was deleting his ass. I'd ignored Eva during the drive to the dress shop while I dealt with his temper tantrum. Not that he could do anything from New York, but I didn't want him taking his frustration out on Noah.

We managed to make it to the sidewalk in front of the shop before D's eleventh message in the last five minutes flashed across my screen. *Why was it necessary for him to be between your legs at all?*

I gritted my teeth as I stabbed out a response. *How many times do I have to tell you? It was a dare, and the video is taken out of context!! Believe me or don't, but stop harassing me. I haven't even seen Noah all week. Don't you have practice or something?*

A few beats went by, then D finally responded like a reasonable adult. *I believe you, Clo. Sorry I'm making things harder. I'll see you at the dinner, brat.*

Crisis averted, I closed out the messaging app and opened the bookmarked video from the coffee shop.

Honestly, I didn't blame D for getting upset. It wasn't exactly a flattering depiction of me, and he'd been there for my breakdown in high school after Vince started spreading rumors.

This was different though. Somehow more invasive and less upsetting at the same time.

I scowled at my screen, where the fuzzy video of Noah kneeling between my legs was ticking closer to one million views. Downtown Addison had great Wi-Fi. I could watch my life unravel in real time while dress shopping for an event I wasn't sure I wanted to attend.

All week, my phone had been blowing up with notifications from my various social media accounts. Mostly from skeezy guys asking for a turn. D had at least waited until mid-morning to come at me with his shouty caps.

He wanted to believe me, so he did. I wasn't even sure I'd lied to him. Noah was currently avoiding me, which didn't lend credence to any warm fuzzy feelings he'd caused. The sharp, achy feelings were even worse.

The soft touch of his fingers on my inner thighs, right over my tattoos, haunted my sleep. Not exactly restful. Luckily, the video didn't catch that part, or the part where I begged him in my mind to move a little higher.

Nope. Some random asshole had filmed just enough to make us look like we were hooking up in public. They'd even included a helpful comment wondering which of my brother's friends I'd choose next.

Oh yes. Noah may be the strong, silent type, but the student body knew who their star football players were, and I'd been lumped in with them, thanks to D.

Eva snatched the phone out of my hand. "Glaring at the video for the thousandth time won't make it go away."

I transferred my glare to her. "This is all your fault."

"Sorry, honey, but you brought this on yourself. My version, which is much nicer by the way, is still safely locked in my cloud. You're the one who dared Noah to step out of his comfort zone. And to my great delight, he rose to the challenge."

I pulled my mass of hair off my face and into a ponytail. "He wasn't supposed to be so sexy—he was supposed to blush and stammer out an invitation."

Eva snorted. "You don't know Noah very well then."

I wondered the same thing myself, but then I remembered the quiet way he stood between me and the trouble that always followed me. In the back of my mind, I'd known he wouldn't back down from my dare.

He hadn't even wanted to ask me to the dinner, but he'd made a spectacle of himself on my behalf anyway. Noah hated being the center of attention. The more I thought about him pushing his boundaries for me, the more I questioned my "no dating, no second chances" rule.

Why couldn't he just be a hot asshole looking for a good time? I knew how to deal with those guys.

Noah was a different beast entirely, and those stupid warm fuzzy feelings wouldn't stop fluttering around in my belly. Worse, I *wanted* to know him. He'd rejected me years ago, and I couldn't stop hoping...

Eva shook my shoulder. "Did I break you or were you just reliving Noah's big moment?"

I shrugged off her hold. "Neither. I was deciding if I wanted to try on the blue dress in the window."

Not entirely a lie—I was good at half-truths—the halter dress would hug my curves nicely and the dark blue color would make my eyes pop. I refused to acknowledge the quiet voice wondering if Noah would like it. He didn't get a say.

Eva sent me a skeptical look and pulled the door open to the little boutique she'd picked as a starting point. Riley was supposed to meet us here, but I didn't see a giant blonde among the racks.

The inside had an upscale thrift store feel with circular groupings of short dresses in the front by the door and slightly taller rows farther into the room. There didn't seem to be any organization, but I was up for a good hunt.

Dressing rooms took up the back wall, marked by heavy velvet curtains in a deep purple. Soft pink poufs littered the floor over shaggy mint rugs. Nothing in the shop matched, but somehow it worked together to create a vibrant, feminine space.

No wonder Eva liked it.

On the negative side, no one else seemed to be there, not even a salesperson. The long glass counter holding jewelry and accessories sat empty.

"Is this place open?"

Eva glanced around, unconcerned. "It's always like this. Honestly, I'm not sure how they stay in business, but they have great dresses at reasonable prices if you don't mind putting in a little effort."

She walked directly to the taller racks in the back and started sorting through clothes. I followed slower, trying to get a look at the blue dress from the other side.

"Where's Riley?" I asked absently, nearly running into a metal pole when I turned back to face her.

Eva pulled out a short magenta number and frowned at it. "She's not coming. Claimed she already had a dress, but I think she just wanted to take advantage of some alone time with Shaw."

I wrinkled my nose. "They live together. How much alone time do they need?"

She propped her hands on her hips. "Are you telling me if Shaw wanted you to stay at home in bed with him, you'd say no thanks and traipse off with your gal pals?"

An image of Parker Shaw, starting quarterback and my brother's protégé, flashed into my mind. Sharp cheekbones, intense blue eyes, and a wicked grin. He was beautiful, I'd give him that, but in the way art or remote mountain lakes were beautiful. Like I only wanted to appreciate him from a distance, I didn't want to partake.

Noah made me want to dive right in. My jaw clenched at the unwarranted thought. There wouldn't be any partaking. No matter how much I craved him touching me again.

I grabbed at a hanger blindly, getting it hopelessly tangled with the dress next to it. "I try not to speculate on booty calls, especially when they involve my brother's friends." Too bad I utterly failed at any kind of separation with Noah.

She sighed. "But they're all so pretty."

"Yeah, and complicated. I prefer simpler relationships where my brother doesn't call me in the middle of the night demanding an explanation for his buddy's drunk tirade."

Her eyes narrowed. "We're going to circle back to that."

"There's nothing to circle back to. I'd rather date a hundred frat boys than one nice guy in the apartment across from ours. They're up front about what they want, and they don't whine when I choose myself over them."

"Hey, I'm all for ladies putting themselves first, but don't you want a relationship that's worth more to you than the toys in your bedside drawer?" She didn't mention Noah, but I didn't think she was talking about Mac or Parker.

"I thought we were here to shop," I grumbled. Hair fell

in my face as I yanked my random choice free—a romper the color of squashed peas.

"I don't think that's the one," Eva deadpanned.

I blew the loose strands back, cursing my impromptu decision to get layers a few months ago. "Why is this even over here?"

"Some people have questionable taste." She shrugged and moved to the next row. "Some need a nudge in the right direction. Some are determined to make poor choices based on past experiences."

I narrowed my eyes at her and shoved the hanger back where I'd found it. "Why does this feel like we're not talking about dresses?"

Eva met my gaze with a raised brow. "Why are you looking through the sale rack when you could have the stunner in the window?"

She couldn't possibly know about my encounters with Noah. Other than the one she filmed, that is. I hadn't told a single person I'd taken a desperate chance with him years ago, and he'd shot me down. Up until this moment, I'd have sworn Noah had kept it to himself too.

My arms dropped to my sides, and I shook my head. "What makes you think I can get the stunner in the window?"

"A hunch." She offered me a small smile and held a navy sheath dress up to her tiny figure.

"No." I shook my head again. "You need something to show off your crazy abs."

I dug through the dresses until I found one close to the image in my head—short, black, with open slashes across the middle. It was sexy and edgy and it would look fantastic on her.

"Here, try this one." I handed her the dress, and her eyes lit up.

"Oh wow..." she breathed.

Eva disappeared behind one of the purple curtains, and I eyed the display at the front. Noah's chance with me had passed, but with the right dress, I could show him what he'd missed. It would be nice to be wanted by someone like him, and after the auspicious start in my classes, I could use the ego boost. I knew what I wanted, why was I dithering?

Other than my need for an actual employee to climb into the store window. I'd never been in a shop like this where the employees weren't constantly watching. How *was* this place still in business?

A door in the back labeled Employees Only was probably my best bet for help. Eva's dressing room curtain remained closed, so I squared my shoulders and knocked. If no one answered, I'd take care of the problem myself. It wouldn't be the first time I'd wrestled a mannequin into submission.

A woman with tortoiseshell glasses and crazy rainbow streaks in her shoulder-length dark hair popped her head out. She looked about my age, but I didn't recognize her from campus. Not a surprise considering I spent all my time with D's crew.

"Crap," she muttered under her breath, then slipped into the main room, pulling the employee door shut behind her. She wore overalls at least a size too big for her small frame over a fuzzy white sweater topped off with a pinched look on her face.

When I stood there staring at her, she raised a brow. "Can I help you?"

I blinked, surprised by the lack of any attempt at a

customer service voice. "Yes. Can I try on the dress in the window?"

Her eyes, a vivid blue-green that didn't look real, flicked to the front of the store then back to me. "Sure."

I followed her, trying to pinpoint if I'd annoyed her personally or if she was simply bad at being a store clerk. "Have you worked here long?"

She sped through the racks without glancing back. "Sort of. This is my mom's shop, but she's at a yoga retreat this weekend, so I'm filling in."

Ah. Bad at being a store clerk. I could work with that. "Your hair is beautiful. Can I ask where you get it done?"

She skidded to a stop, and I nearly ran into her as she turned to face me with her brows furrowed. "If you're hitting on me, I feel I should warn you I'm not into girls."

I snorted out a laugh. "No. I'm just an unrepentant extrovert. My mom says I'm incapable of silence for more than five seconds. I'm Chloe, by the way."

She studied my face for a long moment, as if trying to ascertain my sincerity. "Bluebonnet."

My brows rose. "Excuse me?"

"My name. It's Bluebonnet, but everyone calls me Blue." One of her straps sagged down her arm as she turned to cross the remaining distance to the window. "This one?"

"Yeah. Do you need help getting it down?" I wasn't tall by any means, but she was a couple of inches shorter than me, closer to Eva's size.

"No, Bertha here is a sweetheart."

With efficient movements, she hauled Bertha out of the window display and stripped the blue dress off her.

She held it up to me bunched in one fist. "Just yell if you need anything else."

I took the dress and cocked my head as she left the

naked mannequin splayed on the floor to go back the way she'd come. After a second, I followed, catching up to her near the dressing rooms.

"Do you have any other sizes?"

Blue stopped and peeked at her watch before giving me her full attention again. "No. Everything in here is one of a kind. I can help you look for something else if you tell me the occasion."

The offer surprised me since she seemed sort of inconvenienced at my presence in the shop. Then again, she'd seemed willing enough to talk before.

"It's for a fancy alumni dinner hosted by the athletics department, but I think I'll try this one on before looking for something else."

Her brows drew together. "You're an athlete?"

Under other circumstances, her disbelieving tone would have been offensive, but the confusion on her face made me think she simply didn't have a filter. Or social skills of any kind. I kind of liked her brand of zero bullshit, so I took her at face value.

"No, I'm the arm candy for one of the football players. He cleans up nice, but he's the most anti-social person I've ever met." Except maybe the girl standing in front of me. "I'm there to make him look less feral so the university can schmooze more money out of the donors."

Blue frowned. "That sounds horrible."

I chuckled at her unfiltered comment. "It's not so bad."

She tucked a purple strand of hair behind her ear and adjusted the glasses sliding down her nose. "Statistically speaking, professional football players are among the top alumni most likely to donate back to their schools after graduating, but I suppose non-alumni donors are also more likely to give when presented with introductions to quasi-celebrities."

This girl had a strange way of thinking about things. Before I could ask any of the questions circling my mind, the curtain rattled open next to us, and Eva shouted at me.

"Chloe, you're a genius."

Blue jumped, leading me to think she hadn't known there were two of us in here.

Eva strolled out of the dressing room and struck a pose with her hands on her hips. "I love it. I love everything about it, and I'm never taking it off."

I'd been right about her abs. The guys thought their stomachs were impressive, but Eva could put them to shame. Her core was sheer muscle, which the cut-outs in the dress highlighted.

"I'm thinking a big dramatic braid and shoes that lace up my calves." Eva turned and peered over her shoulder at the mirror.

"That makes sense with the crisscross in the dress." Blue pointed to the straps spanning Eva's bare back.

Eva's gaze in the mirror shifted to my new friend. "Exactly. Good eye."

Blue shrugged, dislodging her overalls strap again. "It's basic shape recognition."

I snickered. "Blue, this is my friend and roommate, Eva. Eva, this is Blue. She works here. Sort of."

Recognition lit Eva's eyes, and she turned to smile at Blue. "You're Hope's daughter, right?"

"Yes. Hope is my mom."

Eva sighed. "I just love her. Best yoga classes I've ever taken, and her choice of dresses borders on psychic."

Blue's face softened. "She'll be happy to hear that. Yoga is her passion. She's been a little depressed since she split with Archer Bolme, but hearing about people enjoying her classes will cheer her up."

My mouth dropped open. Archer Bolme was the super-hot coach for the Dallas NHL team. I didn't follow hockey, but even I knew who he was. Voted most eligible bachelor by Modern Dallas magazine three years in a row. "She was dating Archer Bolme? How? I need to know every detail."

"Why?" Blue's nose scrunched, and Eva burst out laughing.

Eva linked her arms through Blue's. "Okay, it's settled. I'm buying this dress. Chloe is buying that one. And you're coming to lunch with us."

I held up my prize. "Hey, I haven't even tried it on yet."

Blue frowned down at the watch on her wrist. "I suppose I can take an early lunch, but I have to be back here by two."

"Deal." I scrambled behind the curtain next to Eva's, intent on being done before Blue could change her mind.

The blue dress fit me like a dream, hugging my curves and making my boobs look fantastic without threatening a wardrobe malfunction. Maybe Hope was psychic after all. I hurried back into my clothes, and my mind wandered to my unwilling date.

A subtle shiver ran over my skin. The press of Noah's fingers on my thighs wouldn't leave my thoughts. In that moment, I could've sworn I wasn't alone with all the repressed longing. Noah never gave me an explanation for politely declining my generous offer, but I suspect it had to do with D. Just like everything else in my life.

In the end, Noah's reasons didn't matter. Only the result. He'd had his chance, and I wasn't desperate enough to go begging for a second rejection. No matter how many times he looked at me with heat in his eyes. No matter how much I wanted him to follow through on the promise in those hands.

A small part of me knew I was playing with fire. I hoped Noah would lose his shit over the dress—over me—but I wasn't sure I had the strength to turn him down if he touched me like that again.

I wasn't sure I wanted to.

5

Noah

Spring football didn't come with the same obligations as the regular season, and technically, we didn't even start until late February. No one told Parker that. Until Coach took over, our sadistic captain set up a workout schedule to maintain fitness levels over the couple of weeks we had off.

He expected us to be in the weight room at the appointed time, and to his credit, most of the guys showed up. As his roommate, I didn't really have a choice.

Part of me would rather sleep in on a frigid Sunday morning, but my days of being a tall, gangly kid weren't that far behind me. I much preferred the big, tough persona I wore these days. The weight room had helped me find myself, long before Parker and his "voluntary" sessions.

Sweat slicked down my back as I slowed the treadmill to a cooldown jog. Metal clanged in the weight area, and Holbrook's gangster rap leaked from his shitty earbuds across from me. I tossed a towel at his head, but he only grinned at me and turned it up. Asshole.

Mac finished his set and re-racked his dumbbells before

making his way over to me and leaning on my handrail. "How's my favorite movie star today?"

He'd been nonstop since the damn video went viral. I considered duct taping him to his door for some relief, but I was only fifty percent sure I could do it without Shaw's help.

D had already chewed my ass out. He didn't like the media taking shots at Chloe simply because she'd been with me. I agreed. Wholeheartedly.

"I'm trying to ignore the problem in the hopes it will go away." I stared pointedly at Mac, but he remained stubbornly present.

"Did D see the video?"

"What do you think?" I returned my attention to the wall opposite me so I didn't have to see the questions on his face.

"I think D called all of us to make sure we weren't pimping out his sister before Nadia could take his phone away."

I grunted, surprised he'd contacted everyone. "He wasn't happy, but nothing happened. Nothing *will* happen."

Mac shrugged in my peripheral. "Not the end of the world if it did. Chloe is awesome and a smokeshow on top of it. D can't get upset if one of us realizes the opportunity presented."

I glared at him. "You sure as hell better not be realizing any opportunities."

He held up his hands with a wide grin. "Not me, big guy. If that video is anything to go buy, our girl is already taken."

I didn't correct him. A primitive part of me reveled in the idea of putting a claim on her even if I didn't plan to follow through with it. D would have every right to be upset if I took advantage of his sister.

Even if she wanted me to. The video wasn't very detailed, but I remembered the hungry look on her face when she'd stared down at me. Just like I remembered her thighs were firm and supple under her leggings.

Hell, I needed a distraction. "Doing anything after this?"

Mac tilted his head. "Pizza at Johnny's maybe. Alex will be there going over some new stuff, and he asked if I'd come by. Want to join me?"

I grunted an assent, and Mac pumped his hand in the air.

"Yesss. I could use your grumbly sound for some background vocals," he said.

"Nevermind. I'm not going."

"Backup dancing then?" He swiveled his hips in a bastardized version of the Carlton.

"Sure, sounds fun," I quipped.

Mac's mouth dropped open in shock. "Really?"

I sent him a pointed stare. "Have I ever given you the indication I want to be a backup dancer for your talent show delusion?"

He recovered quickly, reaching over to take a swig from my water. "You have hidden depths we've only begun to explore. Who am I to deny your dreams?"

"My dreams involve having food in our apartment the weeks you're supposed to shop." And a certain brunette bombshell whose brother would kill me if I acted on any of those dreams.

Mac threw his hands up. "That's why we're going to Johnny's."

"Your plan is to buy pizza instead of real food for the week?"

He pointed at me. "Yes. Until RJ yells at me. Then I'll activate the puppy dog eyes to distract her."

As if she knew we were talking about her, RJ strolled over from the squat rack wiping her neck with a towel.

"Aren't you supposed to be working something besides your mouth, Mac?"

"Already done. Can you keep Parker busy for a bit tonight?"

She narrowed her eyes at Mac. "Why?"

"A certain wildcat I'm meeting. She's shy."

RJ groaned. "Not a cheerleader."

He laid his hand on his chest with a dramatic gasp. "Why, RJ, what do you have against cheerleaders?"

She smacked his arm with her towel. "I don't want your latest conquest to interfere with Eva's squad. If she decides to torture you, she might throw me in there too since I live with you."

The treadmill beeped, and I stepped on the side rails as it slowed to a stop. I wiped my face on my soaked shirt, then frowned at RJ. "Weren't you supposed to be dress shopping with Eva and Chloe today?"

A faint blush stained her cheeks. "I bailed."

Curiosity ate at me, but I wasn't going to ask her for more information. If she wanted to say more, she would.

Luckily, Mac didn't have any such qualms. "What the hell, RJ? Eva planned this trip around your schedule."

She scowled at him. "I don't need another dress, Mac. Parker and I were dealing with some stuff this morning, and it ran late. Eva understands. I'm sure Chloe will too."

Mac muttered something about Shaw's dick under his breath, but RJ ignored him. I understood Mac's frustration. Chloe didn't have any friends at this university besides us, and despite her outgoing personality, I got the feeling she wasn't looking for any more. I didn't like the idea of RJ abandoning her to spend time with us.

I stepped off the machine and reached for my bag next to RJ's leg. "Did you talk to her?"

RJ tilted her head at me. "Chloe? No, not yet. I'm going over to their place tonight for margaritas and a mini fashion show."

Mac perked up. "Am I invited?"

"No. Eva's orders. What are you guys doing for lunch?" she asked, changing the subject.

"Johnny's for pizza and sweet, sweet tunes," Mac mimed singing into a mic then wagged his brows at her. "You're in, right?"

She laughed. "Not this time. Parker promised me Whataburger. He said it would change my life."

Mac looked pained. "You've lived in Texas for six months, and you haven't been to Whataburger yet?"

"I haven't had time." She shrugged like it wasn't a big deal, but Mac worshipped at the altar of their gravy.

"Blasphemy," he muttered.

"Next time I'll invite the whole group, including Chloe." She raised a brow at me and heaved her bag over her shoulder, waving at us on her way out the door.

Mac shook his head, refocusing on me. "Shower and meet in the front in twenty?"

"Sure, be there in a minute." I grabbed my bag and dug through looking for my earbuds, desperate for some alone time where I didn't have to hide my reaction every time someone mentioned Chloe's name.

Mac whistled on his way to the locker room, but I wasn't in the mood. I found a relatively empty corner of the weight room and sat on a chest press bench with my phone in my hand. Even with my earbuds in, I could hear the conversations of the guys who hadn't finished their workout yet, quieter now that Mac had left.

Five minutes. I just needed five minutes to gather my thoughts.

I scrolled through my playlists, not sure what I was searching for, but a call came through before I could pick something. My jaw tightened at the name scrolling across the top of my screen.

Craig Olsen.

My finger hovered over the *Dismiss* button, but he'd simply leave a passive aggressive message and call again later. Might as well get the frustration over with now.

"Hello, Uncle Craig." I defaulted to the neutral tone I'd used for most of my childhood.

"Noah. How are your classes?" He sounded distracted, and the gentle clink of glass in the background told me he was probably out to his usual lunch at the club.

"No trouble so far."

"No trouble is not the same as excelling." I could practically hear his frown. "You're not slacking after the championship win, are you?"

"No, sir. I'm sitting at As in all my classes, and I just finished up with training for the day." It didn't matter that classes had just started. We'd only had one assignment so far, but Craig didn't want to hear that.

He always went straight to the point, no use wasting time discussing logistics or asking how *I* was doing. As far as he was concerned, my grades and my stats were the only important parts of me. I needed to maintain a certain level of achievement to protect his reputation, and he ensured that expectation by checking up on me with his golfing buddy, the dean of the athletic department.

Craig had raised me, after all. Any failure on my part reflected back on him.

"Good. Good. Not getting distracted by girls?"

My jaw clenched as I thought of Chloe, but no way in

hell would I subject her to my uncle's brand of judgment. "No. Too busy."

A voice murmured something in the background, and Craig sighed. "It shouldn't be this hard to find good service."

I made a noncommittal noise because he wasn't talking to me. He certainly wasn't listening to me either. These calls were purely a way for him to be sure I wasn't following in my old man's footsteps. Easier to cut me off before I drew too much attention if he knew I was on my way down.

The background noise muffled for a second, then Craig was back. "I'm glad to hear you're being responsible. Remember, controlling yourself is a sign of strength."

A bitter laugh escaped, but I managed to choke most of it back. He was referencing my temper, but he was closer to the mark asking about girls. If only he knew how irresponsible I wanted to be—how much easier it would be to take what Chloe offered rather than holding myself back.

Chloe didn't want me for her future, and I couldn't blame her. My own family hadn't made me a priority, maybe ever. Only D and our crew had done that. My promise to D held me accountable, and my feelings for Chloe—because I sure as hell had them—made it impossible for me to walk away.

Of course, Craig wasn't interested in my messy inner dilemmas. "Do you need anything else, Uncle Craig? I need to hit the showers."

"No. You sound like you're on top of things, as usual. I'll talk to you next month, Noah."

He hung up before I could say goodbye, not that I cared. We'd never been close. Craig's schedule as a surgeon kept him too busy for more than a monthly check-in, which was better than his constant monitoring in middle and high school.

At least I didn't have to worry about him coming across the video with Chloe. He didn't concern himself with such pedestrian pastimes as social media. My aunt Melissa might find it—or someone might send it to her—but she'd become an expert on ignoring the events of my life to smooth over her relationship with Craig.

I hadn't said two words to Chloe after my little show in Wildcat Coffee, and my resemblance to Craig's dismissive attitude bothered me.

Suddenly, I was sick of my own company. I didn't really know how to reach out to people, let alone make connections with them. If not for D, I wouldn't have any of the tight friendships I've made over the last few years. He'd brought me into this group—made it a family I *wanted* to spend time with—and I was failing at doing the same for his sister.

She deserved better. I scrubbed a hand down my face. Maybe I could be the one to make it better for her. The first step would be to stop avoiding her.

Mac came out of the locker room, hair still damp from his shower, and pursed his lips when he spotted me. "Your slow ass missed the chance to get clean. Pizza waits for no man. Let's go, Stinky McStinkface."

The big metal doors clanged shut behind him, and I pulled my shirt up to my face for a sniff test. Sweaty, yeah, but not bad. Mac would wait long enough for me to change at least, but what was the point?

I didn't give a shit if I smelled at lunch, and Mac would be busy on the other side of the room with Alex. My job was to guard his pizza, though I was just as likely to eat it if he left me at the table alone too long. I tapped the side of my phone with my thumb.

Nothing said I *had* to be alone.

I pulled up Chloe's contact info and stared down at her

smiling face. When she'd first moved in, she'd stolen my phone and snapped a picture of herself, shifting her gaze to meet my eyes at the last second.

She'd captured the look she saved just for me—the one that broke down my defenses and activated the stupid part of my brain. I'd never admit how many times I pulled up the picture when I lay alone in bed at night.

Before I could talk myself out of it, I wrote a quick text inviting her to lunch and hit send. She probably had plans with Eva, but at least I'd tried.

6

Chloe

E va declared we needed Mexican food to pregame for the margaritas I hadn't been aware we were having later. Blue and I followed along because arguing with Eva was pointless.

Eva's favorite restaurant sat us right away, and I'd just shoved a huge chip in my mouth when my phone beeped. After the video fiasco, I'd set my notifications to close friends only, so I wouldn't be pestered by randos sending me dick pics in the middle of the night.

Probably D with even more life advice I planned to disregard, but I couldn't ignore the message. He'd keep sending them until I responded. I blamed Mac for that particularly annoying personality trait.

I dug through my bag until I found my phone. One new text message.

From Noah.

The chip bits lodged in my throat, and I knocked over my water as I flailed for it. Blue tilted her head at me with a concerned look, but Eva only sighed and pushed her water cup closer before mopping up the mess with her napkin.

I chugged until I could breathe normally again, then pulled up the message.

Lunch at Johnny's. Pizza's on me if you come keep me company.

Girl code dictated I should tell him I already had plans, but I wasn't going to do that because Noah had never reached out to me before. Also because I sucked at being a friend. Something told me he needed me more than I needed to know how Blue's mom had ended up dating the hot hockey coach.

I cleared my throat, just to be sure there wouldn't be a repeat near death experience. "I have to go."

Eva raised a brow. "Important booty call?"

God, I wished. "No. Noah wants me to meet him for lunch so we can discuss the alumni dinner."

Blue's face cleared. "Ah, the football player who needs arm candy."

Eva smiled at my blush. "Need me to give you a ride?"

I shook my head, gathering my bag and coat. "Nah, I'll get an Uber. You guys enjoy your lunch. Blue, it was so nice to meet you, and I can't wait to hang out with you for real."

She nodded. "I'd like that."

Eva patted her arm. "No going back now."

We exchanged numbers, then I pulled up the Uber app while I zig-zagged through the tables on the way out. I didn't realize Eva was behind me until she poked me in the arm.

"*Gah.*" I bobbled my phone and almost dropped it onto the concrete.

"Sorry. I didn't mean to scare you." She didn't look sorry. Her lips pressed together as she fought to hold in a laugh.

"I'm buying you a collar with a bell," I muttered.

"Kinky." Eva scanned the empty street in front of the restaurant.

"Did you need something or were you just trying to make sure I was *really* awake?"

Her eyes flicked toward me then back to the road. "Noah is a good guy."

I waited, but she didn't continue. "I know…"

"I know you know, but I'm not sure you *know*."

"Well, that sentence really cleared things up for me." She didn't laugh, and the uncharacteristic hesitation made my stomach drop. "What are you saying?"

"I've been thinking about our conversation earlier, and I want you to know I support whatever happens."

"But…" I added.

Eva rolled her eyes. "But… try not to break him, okay?"

It was on the tip of my tongue to ask if she'd given him the same warning about breaking me, but I managed to keep my mouth shut for once. After Vince, I'd sworn off relationships, but I wasn't heartless.

I didn't want to hurt Noah. I just wanted to feel good without all the expectations and potential for disaster. A silver Corolla pulled into the parking lot, interrupting my excuses. I confirmed the license plate before stepping in front of Eva.

"I'll do my best." Thus far, my best sucked, but a shitty track record wouldn't stop me from trying.

She nodded, and her teasing tone returned. "I'll take care of your dress. Don't forget to come home tonight. We have plans with RJ."

"Ha ha. As if I'd accept a booty call from Noah," I lied through my teeth. "I expect to hear all about the hot coach later."

Eva went into the restaurant, and I climbed into the back of the car. The drive to Johnny's wasn't long, but a million scenarios flew through my mind. Maybe he was lonely. Maybe he needed money. Maybe it really *was* a booty call.

I snorted at the last one, and the driver glanced at me in the rearview mirror. Noah wouldn't call me if he wanted an afternoon quickie.

The memory of his hands slowly gliding up my thighs made all my inner muscles clench, and I knew if he called me up for afternoon sex, it wouldn't be a quickie. I let out a shuddering breath and told my vagina to calm the fuck down. Lunch. Noah asked me to join him for lunch.

We pulled into the nearly empty bar parking lot, and I thanked the guy driving, giving him a good tip for letting me stew in silence. In the back of my mind, I knew I was over-thinking the moment.

My hands shook as I opened the door. I never gave a guy this much power over me, not in the last three years anyway, but Noah had snuck past my usual defenses. He was *nice*. I considered him a friend—I just wasn't sure if he felt the same or if he only saw me as D's little sister.

It shouldn't matter. I kept telling myself it didn't, but the same hope that crushed in high school lifted my mood. For once, I wanted to be seen as myself instead of a failed exten-sion of my brother—or just a failure.

The bar was a big, dim, open space with tables shoved between a dance floor and a bar. One big booth sat like a throne in the middle of the room. A few of the tables were taken up by groups having lunch, and none of them glanced my way when I came in.

I zeroed in on Noah, who sat alone halfway between the booth and the door. He'd traded his usual workout clothes for jeans and a long-sleeved shirt he'd shoved up to his elbows. The material clung to his broad shoulders, and his dark russet hair stood up in disarray as if he'd been running his hands through it.

He looked up from his phone, and his gaze met mine like a body blow. I stumbled over the industrial rug at the entrance and nearly face-planted onto the floor. Today was not a good day for my coordination.

Noah's lips curled into a slow smile, and for a second, I wondered if I'd hit my head after all. Flutters of sensation coalesced into full-blown tingles. His smile gave me tingles. Naughty tingles. I was in so much trouble.

He stood and pulled out the chair next to him, an automatic gesture that turned my racing heart into goo. "I didn't think you were coming."

I sat, dropping my stuff onto an empty seat at the four top, and belatedly remembered I'd never texted him back. "Right. Sorry. Eva distracted me."

"How did the dress shopping go?"

I sent him a suspicious glance. Noah didn't usually initiate inane conversations. "Fine. We found what we needed at the first place, then Eva strongarmed the sales-clerk into closing the store to have lunch with us."

He chuckled. "That's not surprising. If you were already at lunch, why did you come?"

"You asked. Besides, I believe I was promised pizza—the best of all lunch foods?"

"Luckily, we didn't order yet. Olives and green onions, right?"

I nodded, strangely touched he remembered my favorite pizza toppings, but then the rest of his words hit me. "We?"

"Yeah." He nodded to the DJ booth where I'd somehow missed Mac standing with another guy. "Mac and Alex are working on a singing thing. Thanks for coming."

"No problem." I drummed my fingers on the table, trying to find the right way to ask what had changed without scaring him off, but Noah surprised me by volunteering the information.

"I'm sorry for all the video bullshit, but I'm not going to apologize for what happened in the coffee shop."

Air rushed out of my lungs. "It takes a lot more than internet trolls to bother me."

"What about D?"

I scoffed. "I can handle my brother. He's not in charge of my life, and he rarely factors into my choices."

Noah ran his fingers over the stubble on his chin, and the rasping noise derailed my thoughts as I imagined the rough feel between my thighs. "He factors into mine."

I blinked at him, and realization hit me like a brick to the face. "Is that why you turned me down?"

Noah rubbed the back of his neck, glancing across the room at Mac. "It's one of the reasons."

I frowned at him. "Well now I need a full explanation."

"Let me get the pizza started and I'll explain anything you want."

My pulse sped at the opening he'd left me. "Anything?"

Noah paused halfway out of his chair and leaned forward into my space, close enough I could feel his breath on my lips. "Anything. This round is free, but the next will cost you. Be sure you can handle the answers before you ask."

He walked to the bar without a backward glance, and I laid a hand on my chest, trying to calm my crazy heartbeat. Was I about to make a mistake?

Past experience said yes. I could keep pretending Noah wasn't interested and shore up my flagging confidence with false assurances that I'd never give him a second chance. Except I hated lying to myself.

If Noah had changed his mind about me, I had no good reason to keep myself aloof—not that I'd succeeded at aloof thus far. If he offered me a hookup, I might spontaneously combust at the table. I desperately wanted to prove he wasn't special, but he was. Despite what I said to Eva earlier, I was picky about my sex partners.

By the time he returned, I knew which question I wanted to start with. "Did my brother warn you away from me?"

Noah tilted his head in a half-nod. "Not specifically. He made it very clear you're important to him, and none of us were allowed to fuck with you."

I narrowed my eyes. "Don't I get a say in that?"

He raised a brow. "You want to be treated like a ball bunny?"

"No. I want to be able to make my own decisions."

"Fair enough. Any other questions?"

His easy agreement calmed some of my ire, and I laughed. "Yeah, you're not getting off that easy."

"I'm not getting off at all," he muttered under his breath.

"That was your choice, if I remember correctly."

His gaze shot back to me, and the air between us heated. I raised my chin, challenging him to deny it. Clearly, we had the attraction part down.

Noah braced his forearms on the table, eyes locked on me. "Even if you weren't D's sister, I would have said no."

"Why?" I whispered.

"You and I aren't looking for the same thing."

My brows shot up. "Multiple orgasms aren't good enough for you?"

His lips twitched. "Okay, we're looking for *some* of the

same things, but I'm not interested in a singular experience."

"Why not?"

He leaned back in his chair and crossed his arms. "Hookups are over too fast, and I don't share." His gaze raked over my bare shoulder where my sweater had fallen down. "If I'm with someone, she's the only one I'm thinking about, and I'm sure as hell going to be the only one in her bed."

I swallowed hard, suddenly overheated in the warm bar. "Why did you text me today? Why *me*?"

Noah's jaw ticked, and I thought he might call off our little game. I expected a pickup line, Noah-style—something intense and sexy—but he surprised me again.

"I wasn't in a good place, and you make me feel better."

My brows drew together, and I reached for him. "What happened?"

He flipped his hand to cradle mine, staring down at my palm. "My uncle called and reminded me why I value my friendships here so much, especially your brother's."

I didn't understand the association. "What does that mean?"

"D never made his friendship feel transactional. He and Soren, Mac, Shaw—they all accepted me as is without trying to fix me or wanting something from me in return. I haven't had a lot of that in my life."

My heart hurt for the younger Noah. "There's nothing about you I would change."

"I know, but my uncle would disagree."

The pizza arrived, and I stared up at the server for a long second. I'd forgotten we weren't alone. The entire room had shrunk to this one table with Noah's hand under mine and his eyes on me.

He leaned back, severing the connection so the guy could set the pizza between us. Seconds later, Mac arrived with Alex in tow. I exchanged hellos with the other guys, but my mind was on Noah's revelation as I scalded my mouth with too hot pizza.

Patience was never one of my virtues, along with grace or self-control. I'd always relied on barging through situations with confidence and great shoes. As much as I wanted to firmly put Noah in the too bad, so sad category, I couldn't do it.

I wanted to hear more about little Noah, and I wanted to do it after a sweaty night spent exploring every inch of his sculpted body. Old me would be horrified, but hadn't I decided old me shouldn't be in charge anymore?

You make me feel better... A warm glow took root in my chest and refused to go away. Noah may have started off as D's friend, but he'd texted *me*.

The pizza didn't last long with Mac at the table. He hyped Alex's music project while the other man grinned. Alex seemed nice, a quiet guy with light brown hair, glasses, and an easy smile. Both Noah and Mac dwarfed him, but he was taller than me.

I loved hanging out with Mac because he was the only person I knew more likely to talk to a random stranger than I was. With him leading the conversation, I could focus on other things... like the subtle expressions crossing Noah's face. I played a game with myself trying to read what was happening in his mind. A couple of times, he shifted his gaze to me, and I didn't bother hiding my attention. He knew I was staring, and I didn't care.

After the food disappeared, Alex pulled Mac away again with a wave, leaving Noah and me alone over an empty tray. I had things to do back at the apartment, so I couldn't stay much longer, but I was hesitant to end the rare peek behind Noah's walls.

"Do I still get free answers to all my questions?"

He shook his head with a half-smile. "Nope, round's over."

"What do you want for the next round?" Silence stretched like warm honey, heating my insides until I felt like I could breathe fire.

Noah tilted his head. "I'll let you know when I decide."

I nodded. If I didn't leave now, I'd make a dangerous mistake, like offering myself as a trade. I grabbed my bag from the floor where Mac had put it and stood, slipping on my coat.

"Thanks for lunch. It was enlightening."

"Do you need a ride? I can steal Mac's car."

The temptation to say yes—to invite him into my empty apartment and try my best to convince him casual could be fun—made me press my lips together. Bad decision. Even old me recognized the warning signs.

"No, Uber is surprisingly affordable here. Save your grand theft auto for an emergency."

Noah walked me to the door. "I'll pick you up at six for the dinner."

"From across the hallway?" I teased.

He gave me a smile—a full, beautiful smile—and leaned in to brush his lips across my cheek. "Thanks for listening."

Don't touch your cheek. Don't touch your cheek. My inner voice failed to stop the automatic response of raising my hand to cover the spot where he'd kissed me. Noah's eyes crinkled with amusement as he followed the movement before turning to join Mac and Alex at the DJ booth.

There was a reason I didn't do relationships after I crashed and burned in high school. Too much sacrifice for not enough gain. I liked sex and affection and fun, but two out of three I could get from friends with no commitment or emotions necessary.

No chance the guy will decide some time down the road that my hot mess self was too much trouble. If I couldn't handle my shit, why would anyone else? Why would Noah?

I let my hand drop and shivered in my coat before stepping outside. It wasn't cold enough for the chill to penetrate the thick material, but I wanted the armor of an extra layer.

My spinning thoughts felt dangerously close to fear, and new me struggled to accept that truth about myself. It was so much easier to find another party or convince the men's lacrosse team to go skinny dipping as a way to push the fear deep down. Don't try, don't fail—my motto for the last few years felt hollow compared to the temptation of Noah.

I scheduled a car to take me back to the apartment, ridiculously glad I'd have some time on my own before I had to face Eva and Riley. *Why are you looking through the sale rack when you could have the stunner in the window?* Eva's question circled in my mind, and I thought of the blue dress I'd bought specifically to rock Noah's world.

After today's conversation, I was a little ashamed of the petty urge to make him regret saying no.

Noah wanted me—he wanted *only* me—but he was right. We were looking for different things. At least, I thought I was. The pouty part of me insisted I was being stupid for stubbornly sticking to my no relationship rule. I knew D would never abandon Noah for getting involved with me, but what if *I* scared him off?

The full me experience wasn't for the weak of heart. Old me threw myself into situations without thinking about the consequences. New me wanted to change that pattern, starting now apparently.

That didn't mean I wouldn't eventually screw everything sideways. Something told me Noah was up for the challenge, but was I?

My car pulled up, and I climbed in without a solid answer.

7

Noah

Mac probably didn't know, but I could hear every time he brought a girl into the apartment. My room was the one closest to the front door, and Mac couldn't be quiet if his life depended on it.

I didn't mind. Hell, good for him, but tonight, I wished he'd gone elsewhere. Like every night since Chloe had moved here, I couldn't sleep. My dick didn't need the reminder we were on our own for the foreseeable future.

A giggle came from the hallway, vaguely familiar, but I wasn't interested in playing name that hookup.

The last time I'd invited a girl home, I'd woken up to find her filming me while I slept. I'd been naked, face-down on the bed, with the sheets barely covering my ass. She claimed she wanted something to remember me by, but she didn't stop me when I erased the footage and quickly kicked her ass out.

My skin itched just thinking about it. Monica something. She'd reminded me of Chloe, and maybe my imagination had filled in some of the better traits. We'd gone out a few times before I brought her back here, but getting to know her hadn't stopped her from destroying my privacy without my consent.

It might as well have been a hookup considering my interest was based solely on her resemblance to the girl I couldn't have. I scrubbed a hand down my face. Not a nice move, now that I thought about it, but I'd put *some* effort into separating the real woman from the dream. Then again, if she'd been a hookup, I might not have been so pissed at the breach of trust.

Maybe Chloe was on to something there.

With a groan, I rolled over and shoved my pillow into a more comfortable position. I'd admitted the truth to Chloe yesterday over pizza, and strangely, I didn't regret it. She'd helped distance me from Craig's call, and she'd let me touch her.

A fact my dick hadn't forgotten.

I'd pushed against my self-imposed boundaries by kissing her cheek and spent the rest of the day wishing I could give my mouth free rein. A thud came from the hall-way, or possibly Mac's room, and I shoved my face into my pillow. Nothing good would come from this train of thought. I knew from experience.

Imagining any part of me on Chloe left me desperate and aching. I needed to focus on something else or I'd never get to sleep. Or... I could reach out to her and see what happened. She'd shown up last time I'd texted her, but would she do it again?

I rolled over to stare at the shadows on the ceiling. Only one way to find out. With banked excitement, I unlocked my phone and sent her a text.

Distract me. The message immediately flagged as read,

and I waited to see what she'd do. With Chloe, I was never sure.

The fire in my dorm wasn't entirely an accident.

Mission accomplished. I was suddenly wide awake with a smile on my face. *Ah, so we were right to be concerned about your pyromaniac habits?*

No. Ass. Do you want the story or not?

I did, but I wanted to hear it from her lips with her laying in the bed next to me. *Sorry. Please continue.*

First one's free... next one will cost you.

I could picture her grin as she shot my words back at me. *Understood.*

My roommate and I were using candles to do a sort of ritual. Turns out pictures burn a lot faster than we anticipated, and things got out of hand. My roommate dropped the flaming paper on the rug, then the fire alarm went off, complete with sprinklers.

Tell me you were in skimpy PJs.

In November?

Just trying to get the image right.

Sorry. Tank tops and flannel pants. Worst wet t-shirt contest ever.

I laughed quietly. *What did you do?*

Shivered in the street for an hour, then packed up my soggy belongings and moved here.

The urge to wrap my arms around her, keep her warm and safe, took over my thoughts. *Why were you burning pictures?*

Voodoo curse. Roommate's boyfriend cheated on her. Another strike against relationships.

Maybe she didn't choose the right person for the relationship. What the hell was wrong with me? Flirting with Chloe was the definition of a mixed signal. I didn't expect her to suddenly change her mind simply because I gave her another option. And what if she did? She'd still be D's sister, and I'd still have promised him I'd take care of her.

Chloe responded right away. *Maybe... but now it's my turn to ask a question. What are you wearing right now?*

Before I could come up with a reason to deflect her question, I flipped the camera and snapped a pic of myself in bed—bare chest, hair sticking up everywhere, but smiling. I hit send, knowing we were tipping toward the edge of friendship.

Is that a tattoo?

I took another look at the picture, and sure enough, the very edge of my tattoo was visible on my left shoulder. *How did you see that?*

I definitely didn't zoom in to ogle your chest. What is it?

My thumb hovered over the screen. I'd gotten the tattoo when I first met D, and I mostly kept it covered. People who saw it wanted to know what it meant, and I wasn't inclined to share a painful part of my past for their entertainment.

But Chloe was different.

A phoenix wrapped around my left shoulder.

How did I miss that? I've known you for years. Can I see it? In person, I mean.

The urge to invite her over was a physical ache. I was so hard I thought I'd sprain something, but nothing had really changed. Chloe wanted casual, and I didn't.

Next time, Trouble. Gotta make sure the flammables are put away first.

The negative response didn't slow her down for a second. *Cute, considering you're the one with a flaming bird inked on your body. Got any more tattoos you've failed to mention?*

You mean besides your name on my ass?

Ha! I knew you were pining for me.

Every day. The fast-paced banter slipped past my usual reserve until I realized what I'd admitted. Knowing Chloe, she'd think it was another joke, but I was one hundred percent serious.

I wasn't tired, but the line we shouldn't cross loomed large in front of me. *I should get some rest. Training early tomorrow. Thanks for the distraction.*

Anytime, Noah. Seriously. We're besties now. I'm going to text you every time something makes me think of you.

Goodnight, Chloe.

Sweet dreams, Noah.

If only she knew those dreams were of her. I fought sleep every night because waking up without her sucked ass.

———

CHLOE WASN'T KIDDING. Over the rest of the week, she texted me constantly. Memes. A scrap of conversation. A picture of a giant dog.

I didn't hate it, being on her mind all the time, and I responded to every single message. The ease with which she got me to talk should have worried me. I'd built my walls because I didn't want people to see inside, and Chloe walked right through them as if they weren't there.

By Friday, I'd developed a freaking Pavlovian response to my message notification sound. I walked into the dining hall at the training facility, and on cue, my lips edged toward a smile at the familiar tone. Chloe sent a winking meme with a message.

I have a surprise for you.

She didn't usually text me during lunch since she had class when our crew ate. Because of D's warning, I was surprised to find Chloe took her education seriously. She didn't skip, she had a thing for organizational spreadsheets, and she paid attention, even when I was trying to distract her.

Did her message mean I'd see her sometime soon? I tried to calm down the rush in my blood, but at this point, I might as well get used to the reaction.

The quiet chaos of an entire dining hall of people gathering for lunch didn't phase me. I liked being able to blend in with the rest of the athletes and enjoy the time with my friends. Our usual table was in the corner with a booth on one side and chairs on the other. It helped us accommodate the constantly changing group size.

I was running late today, which meant I'd probably be squeezed into the booth. Even in a place meant for large people, the seating arrangements tended to be too small for me. At least the chairs let me spread out.

The spicy scent of curry wafted to me, and I scanned the food offerings as I passed. My stomach growled, making me walk a little faster. I came around the giant plant wall in the middle of the room and cursed when I saw Mac, Shaw, and RJ had taken the chairs.

My heart tripped when I noticed the curvy brunette sitting in the booth next to Eva. Chloe looked up, and her smile brightened when she spotted me. For once, I didn't mind squeezing.

I slid into the booth next to her and took stock of the table. Mac and Shaw had mostly empty plates in front of them, RJ had a disgustingly chunky green smoothie, and Chloe had a salad she'd barely touched.

Apparently, only Eva had bothered to wait for me. Nothing new. Before I could grab food from the buffet, Chloe dropped a Dallas newspaper in front of me.

"Congratulations, Noah."

I had no idea what she was talking about, but she'd drawn a red circle on the top page around the headline of an article. "For what?"

"You were named one of the top college football players to watch this coming year."

I frowned and grabbed the paper, skimming the article she'd marked. The author basically did a bullet point list of the top twenty-five offensive players in college football. I was on there, with a weird little bio, along with Shaw, Mac, RJ, and Holbrook, our top running back.

The choices seemed arbitrary, though each entry got a paragraph or two explaining why they were on the list. The author was clearly a fan of TU, but our program got written up a lot. Hell, we were the reigning champions of college football.

All that said, I'd never been mentioned in any of the press before.

I held up the paper. "Did you guys see this?"

Mac grinned. "Yeah. Chloe showed it to us before you got here. Not that you don't deserve it, but I was lowkey more impressed she found an actual physical copy."

"What do you mean?"

Shaw pulled out his phone, fiddled with it for a second, then slid it across the table to me. "That article is all over the place. Harper emailed Riley the link this morning. Welcome to the club—benefits include nonstop invasions of your privacy and speculation about the size of your junk."

Mac scoffed. "No speculations necessary. I'll go on record as having a monster cock."

Eva rolled her eyes, and I winced. Not about Mac's genitals, though he wasn't lying. Invasions of privacy ranked right up there with zombie apocalypse and a torn ACL as my worst nightmares.

I didn't know how to respond to being recognized nationally as *good at my job*. There were any number of other talented football players they could have chosen—probably should have chosen. I loved playing football, and I was grateful every day that my skill had gotten me a free ride to college. But I wasn't interested in the fame or the accompanying sacrifices.

The others broke off into a discussion of the other players on the list, and I tilted my head toward Chloe.

"Why aren't you in class?"

She bumped my shoulder. "Cancelled. I thought I'd see why you guys make such a fuss about the food here."

"And?"

"It's fine—a salad is a salad—but the company can't be beat." She nodded at Mac explaining a play using French fries and cherry tomatoes.

Eva reached over and ate one of the defenders as Mac loudly complained. Under the table, Chloe's leg pressed against mine. Her eyes stayed on Mac's drama, but the weight of awareness settled in my chest.

Her gaze flicked up at me, and I knew I wasn't the only one feeling it. Our crew had plenty of women join us for lunch, but only Chloe elicited this kind of response.

Mac swept the rest of his veggie teams onto his plate, setting it back on the table with a clatter. "Okay, enough chit-chat. I have a serious topic."

Shaw groaned. "I'm not weighing in on shaving your chest again. Once was enough."

"Nah, man. I'm working with this 5K for one of my classes, and I think we should sign up." Mac grinned, like he'd presented us with the best idea all day.

Chloe sent him a horrified look. "You want us to what?"

"Run a 5K. It's only three miles, barely a warm-up."

She snorted. "For you. I don't run unless something's chasing me, and even then, there's a solid chance I'll just let it take me down."

RJ snickered, and Mac pouted at her. "You too?"

"Oh hell no. I'll be running. Someone has to keep your ego in check."

Mac held up his hands. "It's for charity—the fourth annual Furry Scurry. All proceeds go to the Lucky Duck Rescue."

Eva linked her arm through Chloe's. "I'm not running either, but I agreed to man one of the booths. You can be my booth buddy."

"Finally, a request in my skill set." Her gaze landed on me. "Are you going to run, Noah?"

Today was the first I'd heard of Mac's plan, but I could get in on it if we didn't have practice or training on race day. "Sure. Shaw?"

Parker stretched his arm behind RJ. "I'll be there watching my girl smoke Mac. You and I can jog along with the rest of the mortals."

Mac raised both arms. "It's settled. Furry Scurry at eight a.m. next Saturday."

Chloe dropped her head onto her arms. "Dammit, Mac. Physical exertion at eight a.m. should be considered torture."

I chuckled, thinking about the years I'd spent getting up early to go work out. "We'll make it worth your while."

She turned her head to peek at me. "Promise?"

Her quiet question sounded innocent, but I could see the speculation in her eyes. Chloe was still playing the game.

Too bad I couldn't resist playing right along with her.

"Yeah, Chloe. I promise."

She gave me a half-smile and nudged my leg. "Go get your food. And bring me some French fries, please."

I nodded my head once and stood, fully aware that she had me wrapped around her finger. If she wanted fries, I'd bring her an entire plate. Halfway to the buffet, my phone vibrated in my pocket with a call.

Everyone I'd actually take a call from was sitting in the corner, which didn't negate the chance that one of them was lazy and wanted me to grab something extra. I juggled two stoneware plates and yanked my phone free.

A random number with an area code I didn't recognize scrolled across the screen. Spam call, probably. I sent it to voicemail, just in case, and went in search of fries.

8

Chloe

I was going to kill Mac. Mornings were the worst, and happy, fit people stretching with big smiles on their faces could fuck right off. A tall, skinny guy wearing shorts only slightly longer than a Speedo blocked my path as he jogged in place. I considered kicking him in the shin, but it seemed like too much effort.

The sun peeked over the trees, warming me a little bit in the cold morning air, and I searched the crowd for Eva's tiny body. She'd said the booth would be next to the warm-up area. Except the booths were actually tents with solid sides, and I couldn't see into any of them unless I drew even with the tables inside.

With no other options, I scooted past shorts guy, who was definitely not wearing enough layers, and started walking along the line of mini-tents set up next to the sidewalk. The first wave of the race didn't start for another forty-five minutes, so I took my time people-watching.

Since I missed the carpool that morning, I kept watch for Noah and the others too. *Missed* was a generous description. I'd thrown a pillow at Eva's head when she tried to wake me up. The rest of them had piled into Mac's Jeep, and I'd gone back to sleep. For a solid fifteen minutes.

Damn Mac and damn mornings... and damn Noah for the naughty dreams that didn't leave me feeling all that rested.

When the negativity threatened to strangle me, I stopped in a patch of sunshine and lifted my face to the warmth. Old me lived on those brittle feelings of desperation and anger. She would have laughed off the prospect of running for fun and gone out clubbing with her girls, stumbling into bed around the time Eva and the others were leaving for the park.

I didn't want to be that person anymore.

My angry tirade was rooted in fatigue and the deep-seated fear of inadequacy I'd struggled with my whole life. No one here deserved my wrath. Might as well try to enjoy the experience.

It was a beautiful morning, despite the chill in the air. My sweater and jeans kept me warm, and I was damn cute in my red peacoat. I had a paper cup of coffee with nowhere else to be. Nothing to complain about there.

In a sign the universe was rewarding me for my improved attitude, a group of broad, muscular guys jogged past me in sweats and TU shirts. I took a sip of my coffee and followed them with my gaze, along with most of the people congregating.

The crowd parted as if royalty were passing, but I didn't think they were football players. For one, I knew most of the football royalty. For two, they moved differently. I couldn't explain the distinction.

One in the back with a beanie pulled low over his dark hair slowed his pace as he drew even with the booths. He zeroed in on one of the tables, frowned, then sped up again to catch his crew. His face looked familiar, but I couldn't place where I'd seen him before.

I moved in the same general direction, dodging a few more groups as I fed my curiosity. The interior of the booth came into view, and my brows flew up at the sight of Eva flirting with another hot athlete type.

Interesting. The running royal seemed personally upset, which made me wonder how Eva knew him. See, new me was already much happier than the crankier, old version. Bonus, I'd found Eva.

I finished off the last of my coffee and eyed the banner hanging from the table. The words *Adopt Me Today!* appeared over a picture of a cluster of ducks that looked like someone had dumped them out of a bucket. What had I gotten myself into?

Eva's latest conquest wandered off with a dazed look on his face, and she finally noticed me, waving enthusiastically. I tossed my empty cup in a trash can close by and joined her in the tent.

She hugged me as if I hadn't tried to decapitate her this morning with flying bedding. "Great coat. It'll really helps draw the eye."

"Thanks," I drawled. "Should I stand out here like a barker pulling the people in?"

"Nah, you're going to take it off soon anyway—it's not that cold. Just stand behind the table next to me and look cute. It doesn't take much more than that."

She scooted over so I could assume my position, and I leaned forward to check how far I could see. "This is a really inefficient set-up. How close are we to the starting and finishing lines?"

Eva pointed, and I caught sight of the giant inflatable arch with the words *START/FINISH* hanging from yet another banner. I blamed the running royalty for distracting me.

"Do they run right past here?"

"Yeah, we're supposed to catch their attention before they leave and right before they finish."

I frowned. "For what purpose?"

She shrugged. "To collect donations? Honestly, I didn't get a lot of information when I arrived. We're working one of the Lucky Duck booths, and the organizer mentioned sample pets."

My brows shot up. "What the hell is a sample pet? Like here, try this one out to see if it's a good fit? That's horrible. Also, there aren't any animals here."

A corner of her lips lifted in a half-smirk. "You noticed that, did you?"

I waved at the empty concrete around our feet. "What's their plan?"

Before she could answer, a frazzled woman in a bright purple Lucky Duck Rescue shirt and neon green sunglasses hurried up to our table carrying a large cardboard box. She set the box down gently and pushed the sunglasses into her hair.

"Thank you so much for volunteering. Usually we'd have some of our regulars at this booth, but three of them came down with the nasty flu that's going around. I'm Alexis by the way."

She shook both our hands and checked her clipboard. "Eva and Chloe, right?"

"That's us," Eva chirped, far too eager. I sent her a suspicious look, and she patted my arm. "I signed you up when I got here."

Alexis nodded, shoving the clipboard back under her arm. "Great. I gave you the easy one. People love ducks. The baby pool is right over there." She pointed through the open back part of the tent to a baby-sized blue inflatable pool leaning against the side of a hut. A black hose attached to the hut lay curled in the grass next to it.

I turned to stare in horror at the box, which was jostling on its own and making peeping noises. "Are there live ducks in there?"

Alexis laughed. "Yes, well, ducklings technically. We had a brood that lost the mother, so we've been taking care of them. John is somewhere..." She looked around and nodded at a short man walking toward us carrying another box. "There he is. John has the playpen and the other goodies. You set up the pen, put the pool inside and fill it with water, then let the ducklings free."

I shared a shocked look with Eva. "What's our goal here?"

Alexis tilted her head at me in confusion as John deposited his box next to the duck box on the table. "You're taking care of the ducks. Let people hold them—gently—and collect donations in the cash box. If anyone is interested in adopting one, send them over to the main tent." She pointed to a large purple tent on the far side of the start/finish arch.

Oh my god, I was going to kill Mac, then Eva. "Isn't it too cold for baby ducks to be out here?"

Her gaze lingered on my coat, and she sent me a reassuring smile, which did not reassure me in the slightest. "They'll be fine. You're going to do great."

With a jaunty wave, she disappeared among the growing throng of runners gathering in the open space. I scanned the crowd, noting the distinct lack of coats or cold weather clothing. Maybe I'd overdressed for the day.

I eyed the box making garbled quacking noises, then

turned to Eva. "Who in their right mind would put a stranger in charge of live baby ducks?"

Eva peeked inside the first box and smiled. "They're not as small as I thought they'd be."

"Don't they just look like those marshmallow Peep things?" I joined her at the table, and she moved over to give me space to peer inside.

Five ducks with fuzzy-looking feathers stared back at me. They had different splotches of brown on their yellow bodies, and they looked like miniature versions of full-size ducks. One of them with an almost entirely brown head quacked at Eva, starting a riot with the rest of them.

"How old are they?" I asked her.

Eva shook her head, pulling her long blonde hair back into a high ponytail. "How should I know? I'm not a duck whisperer. Hush, you."

The last bit was aimed at the duck with the brown head, who seemed to be the leader. His gaze locked on her, and he stopped quacking.

I stood there another few seconds, but they stayed quiet. "Are you sure?"

She flipped me off and walked toward the baby pool. "You set up the pen. I'll get the pool ready."

We worked in tandem, and with the help of the internet, we built a serviceable duck habitat with the supplies provided by Alexis and John. I shed my coat in the first two minutes while I wrestled the pen into place on the grass. By the time we were ready to move the ducks into their vacation home, I was sweating and wishing I'd brought a regular T-shirt like everyone else.

"I could organize this event so much better," I muttered, watching people start to make beelines for us as soon as they realized there were ducklings in the warm-up area.

Eva tilted her head at me while wrangling the baby ducks into the playpen. "Why don't you?"

My gaze snapped back to her. "What?"

The bossy duckling with the brown head quacked at her imperiously. She turned it to face the other babies, but it promptly spun around to try to follow her.

Eva sighed, reorienting it again. "I know we haven't talked about your life goals, but I got the impression from D you preferred to drift. Is he wrong?"

I crossed my arms, fully aware of how defensive I looked. "Yes and no."

She waited for me to explain, crouched in a playpen surrounded by ducks, but I didn't like the answers I had. I held out as the shame and tension built inside me like the world's worst heartburn.

Eva turned the duck around again, then quickly stepped out of the pen before it could follow her. "I know it's easier to hold everything inside, but you might feel better if you talked about it. Especially since I'm already intimately aware of how *not* perfect your brother is. I was in the front lines when he stuck his head up his ass with Nadia."

I snickered. Nadia, my brother's girlfriend, was my favorite. If they ever broke up, I'd probably keep her and toss D to the side. Not that they ever would. They were disgustingly in love, and D would do anything for her.

Yet another example of D succeeding at life while I flailed around lighting things on fire. I scrunched my nose at the bitter thought. Maybe I *should* talk about some of this before it ate me from the inside out.

I bit my lip, unsure where to start. "It's easier to drift than it is to make a plan and utterly fail at it. Ask me how I know."

Eva flashed a smile at me as she picked up a compliant duck for one of the runners to hold. "You're not a failure."

"I'm not a winner either. Unlike D, who is good at everything. College was supposed to be my chance to separate from his sphere of influence, but it turns out I make bad decisions when left to my own devices."

Eva returned the duck and thanked the guy for his donation before responding. "From where I'm standing, you make great decisions. After the dorm incident—" I was grateful for her restraint in describing the fire. "You chose to take the best option given you and continue college. You're making an active effort to befriend us even though I know it has to be hard to come in after the fact. Just so you know, none of us see you as the second-string Asher."

Tears pricked my eyes, but I blinked them away. Eva saw a lot more than I gave her credit for. "Thanks, though I think you're a little biased. As for college, I'm drifting because I'm not sure what I want to do with my life. Not everyone has a clear path like all of you do. A communications degree may seem generic, but it gives me a broad starting point in finding a career. As for staying in school, I'm not interested in throwing my future away because of a stupid mistake, which is why my new life plan involves avoiding future mistakes."

She raised a brow. "How's that going for you?"

I shrugged. "Not bad. Ninety-three days fire free."

"On the plus side, if you *do* light something on fire, we have a whole ass pond right here to put it out." She gestured at the duck pen, setting off another round of quacking.

The ringleader duck waddled right up to the edge of the pen where Eva stood and tried to knock it over with his face. I had no idea how to determine a duck's sex, but Eva tended to have this effect on males. Probably a boy.

I tilted my head at the little duck trying his hardest to get to Eva. "We should name him."

She used her leg to keep the pen upright, and he promptly cuddled up next to her ankle through the mesh. "We *should not* name him."

I grinned. "He looks like a Henry."

"I didn't sign up for this," she cursed under her breath, shoring up the sagging side.

Neither did I, but here we were—working through my issues on a sunny morning surrounded by besotted waterfowl.

9

Noah

"Dammit, Henry, get back here."

I nearly tripped on my own feet as Chloe's voice reached me. Mac, Shaw, RJ, and I were working on some dynamic stretches in the warm-up area, but I hadn't seen her. I'd looked.

"Anyone seen Eva and Chloe?"

Mac nudged my arm and jerked his chin toward a rowdy crowd gathered around one of the booths. Something told me Chloe would be in the center of all that attention.

"How did you get involved in this again?" I asked him.

"Class project. My group decided to run a charity event."

I frowned. "You helped organize this whole thing?"

He laughed and pulled his leg up behind him in a quad stretch, making his eye-searing neon pink shorts ride up to indecent levels. "Nah, we're doing a fictional event based on this one. The Lucky Duck people were nice enough to let us sit in on their planning."

I stopped scanning the crowd for ten seconds to stare at him. "Classes just started. When did you have time to sit in on event planning?"

"Well, not me specifically. Madison sat in on the meetings and took notes. You know how group projects work. Everyone takes a part of the project."

"What part did you do?"

He switched legs, reminding me of a flamingo. "I suggested the 5K. That way I could show off what I do best while also helping animals."

I shook my head at him and started toward the chaos. "I'm going to check on the girls."

"Tell Eva I said lunch is on her if I win." Mac saluted me and hopped over to harass RJ.

I definitely was not passing along Mac's message. Eva had no problem taking out the messenger if she didn't like the message.

One of the benefits of being bigger than everyone else was people tended to move out of the way without being asked. I waded through the crowd with little effort and finally found Chloe, laying on her stomach in the grass as she glared into the gap between the cloth tent walls.

I winced at the mud under her pale green sweater. "Need some help?"

"Oh thank god. Your arms are freakishly long." Eva piped up from my right.

I tore my eyes away from Chloe's ass, molded to perfection in her jeans, and caught sight of Eva crouched next to a soft-sided enclosure full of live ducks. No wonder they were surrounded by onlookers.

Chloe sighed in disgust and kicked out at me with her leg, connecting with my running shoe. "I could use another twelve inches of reach. Henry the escape artist got out of the pen and waddled his little butt between the tents."

I crouched next to her shoulder and glanced into the hole. A small duck was clearly silhouetted by the light shining from the other end. The whole depth of the tent was barely longer than my arm.

"I think I can get him, but I need you to move."

Chloe pushed herself off the ground, muttering obscenities at the duck, the dirt, someone named Alexis, and the race as a whole. It was an impressively long list in a short amount of time.

I got to my feet next to her, moving to the side of the hole so as not to startle the duck. "Having a hard morning?"

She blew a strand of hair out of her face. "I thrive in challenging situations."

"Looks like you might be losing the challenge."

"What?"

I nodded at her chest, where brown and green smears marred the front of her sweater. She looked down and added another curse to her diatribe.

"Here," I muttered, then pulled my shirt over my head.

It wasn't too cold out, and I probably had an extra in Mac's car somewhere. I held the material out to Chloe, but her eyes locked on my left shoulder. As if in a daze, she reached up to trace the tip of my tattoo.

My arm dropped, and I stood still while she circled me, following her with my gaze. Her fingers traced the sweeping lines making up the phoenix's body, trailing down my back in a blaze of fiery feathers and need.

If she kept touching me, I wouldn't be able to hide my reaction from her in my running shorts. I cleared my suddenly dry throat and turned to capture her hand. Chloe looked up at me, lust chasing the questions in her eyes.

"Your phoenix is beautiful—"

Eva whistled from her spot distributing ducks to unsuspecting runners. "Can you stop ogling each other long enough to get Henry, please?"

Shit, we'd completely forgotten about the duck. At her raised voice, a loud quack came from the hole. A second later, a mottled brown head poked out. Henry shook his whole body, then ran with webbed feet slapping the mud straight toward Eva.

She shrieked and tried to put down the duck she was already holding. "Catch him! Catch him!"

Chloe blinked, then lunged for the bird. She scooped him up before he could reach his goal, and he let her know his displeasure by trying to bite her between angry quacks.

"Bad duck." Chloe scolded as she walked him the rest of the way to Eva.

She set him in the enclosure, and he wiggled his butt with his beak in the air. I've never seen a clearer look of disdain on an animal, and I'd met Shaw's cat.

I couldn't hold in the laughter, and I wasn't the only one. Most of the people standing around had seen the show. Chloe took a bow, then stomped over and snatched my shirt from my limp hand.

"Thanks. I could use a wardrobe change since I think we're here for another couple of hours while they go through all the heats."

I pressed my lips together to try to smother my reaction, but my shaking shoulders gave me away.

Chloe narrowed her eyes at me. "Don't you have a race to run?"

People had started lining up behind her, including Mac, who was hard to miss in his ridiculous shorts, but I wasn't in a hurry. Her eyes widened as I drew closer. I touched the bottom of her chin, tilting her head up.

The tip of her tongue came out to wet her lips, and hunger burst to life inside me—feral and completely inappropriate. For an agonizingly short moment, I saw the same wild need on her face, but just as quickly, she hid it behind her sunny mask.

I wiped a bit of dirt from her cheek, lingering longer than strictly necessary.

Chloe offered a breathless thanks and I nodded, moving away for my own sanity. Eva was ten feet away, no doubt taking notes, and I didn't need her getting involved.

Mac called my name from the starting line.

"Don't chase any ducks into the pond," I warned her. "I don't have any more shirts to give you."

"Good luck," she called.

I could feel her gaze on me as I walked toward the rest of the group. Mac took my relative nudity in stride, but RJ grinned at me.

"Couldn't find a way to give her your shorts too?" she teased.

I gave her a bland look. "Shouldn't you be focusing on your boyfriend instead of my ass? He could probably benefit from some advice on how to use his legs in a forward motion."

Shaw shouldered between us. "Hey, I can run."

RJ patted his arm. "Don't worry, honey, I'll bring you something nice back from the front."

"Not all of us sprint for fun, Lorelai. I have other skills." He caught the back of her neck and hauled her in for a kiss.

I looked away, feeling sort of pervy despite sharing a living room and kitchen with them. Now that they could date out in the open, they weren't great about limiting their extracurriculars to the bedroom.

My attention drifted past Mac, chatting at another runner, and over to Chloe. She'd gone back to duck-sitting, wearing my shirt. The soft material draped over her curves, down past her thighs. A faint blush stained her cheeks, and I wondered if I had anything to do with it.

Shaw elbowed me from the other side, and I realized the organizers were doing a welcoming speech, marking the start of the race. RJ had joined Mac up at the front of the group.

The horn sounded, and we all took off. I wasn't a speed demon like Mac or RJ, but I *was* an athlete with a certain amount of pride—I wasn't going to half-assed jog a distance I could run in my sleep. Most of the pack fell behind me, but Shaw stayed even.

He slanted his gaze at me. "I recognize that look."

I grunted, trying to focus on keeping an even pace. My specialty was explosive speed, not endurance, so I liked the challenge of spreading the effort over multiple miles. Shaw ran for fun though. He could afford to waste his oxygen talking, but I needed all of mine.

When I didn't take the bait, he tried a more direct route.

"What's going on with you and Chloe?"

"You want to talk about this now?" I nodded at the people running within easy listening distance.

Shaw shrugged. "Turns out I don't care who hears when we're talking about someone else's love life."

"Lucky me," I panted.

"You don't have to talk if you don't want to, but I'm here to listen if you want to work some shit out."

I focused on the swinging pink ponytail of the girl a few yards in front of us. When Shaw and RJ were going through their stuff last semester, I'd said something similar to him. Had I known the support would come back to bite me in the ass, I might have kept my mouth shut.

But I didn't. These guys were my real family. I could talk to them—about anything—without reprisal. The reminder loosened up some of the tension in my shoulders.

"Chloe is... Chloe." I blew out a breath, then immediately regretted it when I had to suck in air.

"That shouldn't make sense, but I get what you mean," he said.

I highly doubted he knew what went through my mind when I thought of Chloe. Did I really want to clue him in? What did it matter when I didn't plan to follow through on any of those thoughts?

"There's nothing going on with us."

"She's hot," he mused. "In a 'might set fire to your belongings' kind of way."

The fierce urge to both defend Chloe and warn Shaw away took me by surprise. I choked back the angry retort at the last second, choosing deflection over direct confrontation.

"RJ isn't enough for you anymore?" I didn't entirely succeed in keeping the sharp tone out of my voice, but maybe Shaw wouldn't notice.

He snorted. "Riley is it for me, but you're pretty salty for someone who's not involved."

I watched the trees ahead of us slowly creep closer, struggling to verbalize the maelstrom Chloe churned up inside me. Words didn't do the chaos justice.

Shaw took my silence in stride, like he normally did, and kept talking as if I'd responded.

"I admit your poker face is better than mine, but I know you. Every time Chloe is around, you have this caveman protective thing happening."

"She's a magnet for trouble," I muttered. "Am I supposed to let her struggle when I could help?"

He pointed at me. "Ah, but helping isn't all you want."

"No," I finally ground out. Nothing drastic changed with the admission. Lightning didn't suddenly strike me down for having dirty thoughts about my best friend's sister, but another wall crumbled into sand.

I wanted Chloe, craved her. Not only her body—I wanted her smile and her laugh and her willingness to take chances no matter the consequences. If she were interested in a relationship, I'd be fucked because I wouldn't be able to tell her no. I might still be fucked.

Shaw nodded as if I'd said all of that out loud. "That's what I thought. Is D holding you back? Because even he knows Chloe will do whatever she damn well feels like."

"I promised him I'd take care of her."

"We all did, and in that capacity, I'd stop you cold if I thought you'd hurt her." He shrugged. "You won't. I'm more concerned about your feelings... and also your belongings. I don't want to have to evacuate if she decides to light your shit up."

I grunted out a laugh. This was why these guys were my family. Shaw didn't pull punches, and he had a point. I *wouldn't* hurt Chloe. She didn't believe that yet, but maybe if I could convince her, she'd be willing to take a chance on me.

But I wouldn't do shit until I talked to D. I wasn't asking permission, but he deserved to know my intentions for his sister. An image of Chloe on her knees in front of me, dark hair wrapped around my fist, green eyes shining with mischief, nearly made me trip. I winced. Might want to keep the details to myself.

Since Shaw hadn't shunned me for my admission, I might as well unburden myself all the way. "She doesn't want anything serious."

Shaw's brows shot up. "And you do?"

I glared at his disbelieving tone. We all knew Mac had a new conquest every week, but I stayed away from the ball bunnies. Or I tried. Excluding last year's video incident, I hadn't brought a girl back to the apartment in months.

"I don't do all the hookup bullshit."

"I'm not suggesting marriage, man. There's a whole lot of gray area between a hookup and an engagement. You could try exploring some of that with the girl you actually want to be with instead of shitty stand-ins."

My gaze shot to his, and he smirked.

Shaw shook his head. "You thought I wouldn't notice the last girl looked like Chloe?"

"You were busy getting all twisted up over RJ."

"I was busy, not blind. Here's what I think. Tell D you're interested in her, tell *her* you're interested in her, let nature take its course. I'll make sure the smoke detector has fresh batteries."

I shoved him sideways, making him hop off the road where he had to narrowly avoid a bush. His idea wasn't bad. This seemed like a face-to-face conversation, so I could talk to D at the alumni dinner. Bonus, waiting a little longer would give me time to decide Shaw was full of shit and change my mind.

He didn't let a close encounter with the foliage slow him down. He caught up to me easily. What the hell? I could feel my breath sawing in and out of my lungs, despite all the running Coach made us do at practice. How much farther was the finish line?

Shaw didn't seem winded at all, which made me want to toss him into another bush. "Okay, then, new topic. Do you know what's going on with Mac?"

I frowned in his direction. "What do you mean?"

"He's spending a lot of time in his room, but I never see

him bring girls in anymore. And when was the last time he dragged us to a party?"

My unease deepened as I replayed the last few weeks in my mind. Admittedly, I'd been distracted by a certain new addition to our friend group, but Shaw was right. Mac had been with a girl the night I'd texted Chloe the first time.

Normally, the girls don't stay the night, but I never heard her leave. I hadn't noticed any other girls since then.

From the direction of the finish line, Mac let out a shout and zipped past us going the opposite direction with his shirt tied around his head. He'd take any excuse to show off his abs. RJ followed him at a slightly slower pace, waving at us as she passed.

I turned to Shaw. "Seems normal to me."

He shrugged again and picked up the pace, apparently trying to kill me in front of all the people waiting at the end of the damn race, including a smirking Chloe. A tight band across my chest attempted to steal all my air. Maybe I couldn't run this in my sleep, but I wasn't going to finish in a huffing mess.

My phone vibrated in my pocket, but I ignored it. No way could I find extra oxygen to answer it now. I pushed past the weakness, and matched Shaw step for step, valiantly keeping my eyes straight ahead instead of watching a certain dark-haired beauty guard her ducks.

10

Chloe

I smelled like duck shit, which I quickly learned was both pungent and unpleasant. Luckily, all I had to do was lower my nose to Noah's shirt and his scent took over my brain. On the third or fourth sniff, Eva caught me and shook her head.

"You don't have to try to be sneaky about it. If you want to sniff the man, just do it."

The teenage girl waiting for the duck in Eva's hands swallowed hard and very pointedly didn't look at the lanky kid next to her who wanted Henry.

Eva smiled at her and handed over her charge. "Not you. Though if you want to sniff a guy, definitely go for it. Maybe ask first. Consent is key."

The girl's eyes widened, and she slowly backed away cuddling one of the nice ducks—in the opposite direction of the kid next to her. He blushed, confirming my suspicion they'd showed up together. I gave Henry a stern look and set him in lover boy's open palms.

"Don't put him down," I reminded the kid, who followed the girl.

Eva wiped her hands on the back of her jeans and turned to me, completely ignoring the rest of the line. "You and Noah would be good together. He needs someone to pull him out of his head."

My brows drew together. "That's all you have to say? You're not going to interfere?"

"I don't think this is a situation where you need a kick in the ass, but let me know if I'm wrong. I love doing the pushy best friend thing."

A warm little ball glowed in my chest at her off-hand designation of best friend. I had friends from my previous school, but none of them had reached out at all since I'd left. Not exactly a deep connection there.

I'd known Eva for years, but she'd always been in the casual acquaintance category of D's friends. Guess she'd been promoted. Nothing would make me discuss my emotions with my old group of friends, but Eva barely needed me to speak to suss out my issues. She'd helped D with Nadia, maybe she could help new me navigate the foreign land of good decisions.

"I appreciate your restraint, but the situation with Noah is complicated. Maybe after the race we could grab coffee and over analyze everything."

"Sounds good." She nudged me toward the next person in line. "Ducks before dicks."

Our booth was popular, which kept us busy until the guys and Riley approached the end of the race where we were stationed. I was cuddling the smallest duckling and scolding Henry for nipping at one of his nestmates, when I caught my first glimpse of Noah. He came around the bend jogging at an easy lope and smiling.

I almost dropped the sweet duck. Happy Noah was a

sight to behold. Maybe the early morning had been worth it after all.

Mac and Riley finished first, and they took off in the opposite direction for a reverse lap passing Shaw in a neon pink blur. I spared them a glance, but they couldn't hold my attention. My gaze returned to Noah, locked on, and refused to go anywhere else.

He didn't look my direction, but the heat building in my belly made me hyper aware of him. Sweat glistened on his bare chest, and I followed the arrow of dark hair down to where it disappeared into his gray shorts.

Most of the O-line guys my brother had played with were big and hefty, built to use their weight to stop forward momentum. Noah broke the mold. Hell, he might break *me* if we ever gave in to my dirtier urges.

Eva bumped my shoulder, and I tore my gaze away from his crotch, hoping the heat on my cheeks could be blamed on the sun. She sent me a knowing look and exchanged the nearly sleeping duck I was holding for Henry.

"It's your turn to keep him occupied."

The little duck smacked my hand with a wing trying to get back to Eva and let out the saddest quack I'd ever heard. For a fleeting second, I commiserated with him. It was hard to be denied when all you wanted was to be close to the person you... I blew out a breath and purposely changed my train of thought.

Noah veered off from Shaw to come our way. The crowd parted to let him through as he slowed to a walk with his arms crossed over his head. Henry squeaked at me, and I realized I'd been squeezing him a little too hard.

I stooped to put him back in the enclosure, not convinced it was a good idea to be holding a live animal at the moment. My head bent to take a whiff of Noah's shirt, and I caught myself at the last second.

Definitely wouldn't be able to blame my flaming face on the sun now. At least he wouldn't know *why* I was blushing.

"Hey, Trouble. Keeping Henry contained?"

Eva lit up at the nickname Noah had bestowed the night I found out about his tattoo. For weeks, I'd been trying to come up with a way to get a peek without straight up asking him to get naked. Turned out I simply needed to roll around in the mud.

I should thank Henry.

"I'm not sure that's possible. Henry was born for chaos," I belatedly responded.

His lips tilted up in the ghost of a smile. "Sounds familiar."

Eva fanned herself. "Well, this is fun—standing here, also a part of the conversation."

Noah chuckled and he eyed Eva, then the crowd surrounding us in a vague bloblike line. "Can I steal Chloe away from her duties?"

Eva straightened and lifted one eyebrow. "Depends. What are your intentions?"

He crossed his arms. "Not your concern."

"Chloe is my concern, and as her bestie, I take my screening seriously."

I raised a hand. "Chloe is standing right here and can speak for herself."

"Shush, I'm helping," Eva stage-whispered to me.

"I thought you weren't going to get involved?" I hissed back.

She grinned and bent to scoop up a duck. "Can't help myself."

Noah shifted closer, letting a group of little kids scoot

past him. "I promised to make the early morning worth her while."

My inner muscles involuntarily clenched at the naughty potential of his words. The chances of him following through with multiple orgasms was low, but not zero. Eva eyed Noah while she leaned in to fill the food dish with a new scoop of pellets.

"You did promise that," she mused.

As much as I wanted to dive headfirst into the possibility of alone time with Noah, new me had other responsibilities to consider. "I think I have a while longer here."

Noah dropped an arm around Eva's shoulders and pulled her against his sweaty side. "Eva can handle the rest of the day, right?"

She patted his arm with her free hand. "Clearly you haven't been paying attention to the chaos Henry has wrought."

I gritted my teeth, fighting the sudden jealousy at their easy interaction. "I'm happy to stay, Eva."

With Eva's attention elsewhere, Henry squawked in a very un-ducklike manner, flapped his wings twice, and promptly launched himself off the wiggly edge of the pool in an attempt to catch one of the bugs buzzing around. He missed, flinging himself onto one end of the food dish instead and flipping it on top of himself.

Noah shook his head, staring at the mess in awe. "It's like you found your duck soulmate."

Eva waved us away. "It's only another two hours. Go on. You're shit at duck-sitting while distracted, and I'm not looking to chase Henry out of another small crevice."

I snorted, not about to argue the truth. Before I could ask about coffee later, the running royalty from earlier crossed the finish line en masse. Eva's smile shifted into a scowl as she caught sight of the guy in the beanie.

He glanced our way and narrowed his eyes at Eva, or maybe at Noah—the target was unclear.

"Asshole," she muttered under her breath, pulling free of Noah's grasp.

The last time I'd seen him suddenly popped up in my mind. The coffee shop and Eva's weird hatred. Noah followed her gaze with a frown.

"You know the hockey team?" he asked her.

Shit. No wonder they'd looked like athletes. The last thing I wanted was to come face to face with my previous drunken disaster of a hookup—the one who played on the hockey team.

Eva turned her back on coffee guy and replaced her glare with a sunny smile. "Nope. I'm a football girlie through and through."

"Good answer," Noah grumbled keeping his eyes on the group of guys a beat longer than strictly necessary.

I slipped my fingers into his and tugged him in the opposite direction. "You wanted me, and I'm all yours, at least for the next few hours. Studying still needs to happen tonight at which point you will be unceremoniously abandoned."

Noah's lips twitched as his attention returned to me. "Duly noted. I'd better make the best of the time I have then." His eyes flicked to Eva, and he jerked his head at our tent. "Can you grab her stuff when you're done?"

Eva blew a strand of hair out of her face and reached for one of the quiet ducks. "Yeah, but you're getting rid of every spider we come across for the foreseeable future."

"Deal. C'mon, Trouble. We're going for a walk."

Eva dismissed us with a distracted wave, and Noah led me deeper into the park, away from the group of hockey guys congregating around the finish line. He slowed his pace to match mine, allowing our tangled fingers to swing gently between us.

Tingles raced up my arm, and I briefly considered finding a nice hidden area to attempt a seduction. Old me was close to the surface today. I hadn't been with anyone since the hockey guy, not from lack of options—I simply wasn't interested in anyone except Noah.

My lady parts weren't too pleased with the time off, so they were raring to go, even if it meant a sweaty roll in the dirt. Except Noah wouldn't have expectations for a sexy outdoor encounter. Despite his attitude change, I didn't like the chance he'd turn me down for a second time. A prick of apprehension made me have second and third thoughts about whatever it was we were doing.

I snuck a glance at Noah and found him staring at me. "What?"

He smiled slowly. "It's fascinating, watching the thoughts cross your face."

"That's a new one. Most guys aren't interested in my thoughts when they're watching me."

Noah shrugged one shoulder. "Your mind is one of my favorite things about you. I can never anticipate what you'll do or say."

I wasn't sure how to respond, so I didn't. Boobs were easy. Guys liked my curves, some even liked my smart mouth, but no one had appreciated my chaotic nature before. What was I supposed to do with that?

Nothing. The answer was nothing. I tried to tug my hand free, but his fingers tightened.

"Trying to get away already? I thought you were all mine for the next few hours."

I pressed my lips together, not willing to admit that yes,

I'd planned to make an excuse and flee. His gaze dropped to my mouth, and my brain short-circuited, spewing nonsense.

"I don't want to give you the wrong idea. This isn't a date."

His smile widened. "I know. You don't date, but spending the afternoon with a friend isn't against the rules. If you're having second thoughts, I can send you back to Henry and his minions."

"Are you including Eva in the minions?"

"Yes. She finally met her match—a creature she can't control."

A laugh burst out of me, releasing some of the tension. "Don't let her hear you say that. Poor Henry would pay the price."

We strolled in the sun-dappled shade, and I forced myself to stop overthinking everything. It was a beautiful day, and I wanted to spend my time with a friend. It didn't have to mean anything more than that.

"Where are we going?"

"Across the park to a place I know. Speaking of which..." He dug his phone out with one hand, fired off a text, and slid it back into his shorts. "Had to tell Mac not to wait for me."

A quick glance over my shoulder confirmed we weren't heading for the parking lot. The second heat of runners, consisting mostly of families with strollers and wagons full of children, grouped up at the start line in the distance. They hadn't noticed the ducklings yet thanks to the heavy crowd, but I could imagine the rush once the kids caught sight of the babies.

I winced as I realized I'd left Eva alone to deal with the stampede. As pretty as this walk in the park was, mostly thanks to Noah's shirtless presence, guilt twinged in my belly. I had my phone in the back pocket of my jeans, though. If she needed help, she could call either of us.

"Does this place require clothing?" I slid my gaze over his chest—not ogling—and plucked at the material of his shirt covering my torso.

A big part of me wanted him to say no for the sheer pleasure of watching him walk around shirtless a while longer. The added bonus of being surrounded by his scent was pretty nice too.

"We'll be fine."

In true Noah fashion, he didn't offer anything else until the concrete path we were following dumped us out of the park on a side street I didn't recognize. A low wall separated us from the sidewalk, and across the empty road sat a tiny ice cream shop with a walk-up window.

Noah stepped over to the sidewalk and plucked me off the ground as if I weighed nothing. I'd seen him throw full grown men around like drunken dolls, so maybe to him I *did* weigh nothing. He gripped my waist, and my hands landed on his shoulders as he set me gently on the ground.

Neither of us moved for a long beat, and I thought the heat of his skin might sear me. My pulse roared in my ears, deafening with the need to explore. I wanted to drag my fingers down his chest to the ridges of his abs. Instead, I let him go and stepped back.

New me cheered at the restraint, but old me howled with repressed need. The back and forth was getting exhausting. I needed to get all the parts of me on the same page for once.

11

Chloe

"Ice cream?" I asked brightly, trying to mask my sudden retreat.

A flash of regret crossed his face, then he nodded at the squat building. "One of my professors told me about this place. All their flavors are locally made, and they've ruined me for any other ice cream."

I let out a dramatic gasp. "Even Blue Bell? Don't let any native Texans hear you."

He dragged a hand through his hair as he led me across the street. "I don't understand the obsession with Blue Bell. It's good, but so are a lot of other brands."

Up close, the white paint could use a new coat and the window had a crack running from top to bottom. A middle-aged guy with sandy blond hair, a green apron, and a huge smile greeted us from the other side.

"Good to see you, Noah. Who's your friend?"

"Chloe, this is David. He owns the place. David, Chloe."

David leaned his elbows on the counter in front of him and shifted his smile to me. "Nice to meet you, Chloe. Got a flavor in mind?"

"Strawberry?" There wasn't a sign anywhere with the options, so I went with my go-to. Everybody had strawberry.

David winked at me and turned to Noah. "Want the usual?"

Noah nodded, and the man moved away to scoop from the giant freezer behind him.

I raised a brow. "How often do you come here?"

A blush crept up his neck. "A couple times a week."

"Does Mac know?" Mac *loved* sweets. There was no way he'd known about this hidden ice cream stand and kept his mouth shut.

Noah scoffed. "I'm not sharing David's genius with that garbage disposal."

On cue, David reappeared with two cones. I took the pink one interspersed with chunks of strawberry, and Noah got something white with dark chunks.

"Cookies and cream?"

"Horchata and espresso."

I smirked at him, sort of sad I'd taken the easy route. "Fancy."

Noah chuckled as he led me back across the street to sit on the wall since the shack didn't offer seating on the small patch of grass surrounding the building. A breeze pushed warm air past us, and I had the strangest sensation of peace. I had nowhere to be and no responsibilities I was failing to fulfill.

No expectations and no failures. I felt good. Just good. Noah had given me that.

I peeked at him, and my eyes landed on the wing of his phoenix cupping his shoulder. The tattoo was beautiful—sinuous curves stretching across his back accented with vibrant slashes of red and yellow.

"Are you going to eat or stare at me?" he asked.

"I can do both." I took a bite, and my eyes nearly rolled back in my head. "Oh my god," I groaned.

Noah shifted next to me, but when I recovered enough from my sudden foodgasm to look his way, he was calmly eating his ice cream.

"Good, right?"

"I'm not leaving until I've tried every flavor." I licked an escaped bit off my lip, and Noah's eyes flared with heat. The amount of sexual tension between us was getting ridiculous. Time for a distraction. "Why do you play football?"

He blinked at the abrupt question. "TU gave me a full scholarship."

"Do you have fun with it?"

His face softened. "Yeah. Your brother is the reason for that."

I didn't want to talk about my brother, but if it got Noah to open up, I'd take it. "How so?"

"I had offers from several schools, but when I came to tour TU, D kept popping up everywhere. Talking up the program, inviting me out for meals, making me feel like I was a part of the team even though I hadn't chosen a school yet."

"That absolutely sounds like D. He makes every person he meets feel special. If anyone stands still long enough next to him, he'll turn them into family."

Noah laughed, low and rumbly, making me momentarily lose my train of thought. "I haven't had a lot of family in my life, so this one is important to me."

Right. Family. My brother. "Will you tell me why?"

He studied my face for a long moment. "I think I will."

But not yet. The unspoken words hovered between us until he crunched into his cone. "When I factored in TU's excellent post-graduation placement program, nowhere else could measure up."

I frowned. "You're not entering the draft?"

"No. Football is fantastic, but it's not my life."

Something in the way he said it—maybe the way he couldn't meet my eyes—made me think he wasn't telling the whole story. Not a full lie, but a complicated truth.

"What are you doing after college then?" I couldn't believe I hadn't asked before. Very few guys who played college football actually made it to the pros. D thought Noah was good enough to get a rookie contract, so I'd assumed he'd enter the draft with Shaw and Mac after next year.

"Elementary PE teacher."

My brows shot up. I had a lot of respect for teachers, especially ones dealing with little kids, but playing pro football didn't stop him from teaching after he retired. I couldn't imagine passing up on the fame and money associated with playing a sport professionally.

Fame had never been important to Noah, but the money from even a rookie contract would set him up for years to come. Not to mention he'd be doing something he loved. Was he truly not interested or did he not think he was good enough?

"Why?" I blurted out.

"I had a rough childhood, but my teachers made it better. I want to do the same thing. Kids deserve people who *want* to help them."

My insides melted into a puddle of goo at the image of this giant man with the gentle hands helping little kids who were more likely to fall down than play a sport. I remembered his comments about his uncle and desperately wanted to ask for more details.

Noah must have read the intention on my face because his mouth curved up on one side. "You ready to pay the price for asking?"

Suddenly, I wasn't. Noah was already dangerously close to making me think I could make a relationship work. I didn't need anything else weighing on his side, so I swallowed down my questions along with a chunk of strawberry.

"Thanks for bringing me here. This really is the best ice cream I've ever had." An intensity I didn't recognize glittered in his eyes at my strategic retreat.

"You're welcome." He dipped his chin toward my cone. "I've never had that flavor."

I took a big bite of creamy fruit deliciousness and spoke with my mouth full. "Wanna taste?"

"Yes." His big hand wrapped around mine on the cone, but instead of lifting it, Noah lowered his head toward me.

He claimed my mouth in a soul-shattering kiss.

I gasped, giving him access to sweep his tongue inside, while the rest of me freaked the fuck out. His heat countered the cold of the ice cream, and goosebumps raced across my skin. I made a needy little noise in the back of my throat—no regrets, I was a needy bitch—and his free hand slid into my hair.

Noah used his hold to tilt my head back and devour me. Ice cream forgotten, I kissed him back with bare-knuckled desperation. He tasted like the bitter bite of espresso mixed with spiced vanilla, and I knew I'd never be able to drink coffee again without remembering this moment.

He growled his pleasure when I nipped at his bottom lip, and the vibration shot straight to my core, igniting an ache I wasn't sure I could handle on my own. I needed to be full to the brim with him and begging for more.

A cold blob on my leg pulled me back from the edge. My jeans soaked up the remains of my ice cream where I'd dropped it next to me. I pulled back, sucking in air, and he rested his forehead against mine.

Holy fuck, Noah could kiss. If he was this good with his mouth, what else was I missing out on?

"Strawberry is my new favorite flavor," he murmured.

Shit, what had I done? So much for good decisions and sticking to my priorities. The tug of his fist in my hair gave me a subtle preview of things to come should I give in, and I so badly wanted to give in.

But how long before Noah figured out I was nothing more than a shiny bit of fluff floating through life collecting disasters? Long enough to break me when he changed his mind if I let my emotions get involved.

"Not a date," I whispered, mostly to myself.

Noah stiffened and released me, returning to his spot on the wall. "If you say so."

"We can't do this, Noah." My lady parts wailed in anguish, but I was stronger than my urges. "You can't just kiss me and expect it to change anything."

His hooded eyes drifted over my face, and he nodded. "I didn't expect a change, and I won't kiss you again until you ask."

I wanted to tell him I'd never ask... but I think we both knew I'd be lying. How the hell was I supposed to get through an entire evening with him at the alumni dinner without losing my mind?

———

Noah

FOR THE FIRST TIME, I was looking forward to the alumni dinner. Being on display put me on edge, but I'd get to touch Chloe for the first time since our ice cream non-date. I was careful to keep my hands to myself whenever other people were around, and our schedules ensured we didn't have any time alone.

Until tonight.

Mac had suggested we carpool, since all six of us from both apartments were going to the same place, a fancy hotel in the rich part of town. The university had rented out a big ballroom space and informed us there would be reporters everywhere. A not-so-subtle warning to be on our best behavior.

I told the other four to go on without us. We'd be under constant supervision at the dinner, and maybe it was selfish of me, but I wanted Chloe all to myself for the short drive. Which left me alone with her now. In her apartment.

Chloe walked out of her room, head tilted to the side as she fastened an earring. "Eva, can I borrow—"

She stopped abruptly when she spotted me leaning against the wall. Her glossy lips curled into a smile as she gave me a slow onceover. "Wow, you look good, Noah."

The easy compliment slipped right past me as she came all the way into the room and my breath halted in my chest. She licked her lips as I stared, and I couldn't stop the hungry sound that came from me.

She spun slowly in a circle, eyes locked on me. "What do you think?"

I thought I might have swallowed my tongue.

Chloe's long dark hair curled down her back and teased the bare skin of her shoulders. The bright blue dress she wore tied behind her neck with a single bow. My jaw clenched at the image of slowly pulling the knot free and letting the material fall.

She'd worn shorter dresses before, but this one tucked in at her tiny waist and clung to the curves of her hips and ass, wrapping around her thighs to end just above her knees.

The fabric moved with her without budging an inch, and I wanted to see how far I could spread her legs before the material stopped me. I was suddenly sure I'd spend the rest of the night glaring at anyone with eyeballs who dared to look at her the way I did.

"You're always beautiful, Chloe, but that dress..." I shook my head. The half-assed compliment was the best I could do without dropping to my knees and trying to convince her to forget the damn dinner.

A faint blush crawled up her neck. "Is Eva still here?"

"No, they left already."

She eyed Eva's bedroom door for a second, then shrugged. "Girl code says this is an exception to the ask first rule."

I stayed where I was by the door—less likely to incur Eva's wrath that way—while she disappeared inside for a minute. When she came back out, she looked the same. I tilted my head as she approached me.

"You ready?"

"Definitely. Onward to the open bar."

I chuckled and led her outside, waiting while she locked

the door. The weather had warmed enough she didn't bother with a coat for the quick trip to the car, though the intermittent bursts of wind were pretty chilly.

Chloe didn't seem to care. She tucked her arm in mine, taller than usual in her heels so the top of her head came to my chin instead of my shoulder. Chloe had such a big personality I sometimes forgot how tiny she was.

"Why didn't we ride with Mac again?"

"Did you want to be squished into the third row of Mac's Jeep while everyone is imagining their date naked?" Me included.

She shuddered. "No, thanks. Eva probably wouldn't imagine Mac naked, but he's not going to be able to keep his eyes off her in the dress we found."

I snorted as I opened the car door for her. "Mac can't keep his eyes off her anyway. I don't know why he keeps bringing girls home when the one he wants is across the hall."

Chloe shifted to face me as I got behind the wheel, resting her chin in her hand. "Why indeed?"

Her innocent tone didn't fool me. I raised a brow, meeting her gaze for a beat. "I don't bring girls home."

Surprise widened her eyes. "None?"

"Not in a long while. My last experience left a lot to be desired." I'd never planned to share the details with anyone, but I found the story spilling out of my mouth while Chloe stared at me, astonished. Her hand landed on my arm, a soft touch that sent heat spiraling in my chest.

"Want me to set her room on fire?" She asked the question with such glee I burst out laughing.

"Nah, I handled her. The situation just made me rethink my dating strategies."

Chloe narrowed her eyes, still twinkling with amusement. "That's great, but what about me? I'm all juiced up for violence with no outlet."

I removed her hand from my arm before her nails sank in any deeper, linking our fingers together. "Maybe we could save the arson for a more deserving target."

"Anyone who messes with you is going to get a face full of me."

"My hero," I joked, stopping at the valet station.

I had to release her to get out of the car, but Chloe caught my hand again on the sidewalk, pulling me to a halt before letting me go.

"I'm serious, Noah. She was so far past the bounds of decency, and probably breaking the law. I'm sorry that happened to you."

I rubbed my thumb along her jaw, smoothing her frown. "Me too, but it won't happen again. Thanks for coming with me."

She huffed out a breath, and I watched her transform from valiant defender to tease in a heartbeat. Her lips tilted the tiniest bit, and she stepped close to straighten my tie.

"You're welcome."

"What are you doing?" I murmured, unable to resist resting my hands on her hips.

"Making sure you look picture perfect. Can't have the prized football players looking unkempt."

I grunted when her hands smoothed along my lapels, curling behind the nape of my neck. She raised her eyes to mine and fell still. In another life, one where we'd met this year as strangers and she'd been open to a relationship, I'd bend my head and kiss her. I'd claim her mouth—claim her —right here in front of the fancy hotel where I was supposed to be on my best behavior.

The flash of a picture being taken snapped me back to

reality. This wasn't another life. Her brother was somewhere inside, and the college sports world was watching. I urged Chloe up the stairs, scowling at the skinny guy with the press lanyard as we passed.

12

Chloe

"**E**m, stop analyzing the donors I'm supposed to be schmoozing. You're scaring them away with your judgy looks."

Nadia snorted and raised a brow at my brother. "Yeah, and all your glaring is really helping."

I took a sip of wine to hide my smile. D couldn't be more smitten with his girlfriend, and a part of me was really happy we'd ended up at the same table as my brother. Despite Eva's complaints about Noah's previous dates as tablemates, the rest of our crew was scattered over the room, which made me think Noah had pulled some strings for me.

Yet another example of him taking care of me without taking credit for it. I didn't want to be all warm and fuzzy about it, but dammit, he was so *good*.

D curled his hand behind Nadia's neck and pulled her close to whisper in her ear. I felt like a voyeur when a pink flush bloomed on her neck. In my haste to look away, I locked eyes with Noah, who sat between us.

He'd quietly listened during dinner as D regaled us and the couple sharing our table with stories from the professional football trenches. Unlike the gleam I always saw in Shaw's eyes when he and D talked about the pros, Noah showed only a cursory interest.

Why wasn't he gearing up for a fantastic career full of money and non-problematic women throwing themselves at him? I wanted to dive deeper into his loyalty to the family D created for him—and the rough childhood that had made him choose PE teacher over professional football player— but I didn't want to make him feel obligated to answer me in front of all these people.

The threat of whatever price he'd demand also made me hesitate, but I'd spent some time thinking about the options. Noah wouldn't make me do anything I wasn't comfortable with, and there was always the possibility I could convince him to answer for free.

I nodded at the half-empty dance floor. "Dance with me?"

He shook his head. "I'm not a good dancer."

"I don't care." I stood and pulled him out of his chair. "Let's go."

I felt D's gaze on me as we left the table, so I sent him a sassy wink. He could make of it what he would.

Noah edged us to the far side of the dance floor, where a thin line of other dancers offered us a bit of privacy. The music leaned heavily toward slow songs, so I was confident Noah would be fine. Anyone could hold me and sway.

His arm slid around my waist, and his fingers splayed at the base of my spine as he gathered me close. Goosebumps erupted at the brush of his thumb against my skin, but I otherwise tried to remain unaffected.

Noah's gaze roamed over my head, and he maintained a couple of inches between us as we moved stiffly to the music. I might as well have been dancing with my grandmother. Then again, Grandma Edie's short stint with belly dancing had convinced her she could gyrate like she was backing up Beyoncé. She'd put Noah to shame.

I bit my lip, unsure how to tell him I wanted him to pull me closer and stop wasting the moment. "Noah, you're allowed to touch me. We're not at a middle school dance."

Heat flared to life in his eyes, or maybe he let it take the forefront because I could have sworn every tiny touch and accidental brush during dinner came with an accompanying bolt of fire.

The pressure from his hand increased, finally bringing my body into contact with his. I looped my wrists behind his neck, and to his credit, his eyes stayed firmly locked on mine despite the abundance of cleavage available to him.

"Have you heard from your uncle?"

Noah immediately stiffened again, though this time he didn't pull away. "No. He usually only calls once a month."

I played with the short hair at the nape of his neck and phrased my next statement carefully. "You can call me, you know. After. I don't know the history, but I'm happy to take your mind off of it. Anytime, Noah."

He let out a puff of air. "I don't want that part of my life to touch you."

"Why?"

Noah stared over my head for a long moment, and I thought I'd pushed too far, but he started talking. "My dad went to jail for assault when I was six. I haven't heard from him since. That's how I ended up with my uncle. No one else would take me in."

"What about your mom?"

"She died shortly before that."

I couldn't imagine a life where my parents weren't there for me. They never let me doubt they loved me, despite my less than stellar record of falling on my face after my brother proved he could fly.

"I'm so sorry, Noah."

He shook his head, finally meeting my eyes again. "My uncle and aunt never planned to have children, but they didn't have a choice when Dad went to jail. Craig didn't want the negative press that could result from abandoning his nephew while he was trying to build his career. He's a successful surgeon in the Bay Area now."

"You don't think there could be more to their decision?"

"Maybe, but what I told you is what I grew up hearing directly from them. I was welcome in their house as long as I lived up to their standards and reflected well on Craig." He offered me a sad smile. "They gave me a stable home, for which I'm grateful, but he never let me forget where I came from."

My heart hurt for Noah—the man now holding me tightly in his arms, and the boy he'd been. No wonder he was passionate about helping lost kids. He still carried one inside him.

I wanted to go back in time and bitch slap Craig for poisoning Noah against himself. The possibility wasn't entirely off the table in present day either. If Craig ever came to visit, he'd better stay well away from me, especially if I happened to be behind the wheel of a car.

"Fuck Craig."

Noah's lips twitched at my outburst, but I wasn't done.

"Your uncle is the worst, and you should block his number. His opinion is no longer welcome. In fact, give me your phone. I'll do it for you."

I patted his lapel looking for a phone-shaped bulge, but Noah caught my hand before I could move any lower.

"His opinion isn't totally unwarranted. I used to lash out

a lot as a kid, which was a problem when I was bigger than everyone else. My dad's influence lives on."

I snorted. "So you learned to channel your temper into football. You may have noticed I haven't mastered that particular skill yet. It doesn't make me a bad person or someone to be ashamed of."

Noah's shoulders hunched forward slightly. "He's the only family I have left."

I softened, flattening my palm over his heart. "He's not. You have D and the rest of those idiots on the team, Eva, Riley—and me. You're one of the best men I know, and my sainted brother is included in that mix. We're proud to be your family when your blood relations don't live up."

"Chloe...." He trailed off to pull me close again, pressing his face to my hair with a ragged breath.

I hadn't expected the fierce protective instincts rising in me, but I wouldn't change a thing.

"Noah, you're not alone." I could feel my walls crumbling, one by one, but I couldn't do anything to stop it without tossing Noah aside, which I wasn't willing to do. Not anymore.

He raised his head, and a strange light glittered in his eyes. At some point in the conversation, I'd leaned my weight fully onto him and we'd stopped moving. Noah stood with his arm around me, staring at my lips, as the tension built between us.

His head tilted lower, slowly, as if hypnotized, and I held my breath. On cue, the music ruined the moment, changing to a faster pace and bringing more people flooding onto the dance floor. Noah straightened, and I let the air out in a frustrated huff.

He dropped his hands, breaking all contact between us. "I should get you back to your brother."

His words splashed cold water on my perfect lusty daze. I wasn't supposed to be kissing Noah. He'd brought me here because he was a genuinely nice guy trying to do his best to give me time with D. The truth didn't stop me from fantasizing about how far I'd need to push him before he broke his promise to make me ask first.

He led me to our table, pulled my chair out, then leaned back with his arms crossed—grumpy persona firmly in place. D sent me a questioning look. I shook my head at him and excused myself to the bathroom.

Stupid DJ. Stupid cinnamon roll football player. Stupid squishy heart.

I found a secluded spot outside the bathrooms, tucking myself between a giant planter of grasses and a gold velvet bench with tiny paws at the bottom of its legs. My back hit the cold wall as I slouched, staring down at the weird little animal feet.

Okay, yes, I was running. My emotions were officially involved, and the prospect scared the shit out of me. I'd learned from experience when I cared, things went to hell fast. My last serious relationship had taught me not to go all in.

When things came crashing down, and things always crashed down when I was involved, my heart ended up ripped open. Guys didn't want to be cleaning up my problems for the long term. Case in point, I'd tried to show Noah he wasn't alone, and he couldn't drop me off fast enough.

I never should have let Eva manipulate me into coming. Pretending I wasn't interested in Noah only hurt me in the end. Every second I spent with him knocked down a little more of my walls, and I couldn't shore them up fast enough.

My track record of choosing guys—or making major decisions, really—wasn't all that great, and Noah had the potential to destroy me. Worse, I had the potential to destroy him. D would never abandon him, but if things didn't work out between us, Noah would distance himself from the group.

I didn't have a good reason for believing that, but I sensed the truth the same way I sensed spending the night with him would never be casual.

"Hey, beautiful. What are you doing out here by yourself?"

I raised my head, surprised to find a slim guy in a nicely tailored suit standing way too close. He smelled rich, like the inside of an expensive spa, but the predatory way he dragged his gaze over my dress and down to my stilettos raised my hackles.

"Just looking for some fresh air."

He smiled, showing off too-white teeth. "Why don't I show you the balcony on the penthouse suite?"

"No, thanks. I'm about to head back into the ballroom." I offered a tight smile and tried to slip past him, but he side-stepped into my path.

"What's the hurry? We could have some fun together."

I sighed, suddenly tired. The guy wasn't unattractive, and he was probably used to having women fall at his feet. Old me might even have gotten a little thrill from catching his attention. Too bad for him I was done making bad decisions.

"The answer's still no." I angled myself to move past him.

He stepped forward, crowding me so my back hit the wall again. "I can change your mind."

Anger started to push away the emotional fatigue. Apparently, even when I didn't choose the bad decision, it chose me. I could have told him my boyfriend was waiting for me, but fuck that. "Listen, dickwad—"

I didn't get any farther before his hand snapped out to wrap around my wrist. He yanked me forward off balance, and I yelped as I fell against him.

For a split second, his free hand landed on my lower thigh just below where my dress ended, then he was roughly hauled away from me by a scowling football player twice his size gripping his lapels. The jackass let go of my wrist to try to free himself, and I quickly moved out of his reach.

The animal bench nearly took me out in my hurry. "Noah..."

I wasn't sure what to say because I didn't particularly want him to let the guy go, but I also didn't want him to get in trouble for murdering an entitled asshole.

Noah's green eyes took in my disheveled state with a dangerous glint. "Are you okay, Chloe?"

The asshole glanced over his shoulder at me, then glared up at Noah... and chose death. "She's not worth it," he sneered.

In one large step, Noah slammed the guy into the wall, with his toes dangling a good two inches off the floor.

"She's worth two of you, now apologize." Noah's quiet order belied the fury in his eyes. He held the guy there, in complete control, and a flicker of unease cracked the mask of false bravado on the asshole's face.

"Whatever you say, man." He turned his head to meet my gaze. "Sorry. I must have misunderstood."

Misunderstood, my ass. He'd seen me standing alone and assumed I must be in want of a good dicking. I raised my chin and would have seriously considered kicking him if Noah's body hadn't blocked my shot.

"Next time listen when a girl says no."

A growl rumbled from Noah, and the guy blanched. "Yeah, I get it."

Noah gave him a little shake before lowering him to the ground, but he didn't release his hold immediately. "Chloe, do you want to press charges?"

I hadn't even considered getting the police involved. Guys like him were everywhere. Once upon a time, old me might have even taken him up on the offer. He'd chosen the wrong night to approach me, but hadn't I just been telling Eva I preferred these guys because I knew exactly what they wanted?

Fuck, I didn't want to deal with this tonight.

"No, I think he learned his lesson. Let him go."

Noah nodded and released the asshole, stepping back while simultaneously putting himself between us. By some miracle—probably Noah's calm delivery and the large grassy decorations next to us—we hadn't drawn much attention from the people mingling outside the ballroom. I wanted to keep it that way.

The guy smoothed his suit and walked away without a backward glance. I highly doubted he'd learned anything. I watched to make sure he actually got into an elevator— alone—before relaxing.

When I turned to face Noah, he was staring at me with his arms crossed. I opened my mouth to thank him for his good timing, but he gave his head a sharp shake.

"Outside. Now."

13

Chloe

I raised my brows at Noah's brusque order, but I moved toward the double doors at the end of the hallway. He followed close behind until we reached the relative solitude outside the hotel. Bright lights lit the side entrance, but Noah moved us around the building until no one could see us through the glass doors.

His jaw ticked as he stared down at me. "What happened?"

Shock had me taking a step back. Was he blaming me? I hadn't expected Noah to jump to that conclusion, especially after his words to the asshole inside.

"That mess was *not* my fault." Frustration made my words sharper than I meant.

Noah cursed quietly, walking to the edge of the sidewalk and back. "I know, Chloe. I wanted to know what he did to you. Are you hurt?"

I flexed my hand without consciously meaning to, and Noah's gaze dropped to my wrist, circled by angry red marks in the distinctive shape of fingers. With the adrenaline fading, I noticed a dull ache radiating up my arm, but I wasn't about to say anything to Noah.

Under all that quiet contemplation lived a beast on a short leash. He didn't scare me, but I wasn't sure he wouldn't chase the guy upstairs if I admitted I might be hurt.

"I'm fine," I lied. "You have to stop running to my rescue."

Noah's jaw ticked, and he stalked toward me. "Stop needing rescuing."

I shoved at his chest. He took a step back, but not because I'd moved him. "I had the situation under control."

Noah slid his fingers under my wrist, lifting my arm until the red part was clearly visible. "He left a mark on you."

I inhaled, willing myself to think past the tingles rippling up my arm. "I know."

He lowered his head to kiss the inside of my wrist, and I gave up on trying to resist. Noah just hit different. His gentle side lulled me into feeling like nothing could possibly hurt me, and the feral side I'd just seen backed it up.

"What were you doing in the hallway?" I asked quietly.

His eyes shifted from my arm to my face. "You seemed upset when you left. I wanted to make sure you were okay."

"I wasn't."

His brows drew together. "Did I say something during the dance?"

This was my chance to admit the truth, but fear made me hesitate. Memories of the last time I'd allowed my feelings free rein encouraged me to clam up and find an escape. When I didn't answer, Noah used his grip to draw me forward. His other arm curled around my waist, almost like we were dancing again, but without the audience.

"What happened?"

One minute we'd been raw and honest, on the verge of crossing a line in front of everyone, and the next he'd relinquished me to D. Like he'd suddenly remembered who I was, or at least who I was related to. I couldn't decide which part had been the mistake.

My frustration at the whole situation finally reached a breaking point, and I shook my head. "I'm tired of this back and forth. Do you know why I don't do relationships? Because no one ever wants me. Just me. They want the connection to D, and barring that, they want someone easy and compliant. Expectations of devotion lead to binge eating queso and French fries when the truth comes out that what I had to offer wasn't good enough."

"Those guys were idiots if they didn't show up for you."

"No argument there, but it's easier if I set reasonable expectations. A good time with no promises on either side, and usually no mention of my brother. At least I know those guys want *me*, and not D's problematic little sister. I'm adequate for an average human, but it's hard not to find myself lacking compared to the perfection of my brother."

Noah choked on a laugh. "Your brother is *not* perfect."

"You could have fooled me. I was right there, and you couldn't wait to get back to him."

He stepped closer, amusement forgotten. "I would have stayed on the dance floor with you all night, but you never get to see D. Besides, I didn't want him to find out about my interest in you by watching me make you come in a crowd of alumni donors." His thumb dragged across my lower lip, making me swallow hard. "D has his blind spots—you're one of them. I can like someone while still acknowledging their faults. I like you, and I'm well aware of your penchant for finding trouble."

I pursed my lips at him, trying to ease some of the

tension before I dove headfirst into his pants. "I'm baring my soul to you, and you think this is a good time to talk about my unfortunate habit of destroying things, which is entirely not my fault?"

A chilly breeze blew through the side street, making me shiver, and Noah walked us back into a corner. With stone walls on two sides, and Noah taking up all the space in front of me, I had trouble remembering why I was supposed to be holding back.

"Why were you upset tonight?"

"Because you danced with me, treated me like a real person you wanted to spend time with, then passed me along like a package. I don't like being dismissed, and I definitely don't want to feel that way from you."

"Chloe, when I was dancing with you, I forgot anyone else was in the room, including your brother—which is the problem. He was watching us."

Not surprising considering D wasn't stupid or oblivious. "He doesn't scare me. You do. I don't want to like you this much."

He trailed his nose along my cheek to speak into my ear. "Catching feelings for me, are you?"

"What does it matter? You'll still pull back because I'm D's untouchable sister."

Noah nuzzled my hair. "I pull back because I don't want to be another throwaway boy toy to you. I want more."

The description wasn't entirely inaccurate, but a heavy weight sat in my stomach as I realized he'd nailed old me's hopes for him. Football players were supposed to be into casual hookups. New me was more open to an intriguing second option. With him.

"What if I might possibly be willing to try a less casual... thing?"

He chuckled and moved far enough away to study my face. "You can't even say the word relationship?"

I squared my shoulders and met the challenge in his eyes. "Situationship. No more boy toys."

He nodded slowly. "What if I might be willing to remove your brother from any consideration of a *relationship* with you?"

Were we really talking about this? I'd been burned before. Bad decisions, bad choices, bad boyfriend. The thought of giving part of myself to another person again—one who could do as they wished with my feelings and independence—freaked me out, but when the person was Noah, my misgivings mostly disappeared.

I had no doubt he wanted me—the evidence pressed against my abdomen in a hard line. He was intimately familiar with the bad decisions I'd made. Hello, drunk night with the hockey boy. Noah had nailed it when he said I'd chosen the wrong guys before, but was I willing to take a chance that Noah was the right guy?

"What are your ground rules for the situationship?" I asked.

Noah tucked a strand of hair behind my ear. "Relationship. I want exclusive access to you. No other guys while we're together."

That one was easy. I hadn't been interested in another guy since I transferred to TU. "Okay. No girls either."

"Agreed. My schedule can get crazy, even in the spring. I'll do my best to make you a priority, but sometimes football or my classes have to come first."

"Same goes for me. Actually, let's just assume that any rule we decide on goes for both of us."

He nodded. "That's fair. You have to talk to me if I do

anything that makes you uncomfortable. No keeping things inside until they explode."

I could have simply agreed, but I had one more thing I wanted to be clear about, even though I knew from experience it could be a deal breaker. "Okay, but you can't tell me what to wear or how to act or otherwise try to change me. Accept me for who I am or fuck off."

The words came out more confrontational than I intended, but I had some complicated emotions mixed in with those experiences. Even limiting myself to hookups hadn't spared me from the misogyny.

Noah frowned. "I'm going to repeat myself for emphasis: you were dating the wrong guys before."

"No shit. Remember the part where I decided to stop dating? And it was mostly the one guy." I muttered the last sentence, but he heard me.

His gaze sharpened. "Did he hurt you?"

"Besides my pride, no. Despite recent events, most guys aren't out to leave bruises, at least not physical ones."

The intensity cloaking him faded a little, but not entirely. "If we're doing this, I'm not hiding it from D. "

I raised my brows. "You're going to ask him permission to rail his sister?"

He sent me a quelling look. "I was going to tell him I was interested in you, but if you want me to go into detail, I can."

I curled my arms around his neck. "How about this? We test the waters so to speak before we tell anyone. Not a secret so much as a chance to get used to the new dynamic before Mac breaks into song and dance."

"Do I still get to rail you?"

A giggle tried to break free, but I managed to keep my face solemn as I nodded at him. "Part of the deal."

A frisson of excitement shivered over my skin. After two

years of what I won't admit was pining, I was finally getting a taste of Noah. Not a second chance since we'd never had a first chance thanks to D. And maybe some of our own holdups.

"How long are we hiding this from D?" he asked.

"Until we're both sure?"

"That's a pretty loose bar."

I ran my hands down his chest, exploring the broad expanse of muscle under his suit. "Take it or leave it."

"I'll take it." He released his grip on my waist to flatten his hand over mine.

We'd both abandoned any pretense of a platonic friendship. I wanted to touch him, so I did. His heart thrummed steadily under my palm—a fast beat repeating in my chest. In the years I'd known him, seeing him regularly with D and the others, I hadn't noticed the barriers I'd made to hold myself back until I let them drop. With them gone, I burned.

My nipples pebbled through the silky material of my dress, sending shudders down my spine when they brushed against Noah. He pressed a kiss to my forehead, trailing his lips across my temple and down my cheek to the sensitive spot under my ear.

The curl of his tongue, warm and wet, set off a series of tiny explosions like fireworks erupting in my chest, my belly, my pussy. I dug my nails into his shoulder and dropped my head to the side, giving him greater access.

One big hand smoothed over my hip to my ass, pausing long enough for a groan to rumble out of Noah. With slow, careful movements he gathered the material of my dress in his hand, inching the hem up my thighs.

When he hit bare skin, he whispered my name against my neck. His fingers slid between my thighs, brushing the tiny scrap of soaking wet lace I wore. I spread my legs, as much as my bunched-up dress would allow, and tried to shift so his fingers hit the place where I ached.

Noah moved with me, staying just out of reach, teasing me with light touches until I whimpered.

Behind Noah, completely hidden by his body, the double glass doors burst open. A high-pitched giggle and low murmur pulled me out of my smutty fog. Noah stiffened but held his position—dress up around my ass, fingers a strong breeze away from my pussy—until the other couple wandered off.

To my eternal regret, he eased back, returning my dress to the pre-sexy times position. Noah didn't let me go completely, keeping an arm around me while I leaned against him. I let my head drop to his chest and sighed.

Noah curled a hand around the back of my neck, squeezing the tense muscles there. "Do you want to go back inside or somewhere else?"

He didn't give me the option of leaving on my own. I understood, since I had no intention of ending the night alone.

As tempted as I was to drag him back to his car, and hopefully back to his apartment, I wanted to say goodbye to D and Nadia since I wasn't sure when I'd see them next. Dammit, my brother was cockblocking me again.

I took a deep breath through my nose, inhaling Noah's scent, and leaned away from him. "Inside, but I have one more question first."

Interest gleamed in his eyes. "I told you the next one would cost you."

"What do you want?"

His fingers tightened at my softly spoken question. "A date."

My pulse took off. "Didn't we just agree to take things slow—test the waters first?"

"Slow is relative, and a date is the usual first step in a relationship," he said dryly.

"What do I know? I had one disastrous relationship in high school and a series of mostly disappointing hookups."

"At least I can guarantee one benefit to our relationship."

"What's that?"

"You won't be disappointed." His gaze locked on my lips, and my core clenched at the promise in his smile.

His hand splayed over my hip, as if he couldn't seem to stop himself from touching me, not that I was complaining. If that couple hadn't interrupted us, I would have happily ridden him—any part of him—until I couldn't stand. Suddenly, saying goodbye to my brother seemed significantly less important. It wouldn't be the first time I'd disappeared on him. He'd understand. Someday.

"I think I've changed my mind. We should just go home and enjoy our new situationship. Very little risk, lots of reward."

Noah caught my chin between his thumb and forefinger, then traced my jaw with a knuckle. "It doesn't matter what you call it, Chloe. I won't rush you, and I won't hurt you. Spend the time with your brother."

His confidence shot right through my attempt to edge us back to friends with benefits territory. In the end, did I really want to let fear—an unsupported fear, at that—control me?

Noah had proven over and over again he could be relied on, even when he got grumpy about it. He hadn't run away yet. I trusted him to rescue me every time, but could I trust him not to break my heart?

As long as I didn't fall for him, I didn't have to trust. I could protect myself.

I smiled, pushing the unease away in favor of the delicious ache between my legs. "You can have your date."

He rubbed his nose along the length of mine. "What's your question?"

"Will you kiss me again, Noah?"

With a possessive growl, he finally closed the last of the distance between us.

14

Noah

I kissed Chloe like a starving man, desperate for her after the taste I'd gotten at the ice cream shack. Two years of pent-up hunger made my mouth rough, but I kept my hands gentle. It would be so easy to leave my mark on her skin—a claim made though pleasure instead of pain.

She opened for me, and I swept my tongue inside as her hands fisted on my dress shirt. I wanted the shirt gone. The dress gone. I wanted to plunge into her heat—take the easy release she was offering—but I caught the jagged edge of restraint, pulling myself back from the brink.

I eased away before I lifted her against the rough stone. In all my fantasies, none had started with fucking her like a wild animal in a semi-deserted alcove outside a hotel. Considering how damn hard I was, they probably should have.

"Sure you want to go inside?" she asked with a raised brow.

"Yes." I rubbed my thumb across her swollen bottom lip. "No one's going to believe you weren't out here kissing someone."

She lifted to her toes, smoothing the mess I'd made of my hair. "Let them talk."

The gentle tugging shot directly to my cock, and I caught her wrists, moving them between us. "I thought you wanted to keep this quiet for now. Test the waters?"

Chloe grinned at me. "No one said I had to be kissing *you*. Go in first, I'll follow in a little later. I have to go to the ladies' room anyway."

I held her wrists captive a moment longer, fighting the urge to simply run away with her. I hated the idea of anyone thinking she'd been kissing another guy while here with me. This level of possessiveness was new to me, and Chloe had made it clear she didn't appreciate the trait.

With reluctance, I let her go, stepping back to shove my hands in my pockets so I didn't grab her again. Immediately, a sense of loss rocked me. I'd barely had the chance to touch her, and it wasn't enough.

I suspected it would never be enough.

The wind kicked up again as I backed toward the door, watching her straighten her dress. "Try not to kick anyone's ass in the next five minutes."

Her lips quirked. "I'll do my best."

I shook my head and headed back into the hotel, utterly changed. What had I just done to myself?

D was one of my best friends, but Chloe was... I couldn't find the words. She scared me and tempted me, and after having my hands on her—my mouth—I couldn't imagine going back. She could slice me open and destroy my relationship with her brother, but I still wanted her to walk back into the ballroom with swollen lips and sex hair.

A clear signal to everyone she was taken. She was mine.

Maybe she'd leave a mark on me too.

———

THE REST of the dinner passed in a blur of trying not to advertise my erection, which meant I stayed safely seated at the table. A couple of donors came by to tell me how much they enjoyed watching me play and quickly moved on to D.

Shaw brought me a beer at some point, but I only took a few sips, needing my wits about me to counter Chloe's constant flirting. No one seemed to notice her extended absence, and every time she turned those green eyes on me, I wondered why she'd bothered to ask for a secret trial period. Fortunately, I'd spent years perfecting my poker face. I might have to thank Craig the next time he called.

She flirted mercilessly, but she'd always flirted with me. And everyone else. Tonight, I got to monopolize all of her attention. The harder she tried to get me to smile, the harder I resisted. They were used to my dour attitude, but Chloe knew what lurked underneath.

D sent me a questioning look at one point, and I shrugged at him. The ruse didn't feel great, but it wasn't a direct lie. I *didn't* know what Chloe was up to, other than torturing me.

By the time we said our goodbyes, I'd come to a decision. She wanted a trial period, so I'd give it to her. No sleepovers, no sex. It wasn't even about D—okay, not only about D.

I liked her.

Chloe was warm and open on the surface, but she resisted letting anyone deeper. I wanted past those walls. If I gave in to my need for her, she could fall back on the habit of seeing guys as casual hookups.

I had no intention of letting her relegate me to the same category.

She grinned at me for the entire drive back to the apartments, probably expecting a continuation of our time outside the hotel. I didn't enlighten her. Safer that way. If given half a chance, she could convince me to do just about anything.

Her hand landed on my leg when we pulled into the parking lot, and I scooped it up to kiss her fingers. Partly because I wanted my mouth on her, partly because I wanted to prevent her from taking it any farther.

Outside her door, I pressed a chaste kiss to her cheek and stepped back.

Chloe frowned. "Aren't you coming in?"

I slipped my hands in my pockets to remove the temptation to reach for her. "Not tonight."

Her head tilted. "Is something wrong?"

A small laugh burst out of me, borderline desperate. "No. In a possibly insane attempt to take things slow, I'm clinging to restraint with my fingertips."

"I thought we went over this. You don't need to restrain yourself. Full permission to rail me." Her head tilted with a frown. "Unless you're having second thoughts?"

"No, Chloe. I want to do this right, which means I'm not going to jump in bed with you the first chance I get. No matter how much I want to."

She stepped closer, her voice going husky. "How much do you want to?"

"Chloe," I growled.

Her fingers slid down my arms, curling around my wrists and pulling my hands free with a soft touch. "I get it. Testing the waters, remember?" She slipped my arms around her waist, only letting go when I locked in place. "This situationship is new, but I've known you a long time— most of it thinking you weren't interested. Can you blame me for wanting to take advantage of the fact that I can touch you like this now?"

I tugged her a little closer, and she wrapped her arms around me in a hug. Just a hug. She snuggled against my chest, and I rested my chin on her head. Chloe never failed to surprise me.

"I'm not going to pressure you to do anything, Noah. I just like touching you, and I really like it when you touch me."

I relaxed, amused by the situation—this tiny woman reassuring me she only wanted a hug. A complete lie I was totally comfortable running with for the sake of my willpower.

"I'll touch you any time you want, Chloe."

"Good to know," she murmured. "When do you want your date?"

An inexplicable warmth filled my system, not the electric-filled kind my cock liked, but a happy glow from her effort to take the change in our relationship seriously, to take me seriously.

"I'll text you when I know Shaw's torture schedule for the next week," I told her.

"Text me anyway. Every day. All the time. Especially snaps of you half-naked. Or full naked. I'm not picky."

My arms tightened at the thought of her sending me nudes, not out of the realm of possibility with Chloe. We already texted constantly thanks to her endless collection of memes. I'd have to be careful when I checked my phone from now on.

Chloe shifted, and her hair caught on the stubble I was too lazy to shave. She smelled like rain—crisp and fresh, with an undertone of something dark. I hadn't noticed before in the chaos of the dinner, but with everything still, her scent drifted up to me.

Why was I doing this again?

She wanted me to come inside, and I'd already pushed us across the line into a murky relationship. Would holding off really make a difference in the long run?

As if she could read my thoughts, she tilted her face up to me with a saucy grin. "Let me know if you change your mind. I'll make it worth your while."

Her lacy thong had been soaked when I'd teased her earlier, and I desperately wanted to follow through on my promise to make her forget her disappointing history. The other guys she'd been with would have taken her up on the offer without question.

I wasn't those other guys.

"Goodnight, Chloe." I dropped a kiss on her hair and backed out of the embrace.

Regret flashed in her eyes, but she held her smile. "Night."

I stayed in the landing until Chloe's door closed and the lock engaged. At Eva's demand, Mac had removed the door cams a few weeks ago, but it wouldn't have mattered. I was rooted to the spot.

My body begged me to change my mind.

I tucked my hands behind my head, linking my fingers together as my jacket pulled taut across my shoulders. All the others had gone to Johnny's—except D and Nadia, who'd had to fly back to New York tonight—leaving me an empty apartment.

The night air teased my open jacket, helping cool some of the heat rushing through me, and I filled my lungs with the faint pine scent. I'd never admit it to Mac, but I liked the noise and insanity he brought.

The silence reminded me too much of years spent in forced quiet because Craig couldn't afford any distractions. I'd never been an extrovert, but I remembered being an affectionate kid. My dad had never turned down a hug. Even on his worst days, he'd squeeze me so hard I thought I'd pop.

The memory left a bittersweet ache. I couldn't change my past or the way it had shaped me, but I could choose chaos now if it made me happy. Mac made me happy. Shaw, D, Eva, even RJ. They made me happy.

Chloe made me happy.

I stared up at the stars visible past the trees and let the crazy night wash over me. Chloe knew the worst part of me, and she'd offered comfort. I hadn't expected to test my limits so fast, but seeing that asshole with his hands on her had forced me to claw back control by the barest margin.

She hadn't shied away or tried to stop me. Chloe had seen my temper firsthand, and she'd still let me touch her—still invited me inside.

What the hell was I doing making boundaries like I couldn't trust her? As if I had the right. She agreed to a relationship, a *situationship*, and I'd insisted on taking things slow like it would provide some kind of security.

Fuck security. I didn't need reassurance—I needed her.

I shook out my hands and headed for her door. Chloe answered mid-knock, like she'd been waiting. I stared at her, letting the space between us fill with the good intentions I'd abandoned. The weight of what I should do threatened to crush me, so I let it all go and stepped toward her.

"Changed my mind."

"Thank god," she breathed as she launched herself at me.

15

Chloe

Noah caught me with ease, and kissed me like he'd never let go. I'd been willing to do things his way —slow and steady—but this was a million times better. My dress hiked up to my hips as I locked my legs around his waist.

His fingers tightened in my hair, tugging my head back so he could slide his mouth down my throat in a burning caress as he maneuvered us into my apartment. The door slammed, then my back hit the cool wood with the solid breadth of Noah holding me in place.

I yanked off his tie and clawed at the buttons of his suit shirt. The pants stopped me because I couldn't figure out how to get them open on my own with his tongue tracing patterns across my collarbone.

All at once, the bow behind my neck came untied, leaving my breasts as the only thing holding the top up. With one nudge from Noah's chin, the silky material slid away to pool around my waist with the rest of the dress.

A pleased rumble came from Noah as he captured one nipple in his mouth. He flicked the tip with his tongue and an electric jolt shot through me. I abandoned his pants to bury my hands in his hair. As I writhed against him, Noah shed his jacket and shirt in a pile on my living room floor.

Distantly, I wondered if I should warn Eva in case she came home tonight, but the concern quickly floated away on a wave of pleasure caused by Noah's wicked mouth. He moved to the other breast, dropping his pants and whatever else he was wearing.

I didn't check. I slid down Noah's gloriously naked body until I came in contact with the hard length of his cock. He shifted forward, pinning me to the wall, and my mouth dropped open with a nearly silent moan.

My body was an inferno, and Noah's touch drove the flames higher and higher. He knew just how to kiss and suck and move. I couldn't hold a thought in my head, rapidly cycling through prayers to various deities and nonsense phrases like a short-circuiting toy.

The only thing between us was a scrap of lace from my thong, and at this point, it was so wet I might as well have worn nothing. I tilted and rolled my hips, panting as I hit the bundle of nerves with every upward stroke.

"God, Noah, don't stop," I moaned.

He chuckled and released my nipple to blow on the wet heat he'd left behind, all the while maintaining the tortuous rhythm against my clit. My body spiraled tighter and tighter, and right when I hit the peak, Noah plunged two fingers inside me.

"I'm not going to stop, and you're going to come all over my hand like a good girl, aren't you?"

His rough voice in my ear sent me over the edge. My nails dug into his scalp, and white starbursts exploded behind my closed lids. I rode out the orgasm squeezing

Noah's fingers as he fucked me with an unrelenting pace, sighing his name on repeat.

When the last shudders stopped, he didn't let me down, despite my legs turning to jelly. Simply slipped his fingers free and palmed my ass again to hold me up with one arm. The benefit of lusting after a guy who could bench press two of you.

I opened my eyes to his cocky grin, not a sight I got to see often, though he'd definitely earned it in this case.

"You're beautiful when you come, but nothing beats hearing my name on your lips when you tighten around me."

"I can think of something." To illustrate my point, I reached between us to grip his rock-hard shaft, spreading a drop of liquid across the tip with my thumb.

"Bed," he grunted, hauling me away from the wall and carrying me into my room.

Another slammed door, and seconds later, my back hit the mattress. Pillows and my stuffed llama bounced onto my face from the force. I swatted away the attacking bedding and ran my hand down the hard planes of Noah's chest until I wrapped my fingers around his straining cock.

"You're right."

"About what?" he growled, covering my hand with his, showing me the right pressure and speed.

I stroked him as he moved his hips slightly in tempo. "So far, not a single disappointment."

Noah flashed me a grin, nearly hidden in the deep shadows of the room, and dropped his head to my shoulder for a brief second. "Should I say I told you so now, or wait until later?"

"Definitely later," I gasped when he slicked his thumb over my clit.

He levered himself farther away to yank my dress and thong down my legs. They landed somewhere behind us with a dull thud. Past experience said with both of us naked his focus would shift to his own pleasure, but he surprised me.

Instead of settling between my legs where he was one hundred percent welcome, he lay on his side next to me and trailed his fingertips along the curve of my shoulder, over one breast, dipping in at my waist, and flaring out at my hips. A physical silhouette with a barely-there touch I felt in my soul.

My breath hitched when he glided along the crease of my hip to my inner thigh, tracing the tiny trio of hearts I'd inked there last year on a dare. The streetlights outside weren't bright enough to do more than lighten the shadows a little, but Noah unerringly found the matching shield on the other thigh. I watched him follow the outline twice, transfixed at the sight of his large hands on my skin.

The tattoos were my secret. Even the friends who'd dared me to get them didn't know the real meaning. Would Noah figure out they represented him and my obsession with wanting what I couldn't have?

His palm grazed over my hip on a return journey north until he flattened his hand over my throat, lifting my chin. I met his gaze, burning with intensity as he watched me—his guard forgotten.

I'd done that. I'd breached his reserve and found the real Noah underneath. Turned out, I liked the real Noah. He kissed me again, an exploration in place of the desperate claim from before. Slow and deliberate.

"What are you doing?" I whispered against his mouth.

"Taking my time. I plan to enjoy every inch of you tonight, over and over again."

He'd blunted the sharp edge of my hunger in the living room, but his words brought the need back to a razor peak. I wiggled closer, and he laughed, low and rough in the near darkness.

I reached for him, hard and ready against my leg, but he intercepted my hand and brought it above my head. He trailed his lips across my cheek to suck on the sensitive spot below my ear.

"Noah..." I sighed, clenching my thighs together.

He collected my other hand and pressed my palms to the headboard, curling my fingers around the metal slats. "If you let go, I'll stop, understand?"

I wanted to touch him, explore his body the way he was learning mine, but no way in hell was I risking him stopping his current trajectory. Bossy Noah was sexy as fuck, and the little growl he gave me when I didn't answer immediately sent a spike of molten heat through my blood.

Noah shifted over, pinning me with his weight as he started to move lower. "Do you understand, Chloe?"

I pressed my lips together, determined to see how far I could push him. The short hair on his chin rasped over my breast, and I yelped when he nipped at the sensitive skin there, soothing the sting with his tongue.

"I know what you're doing, Trouble, and I promise you, I'm going to enjoy making you beg."

Noah kissed his way down my body, spreading my legs with his broad shoulders until he could kiss the tattoos on both thighs. He teased me with soft touches and abbreviated strokes until I whimpered under him.

"Please, Noah," I pleaded.

"Please what?"

He didn't let up, and I was going to explode if I didn't come soon. "You win. I understand. Please fuck me."

I felt his smile of triumph on my skin, and the metal headboard dug into my palms as my hands tightened.

"How many times are you going to come for me, Chloe?" He punctuated his question by swiping his tongue over me and fastening his mouth on my clit.

My hips jerked off the bed, but I held the headboard in a death grip. God, I regretted all the time I wasted thinking Noah wasn't interested. For the first time in my life, I exploded a second time under his relentless attention. My heels dug into his back, riding out the shockwaves racing through my system.

The books were right. Multiple orgasms were magical. And tiring.

Noah withdrew his hand and pressed a final kiss on my hip, gently moving my legs so he could finally settle between them. His cock slid against my entrance, and he flexed his hips with a groan, parting my folds.

He reached up to pry my fingers off the headboard and link our hands as he buried his face in my neck. I curled my leg around his hip, more than ready to feel him inside me. Noah hesitated, then shifted back an inch.

"Condoms?"

Fuck. I hadn't planned on entertaining tonight, so I was woefully unprepared. "I don't have any. You?"

He cursed quietly. "Not here." Noah's weight shifted off me, and I thought for sure he was going to haul ass across the landing to his apartment. Instead, he rolled to the edge of the bed with a pained expression on his face. "Not at my place either. It's been a while."

I let my head fall back on my pillow, and the mattress jiggled as he stood. The night was cursed, that had to be it.

No way was I letting Noah leave this apartment. Knowing my luck, a meteor would strike him down in his undies, or worse—he'd come to his senses. I wanted Noah to wreck me in the best way possible.

For a split second, I considered going without protection. I wasn't on the pill, but I'd gotten tested when I moved to TU. Thanks to the brooding giant in front of me, I'd been going solo since then.

Judging by the clear frustration on Noah's face, he wouldn't go for it though. Oddly, the fact that sex without protection never crossed his mind softened my already dangerously squishy heart.

Noah's eyes trailed over me, still splayed out on the bed in all my naked glory, and he grimaced. "Don't move an inch. I'll run to the store and be right back." He glanced around at my floor. "As soon as I find my pants."

I giggled at the image of him checking out at the closest gas station with a box of condoms and a massive hard-on that couldn't be contained by his suit pants. Nope. I couldn't let him do it.

"We don't *need* a condom." His brows drew together as I slid off the bed and crawled across the couple of feet of distance between us, coming to my knees in front of him. "There are other ways to take care of this."

A low groan rumbled in Noah's chest as I wrapped my fingers around his cock. He brushed my hair back, holding it in a tight fist.

"Chloe, I would love nothing more than to fuck your smart mouth, but I'm pretty dedicated to making you come at least twice more."

I didn't hear a no, so I slowly licked up the length of him. "I have it on good authority that you're talented in that area. I think you'll be able to achieve your goal."

His hips hitched forward, like he couldn't help himself.

"Eva's going to need headphones tonight to block the sound of you screaming my name."

Eva. Thank fuck for my generous roomie.

I laughed and kissed his tip before climbing to my feet. "New plan. You can fuck my mouth later. Eva has condoms. I saw them earlier when I was using her deodorant."

His brows furrowed. "What does the girl code say about this instance?"

"Nothing specific, so I'm going to go with 'girl, get you some' and borrow one."

"Borrow?"

"Yeah, I'll replenish her stash." I patted his chest as I walked past. "Besides, she offered to share her coffee and it's basically the same thing."

His gaze slid down my body. "Better grab a couple."

16

Noah

Chloe disappeared into Eva's room and returned in no time with a handful of square packets. She closed and locked her door, then flashed a quick grin as she hurried past me to dump them on her bedside table. Before she could turn around, I wrapped my arm around her waist and hauled her against my chest.

She stilled and her hands landed on my forearm where it crossed in front of her. "I'm glad you changed your mind," she whispered into the dark.

"Me too."

Now that I'd tasted Chloe, there was no going back. The need for her sang in my blood, demanding I take what she offered with the delicate shudder across her back. I kissed her shoulder and swiveled her to face the bed.

"You're so beautiful," I breathed into her hair, pulling it to the side. "Do you trust me?"

"Yes."

She answered without hesitation, completely willing to follow my lead. Her immediate submission made me let out a shallow breath. I was holding onto my control by my fingertips. Chloe's personality was so big I sometimes forgot how small she was compared to me. I could easily break her in half if I was careless.

As if she could read my mind, she reached up and pulled my head down for a kiss. "I'm not afraid of you. I like everything you do to me, Noah."

Her words banished the last of my doubts. I quickly sheathed myself with a condom and gripped the back of her neck, urging her upper body down onto the bed. She twisted her head to send me a wicked smile over her shoulder. A buzz of excitement started at the base of my spine and spread through my body. Chloe liked when I took charge, so I stopped trying to hold back.

Even after our brief hiatus, she was still soaking wet for me. I gripped the base of my cock and teased her entrance.

"You ready for me, Trouble?"

I didn't wait for her to respond. With a tight grip on her, I plunged in to the hilt—a long, slick slide marked by her gasp. Chloe squeezed me tightly as I held myself still, giving her time to get used to my size. When she tilted her hips looking for more, I pulled back slowly and snapped my hips forward again. I kept up the deliberate pace until she was straining to meet each thrust.

"Fuck, Noah...," she groaned into the mattress, grasping handfuls of the sheets in her fists.

We fell into a rhythm that had us both panting, racing for the end. I palmed her ass, stroking a line down between her cheeks. Chloe sucked in a breath, and her gaze darted to mine. With a raised brow, I pressed my thumb against her puckered hole, asking permission.

Her lips curled up, and she pushed back into me, squeezing me impossibly hard. "Yes. Harder. Fuck me like you mean it."

Yes. The real Chloe was so much better than any fantasy I conjured up. I swiped some liquid from her pussy onto my thumb and wet the skin before pushing inside her ass—just enough to make her fuck herself every time she met my thrusts.

My other hand disappeared between her legs to rub her clit. If I had my way, she'd think about me, about this, every time she moved tomorrow—every time she moved and felt the pull of what I'd done to her, what we'd done together.

I wanted to put a claim on her so deep it would never leave her... just like she did to me.

As promised, she came twice more before I finished with my mouth against her neck, whispering words of praise. Chloe let out a satisfied hum, and inside me, something vital shifted and slid into a new configuration.

A burst of rightness, of belonging, tightened into what was probably an unhealthy attachment to the woman underneath me. I dragged my lips across her shoulder blade, reveling in her salty taste.

"Is this the part where I tell you good girl?" I murmured, loosening my hold.

Chloe collapsed onto her belly and shook with laughter for a long second. "Damn, Noah. As soon as I can move, I'm going to give you a high five. Ten out of ten. Would recommend."

I chuckled and headed for the bathroom. Her apartment was a slightly smaller copy of ours, with each room having an en suite. I tossed the condom, washed my hands, and flipped on the hot water in the shower. Chloe may have been singing my praises, but she would probably be sore. The heat would help.

When I returned to the bedroom, she hadn't moved from her face down position sprawled diagonally across the mattress. I sat next to her, trailing my fingertips down her spine.

"Come get clean with me before we get dirty again."

I watched the subtle movements of her back as she flopped over, then I couldn't tear my eyes off her breasts.

"I'm too tired for another round. Seriously. I've never come so many times in a twenty-four-hour period."

I raised a brow. "I haven't had you in here for nearly that long."

"I know. I was counting when I fucked myself silly this morning to try to take the edge off before going to the alumni dinner with you."

The loose, warm contentment swimming in my system sharpened to painful need in the space of a breath. My gaze lifted to her face and the knowing smirk on her lips. She reached out to stroke my now hard cock.

"Your recovery rate is ridiculous. Are you sure you're not part superhero?"

I scooped her up and carried her into the steamy bathroom with me. "It's all about the incentives. Any time you're near me, my dick is ready to go."

"I like this superpower." She sucked in a breath when I stepped into the shower with her, then tilted her head back to wet her hair. "I could get used to dick on command."

"It's a big responsibility, but I think you're up to it," I deadpanned.

Chloe laughed and patted my arm until I let her down. "Let's find out."

She maneuvered us so my shoulders blocked the spray of the water and sank down to her knees. My heart tried to beat out of my chest when her eyes flicked up at me, her mouth full of my cock.

"Yeah," I gasped, spearing my fingers into her wet hair. "You're definitely up to it. Deep breath now."

After the best blow job of my life, I washed her, *thoroughly*, and she dragged me back to her bed. I couldn't stop smiling. Chloe wriggled around until she was comfortable, using my arm as a pillow with her back pressed to my chest.

Once she was settled, I held my hand out in front of her face. "I believe I'm owed a high five."

She snorted out a laugh and slapped her palm against mine. "This is for both of us. Giving in was the best idea ever."

I tangled my fingers with hers and brought her hand to my mouth for a kiss. "Stay or go?" My breath caught in my chest while I waited for her answer. She'd told me she didn't invite guys to stay the night—not her hookups anyway—but I hoped we'd stopped pushing each other away.

"Stay," she whispered.

Relief flooded me as she cuddled closer and let out a happy sigh. I'd waited years to hear her say that. Tonight might as well have been a dream, or a fantasy. I never wanted to let her go.

"Are you sure you want me to stay? The others will notice if we're having sleepovers."

She snorted. "Not Mac. He's preoccupied with his own ego."

"Maybe not Mac," I conceded. "But Eva's probably going to trip on my suit the second she walks in the door. I wouldn't be surprised if she was having a psychic flash right now."

"Eva won't say anything if we ask her not to."

"I don't *want* to ask her not to. If D is going to take a swing at me, I don't want to add lying to his face for an undisclosed amount of time to the list of sins."

Chloe turned to face me with a frown. "Do you regret tonight?"

I hesitated, and she stiffened, scooting back a little.

"Are you serious right now?"

"No." I hooked an arm around her waist, anchoring her against me before she could move away again. "I don't regret any of things I've done with you other than waiting so long to do them."

Slowly, her posture softened. "I'm not ready to share you with D yet. Please?"

I couldn't deny her, even though the omission stuck in my gut. "Whatever you need, Chloe."

"Do you ever do anything only for you? Simply because you want to and it makes you feel good?" she asked.

I brushed her hair away from her face, grazing her cheekbone with my thumb. "Pretty sure I just did."

Chloe fell silent, but she wasn't sleeping. Her fingers traced patterns on my arm until she figured out what she wanted to say a few minutes later. "This is new for me. I don't know what the right move is, and I'm terrified of screwing everything up. You might have noticed my unfortunate track record of bad decisions. How am I supposed to know this isn't another one?"

I winced as the echo of my uncle harping on my dad's bad decisions, me included, circled in my mind. Her fear wasn't about me though. Chloe was scared she wouldn't be enough for me to risk my relationship with D, and I couldn't fault her for that response considering my initial reservations.

"I can't tell you everything is going to be okay, but I *can* say I want to be here, right now, with you. Not with D's little sister or a convenient ball bunny. With the Chloe that thinks strawberry is an adventurous ice cream flavor, and laughs at every single cat meme on the internet, and does her best to protect opinionated ducks even when they don't deserve it."

Her lips curved up and the shadows left her eyes. "Henry wasn't so bad."

"You make me happy, and nothing short of a blazing inferno would convince me to leave your bed." I kissed her temple, then added, "Please don't light anything on fire."

Her body shook with laughter. "I make no promises." She yawned loudly and rolled over to curl into a ball tucked into my side. "Thanks for being you, Noah. Also for the very not disappointing orgasms."

No one had ever thanked me for getting them off before. I closed my eyes and pressed my face into her hair, breathing in the sweet smell. No going back now. Chloe was mine, and the thought of returning to only being friends clawed a hole in my chest.

CHLOE WAS NOT A MORNING PERSON. I knew that already, but when I kissed her shoulder, she straight up growled at me. Full demon voice. The only words I caught were *murder* and *sleep*. She burrowed deeper into the covers, wiggling her ass against my morning wood, and I sighed.

I could probably change her mind with very little effort, but the sun streaming through her window meant I was most likely late for Shaw's training. Spring football may have been less demanding than the regular season, but Coach still expected us to maintain a high level of discipline.

With a quiet groan, I slipped away from Chloe's warm body and started the search for my clothes. After peeking out her door to make sure I wouldn't surprise Eva, or worse Mac, I strolled naked into the living room.

My suit was neatly draped over the couch with a sticky note of a smiley face attached to the crotch. Eva must have come home at some point. I slid on my pants and gathered the rest of my clothes, intending to run across the hall for a clean outfit, talk to Shaw, and maybe come back over here to coax Chloe into the shower with me after training.

I checked the time, relieved when I still had fifteen minutes before I was supposed to hit the weight room with Mac, Shaw, and RJ. They'd have questions, but I'd spent years honing my no comment skills.

Before I could make it out the door, my phone vibrated in my pocket. I pulled it out and frowned at the screen. Another unknown number.

As a matter of habit, I didn't answer any calls from people not in my contacts list. It wasn't usually a problem, but ever since I was featured in that article, I'd been getting a lot of spam calls. Weirdly, this one had called me a couple of times before. Most recently, last night.

Nope. I wasn't interested in whatever they were selling. I sent whoever it was to voicemail and picked up my clothes again.

Next to me, Chloe's door swung open with a slight squeak I hadn't noticed earlier. She stopped in surprise when she spotted me and smiled smugly as her gaze dragged over my naked chest.

"I wondered if you were going to remember your pants or if I missed a true walk of shame across the landing. I admit I hoped for the latter." She leaned against the doorframe, dark hair wild around her face and a red mark on her neck barely visible over the collar of her robe. Hunger licked at my gut.

"I'll get naked for you anytime you want, Trouble." I dropped my stuff on the floor at my feet and took a step toward her, ignoring the hand Chloe held up. "Miss me already?"

She pressed her lips together, smothering the smile I saw lurking there. "Don't look at me like that. I know you have training today, and I know how important it is. Your spring practices just started, and I'm not about to be the reason you get injured."

I ran a hand through my hair, clawing back the overwhelming urge to say forget training and practice in favor of locking both of us in her room for the foreseeable future. "I expected you to sleep longer."

"Yeah, well, the bed lost a lot of its appeal when you got out of it."

A grin took over my face. "I'll only be a few hours, but you could try my bed. I wouldn't say no to finding a beautiful woman hogging all the covers in there when I get back."

She propped her hands on her hips. "I *do not* hog the covers. It's not my fault my blanket isn't big enough for your massive—"

I cut her off with a kiss. Chloe curled her arms around my neck and opened her mouth with a sigh. For a minute I let myself sink into her, drowning in memories of last night and fantasies of what I'd like to do to her next.

All too soon, though, I eased back. "I can't get enough of you."

Chloe's lips twisted as she tilted her head. "You need to go or you're going to be late. Eva wanted me to do a karaoke thing later, despite my insistence I had no interest in singing. She invited Blue, so I might be able to get out of it."

Mac had cornered me with the same karaoke thing,

though I'd forgotten until just now. Alex was hosting a Sunday Funday to test out his new material. Mac wanted to go right after training. Well, after he'd primped after training.

I'd much rather have Chloe all to myself in my big bed, but Mac was proud of his contributions. Besides, there was always after.

I kissed her nose and stepped back to collect my things for the third time. "Don't worry about it. We'll go to karaoke, and maybe I'll finally get to meet this friend you and Eva keep mentioning."

Her eyes narrowed. "You don't like meeting new people."

"Not particularly, but you smile when you talk about her. Even better, I like spending time with you."

She flapped her hand at me. "When did you get this good with words? Go. Build bigger muscles. I'll meet you at Johnny's with the rest of the crew."

I waggled my brows at her, backing across her living room with my clothes clutched in my hands. "And you'll come home with me after?"

Chloe let out a little laugh, and her smile hit me right in the chest. "And I'll come home with you after."

I couldn't ask for a better night.

17

Chloe

Karaoke was a gross understatement. When Eva, Blue, and I stepped into Johnny's that afternoon, nothing could have prepared me for the sheer amount of glitter covering every conceivable surface.

"What the actual fuck," Blue breathed out next to me.

I'd only been in there the one time before, so it wasn't crazy to think this was normal décor for a Sunday afternoon. Blue's wide eyes and vaguely defensive stance made me reconsider.

The dark interior had been transformed into something that resembled the inside of a disco ball. Bright lights reflected off curtains of shiny fringe hung over the walls, and each table had a different colored sparkly tablecloth. People were packed in every bit of free space, most dressed in normal clothes like us, but I spotted a full three-piece suit and someone in Houston Stallions pajama pants.

Too bad I couldn't get a picture. Soren would get a kick out of someone repping his team at Sunday karaoke.

I stood on my tiptoes and scanned the faces for a group of tall, stupidly attractive guys. My gaze landed on Mac almost immediately, talking violently with his hands next to a large booth in the center of the room.

With so many people standing between me and the booth, I could only see glimpses of the occupants.

Blue still looked shell-shocked, but Eva was smiling. I nudged my self-proclaimed best friend and nodded toward Mac's booth.

"They're over there."

"I know," she said, then pointed to the bar. "But I see a soccer player in that direction who deserves to buy me a drink."

She sauntered away, and within seconds, a sandy-haired guy in blessedly normal clothes smiled down at her. I shook my head. Eva had a strict rule about never buying her own drinks. I hooked my arm through Blue's and led her into the chaos.

"Is it always like this?" she hissed at me.

I shrugged. "No idea. This is my first time, but knowing my luck, something will go horribly wrong, and we'll end up drenched and eating tacos for disaster brunch."

Blue's brows scrunched together. "I like tacos. Brunch tacos sound great, so that doesn't qualify as a disaster. Why do you think a disaster would be tied to you?"

A sigh escaped, louder than I meant it to be. "I make decisions, often bad, that lead to worse consequences."

"Like what?"

"Like waking Noah up to come remove a naked, passed out teammate from my bed."

She scoffed. "Eva told me he got drunk at her birthday party, which you cleaned up after. You didn't make him drink or invite him into your bed. The only decision you made was asking Noah for help to take care of someone else's problem. Those consequences weren't yours, but you're taking ownership of them. Have you considered your strength lies in cleaning up messes rather than making them?"

I opened my mouth and shut it again. I'd spent so much time focusing on navigating the challenges in my life—from asshole classmates to belligerent ducks to handsy strangers in a hotel—that I hadn't spent much time analyzing the cause of the challenges and how I reacted to them.

It wasn't in me to back down, but was I adopting other people's messes? A pattern of trouble meant I had to be involved though, right?

Blue didn't say anything she didn't believe to be one hundred percent true, but I'd had years of practice seeing myself as a troublemaker. Had Vince fucked with my self-perception that badly?

I set aside the thought to be examined later, when I wasn't steps away from Noah and the rest of the crew.

Blue scanned the room, and I could see the calculations happening in her head. "What do you think is the max capacity in here?"

I laughed, relieved to change the subject. "I'm sure Mac will be happy to answer your questions."

She stiffened, nearly pulling me to a stop, then relaxed as we rounded the last group of people. As expected, we were the last to arrive. Shaw and Riley took up the middle of the booth with Noah sitting on the side closest to us and an empty spot opposite him big enough for my two friends. Mac had already moved on to his next verbal conquest.

Noah's lips twitched as his gaze raked over me, taking in my jeans and white cropped sweater. "No danger of duck-related mud shenanigans?"

I shoved him over, claiming the sliver of booth next to him and digging my elbow into his side. "Not funny. I'm still trying to get those stains out of my green sweater. We've been ordering a lot of Peking duck from China House in retribution."

Blue grimaced and slid into the open spot across from us, tugging at her dress. "Do they have actual food here? I'm starving."

She reached for one of the plastic-covered menus sitting in the middle of the table, and I spotted Mac weaving his way back to us. People stopped him every few feet, but he gave each of them his full attention. Noah shifted, immediately yanking my focus away from the room and narrowing it to the quiet giant next to me.

Eva beat Mac to the table. She didn't have a drink with her, but she flashed a smile over her shoulder as she waited for Blue to move—our new friend had a preference for always sitting on the end of booths. Something about statistically being the safest in case of emergency.

I followed Eva's gaze to the soccer player, who nodded toward us while talking to the bartender. Blue reclaimed her seat as Eva slid in next to Riley, and Eva's smile turned feline.

"He's here with his friends."

Blue snorted and lifted the menu again. "Our table is full."

She wasn't wrong. With three broad-shouldered football players taking up most of the space, I was pressed against Noah's side. Not that I was complaining.

Eva lifted one shoulder and let it drop. "He's happy at the bar. I was simply offering the opportunity of a fine athletic specimen."

Mac arrived in time to hear the last part. "Talking about me again, Wildcat?"

She looked him up and down. "I'm not sure you qualify. Maybe if you took your shirt off."

Challenge filled his gaze, so I jumped in before he started stripping. "Mac, what did you drag us to?"

He spread his arms in welcome. "It's Sunday Funday! Happens every last Sunday of the month. Boozy brunch and invite only karaoke. Alex and I started it, but he does most of the work."

"Did you decorate too? It's like a unicorn exploded in here."

Mac's brows drew together as he looked around. "Alex always lets the drama department do what they do, so for all I know, that might be accurate. I just show up where they tell me."

I took in Mac's outfit, low-slung dark jeans and a black, long-sleeved dri-fit shirt clinging to the muscles in his arms and chest. The lack of color made him stand out against the rainbow around him, and I'd bet my new earbuds he'd been advised to wear something along those lines.

"You're singing today, right, Mac?" I asked him.

He grinned at me. "Hell yeah, Baby Asher. Alex and me been working on something special."

My smile turned brittle at the unwanted nickname, but I was determined not to make a big deal out of it. Noah, on the other hand, had no such qualms. He reached around me to punch Mac in the arm with a scowl.

"Don't call her that."

Mac yelped and rubbed his arm. "What? Baby Asher? But it's one of my best nicknames. Almost as good as RJ." He jerked his chin at Riley, but she was busy trying to swallow Shaw's tongue.

The lack of backup didn't faze him in the least. He

shrugged and his gaze landed on me again. "I can come up with something else if it bothers you."

I opened my mouth, intending to change the subject before the name caught on, but Noah responded before I could.

"It bothers *me*," he grumbled. "She's not a fill-in for D."

Mac's brows went up and he laughed. "No shit, man. I'd pick the Clo-ster here any day over her brother." He winked at me, and despite his egregious overstatement, a warm glow filled my chest.

"I'm going to veto Clo-ster," I said with a wince.

"Yeah, they're not all winners. We'll keep working at it." He nodded at Alex, who was waving at him from behind the sound booth. "That's my cue. Gotta go to work."

Noah pulled me closer and pressed his mouth to my ear. "You could come up with a nickname for me. Give you some variety when you make those breathy little noises."

I sucked in my cheeks to keep from voicing the naughty thoughts invading my brain. Across from me Eva met my eyes and shook her head. We hadn't had the chance to discuss the pile of clothes she'd found in the living room, but I hadn't missed the smiley face on Noah's suit this morning.

She raised a single brow, promising a full inquisition later. I shifted my gaze to Blue, but she was still silently buried behind the menu. No pressure there. She didn't know D, or anyone else here really, and I liked the fresh perspective. Once again, I was thankful for Eva's powers of persuasion.

No one else paid us any attention for once. Either the other patrons were used to seeing the football elite tucked away in the booth, or they were watching Mac stride across the makeshift stage to the mic. Noah took advantage of the relative anonymity and tucked his hand under my loose top to caress my rib cage, rubbing his thumb along the bottom edge of my bra.

I wasn't self-conscious about my body—my curves were awesome, thank you very much—but a series of giggles from the next table made the hairs on the back of my neck stand up. A covert glance showed three girls dressed for a club. Dark makeup, short skirts, stilettos, the works, and all three of them were looking at Noah.

More accurately, they were looking at the spot where Noah's hand disappeared. I tried to tune them out, but my brain had other ideas despite the level of ambient noise in the room.

"Probably another ball bunny," one of them said.

"No, I know her. That's D's sister."

My brow furrowed at the quick identification, and I took another look. Yep. The girl in the leather skirt was from my shitty math class. They'd stopped staring to huddle together instead.

"Isn't she some kind of psycho? I heard she got kicked out of her last school."

I rolled my eyes. Ridgegate University had asked me to leave voluntarily. It was all very polite.

"How lucky she gets her choice of her brother's friends. Have you seen the size of Noah's hands?"

Leather skirt girl snuck a glance at me, and I raised a brow when our gazes met. Her attention flew back to her friends, and I tried not to feel a petty sense of joy for the quick retreat.

"Shh. She can hear you, Lauren."

Yeah, Lauren, don't want to spread vicious rumors if the subject can hear you. I didn't hate the idea of them fearing me, but a year ago, those girls might have been me and my friends. Petty as fuck, jealous for the wrong reasons, craving attention from the wrong guys.

I frowned as Mac cleared his throat, quieting the room. He thanked everyone for turning out to hear Alex's hand-picked singers, and my mind wandered. Didn't Lauren and her friends realize they could *also* have a shot at the guys in my booth if they simply came over and said hi without any ulterior motives?

Riley came up for air long enough to cheer with everyone else when Mac introduced the first singer. Shaw couldn't take his eyes off his girlfriend, so maybe their chances with him were unlikely. I glanced at Noah, surprised to find him watching me.

"What?" I asked.

"Why don't you wear your glasses anymore?"

I shifted to face Noah, giving the mean girls my back, and wrinkled my nose. "Contacts are a lot easier. Especially the ones I have. They last a month, so I barely have to think about it. You know how much I like easy things. Why?"

He gripped the back of my neck and leaned in to whisper. "I kind of miss the glasses. They gave you a bad librarian vibe that drove me crazy. Made me want to bend you over my knee."

My cheeks warmed, and I was glad none of our booth-mates were looking our way. Spanking had never appealed to me, but I was willing to try just about anything with Noah.

"Should've realized you had a dirty side hidden under all that quiet muscle," I murmured.

He smiled slowly as I ran my hand up his arm, over the dips and ridges, until I could hook my wrist over his shoulder. I loved Mac, but I was going to have a hell of a time waiting for the *after* Noah had promised.

From across the booth, Blue cleared her throat. "Am I wearing the wrong clothes for this type of thing?"

I shared a confused look with Noah, then shrugged. "I don't think there's a dress code or anything. You look different than normal, but nice."

She grimaced at my answer and slid lower in the booth. "I knew it," she muttered, almost too quiet for me to hear over the sounds of an Adele remix.

Earlier, she'd shown up at our apartment in a sexy black dress, her hair curled in a way that hid her rainbow streaks with her glasses nowhere in sight. She'd even traded her beloved All-Stars for a pair of low-heeled booties. Without the riot of color and the thick rims covering her face, her blue-green eyes looked huge. Honestly, she was hot in an unexpected, awkward way.

"Thanks, Mom," she continued to herself, sounding bitter. In the almost month that I'd known her, she'd never shown any signs of self-consciousness. Something was clearly bothering her, and at some point I'd missed, Eva had left again to flirt with her soccer player. Time to step up.

Somewhat reluctantly, I leaned forward, abandoning my sexy talk with Noah. "What's going on?"

Her eyes flitted to the side of the stage, where Mac grinned at a group of pretty co-eds in jeans. "I'm not comfortable with... all this." She gestured at herself, and I tried to keep my face neutral. "My mom said I should try something new."

"You look hot as fuck, so if that's your goal, you should be thanking your mom."

Her lips twisted into a scowl. "Do I look like being hot as fuck is one of my goals?"

Noah grunted behind me, but I suspected he was trying to hide a laugh. I smacked at him with my palm without looking, connecting with solid flesh somewhere in his abdomen.

"If you're not having fun, I can take you back to the apartment."

She sighed, losing the air of intensity she'd momentarily adopted. "No, you're busy with your football arm candy."

Noah's laugh couldn't be disguised this time. I glared at him over my shoulder, but he smiled at my disgruntled expression. No help there.

I returned my attention to Blue just in time to see her lift the menu again as Mac approached our table. I didn't miss the way his gaze lingered on the expanse of leg visible on her side of the booth, but he quickly moved on, looking around until he spotted Eva across the room.

His easy smile tightened, and he tore his eyes away to focus on me. "Alex wanted me to tell you he changed the tempo of the next song like you suggested. He wants you to let him know what you think."

My brows shot up at the reminder of a throwaway comment I'd made during my fateful lunch with Noah. The same day we'd met Blue. I'd totally forgotten, but nice to know I made an impression.

"Uhh, thanks?"

Mac nodded with none of his usual flair and made his way back across the room, pointedly avoiding the bar area. Weird. Why was everyone being so weird?

Blue lowered the menu and stared longingly at the door. "I'm going to call an Uber. Can you tell Eva I left?"

I nodded. "Text her when you get back. You know how she worries."

She frowned and slid out of the booth. "Unnecessary. I've lived in this town my whole life."

"Please, Blue." I tried to keep the exasperation out of my

tone, I really did, but sometimes I felt like I was dealing with obstinate children.

Blue's eyes darted over to Mac as he climbed onto the stage at the end of the song, and she sidled around us. "Fine. You can tell her I'll text her when I get home."

A second later, she disappeared into the crowd. I rubbed my temple until Noah caught my hand and kissed my fingers.

"She's interesting—and nervous about Mac for some reason."

I shook my head. "It really seems like it, but Mac is such a..."

"Child? Pain in the ass? Golden retriever in human form?"

I snorted out a laugh. "He's not scary, that's for sure." My mind jumped from Mac's non-threatening self to the much scarier situation between me and Noah.

"What are you thinking, Trouble?" he murmured, breaking into my doom spiral.

Eva slid into her abandoned spot with her eyes twinkling and two frozen pink drinks in her hands. "Now *that* is a perfect nickname. Where's Blue?"

I tilted my head toward the door. "Left. She'll text you when she gets home."

"Good. She has to be the most confident person I've ever met, and I grew up with Mac. A serial killer could kidnap her, and it would never occur to her that she was in danger." She slid one of the drinks toward me. "I don't know what's in it, but the cute bartender said it was a smoothie. Non-alcoholic."

Noah raised his brows at me. "Not drinking today?"

I took a long pull from the straw and let the sweet taste linger on my tongue for a long moment before I answered him. "Nah, I have plans tonight for which I'd like to be completely sober."

Eva rolled her eyes. "This is why I invited Blue. I needed a wingwoman to counter all the sexy eyes happening over here." She jerked her thumb at Shaw and Riley, who were oblivious to the room and trying to meld into one person in the middle of the booth. "Are they like this at practice?"

Noah chuckled. "No. They're serious at practice. Mostly. The eye-fucking is unreal though." He stretched his arm along the fake leather behind me. "After the shit they went through during the season, I figure they've earned the right to ignore the rest of the world in their off time."

"We can hear you," Riley muttered from her spot in Shaw's lap.

Eva toasted her with the other smoothie. "I'm just glad you're past trying to drown yourself in the shower."

Shaw snorted and poked Eva in the side. "Where's your flavor of the month?"

She raised her chin, one hundred percent a princess staring down at a peasant. "I'm taking a hiatus from the tasting menu. Mind your business."

Riley laughed so hard she had to steal some of Eva's smoothie, sucking down a long drink then handing it back. "When have you ever minded your own business?"

Eva sent her an arched look. "It's a public service. I do what I do for the good of the community."

Shaw coughed into his fist, and even Noah shook with laughter behind me.

"I hate you all," she muttered, ignoring us to cheer for Mac as he took his turn at the mic.

Noah cupped my hip, tugging me nearly into his lap. "I'm ready to leave whenever you are," he whispered into my hair. "I have plans for your mouth that don't involve singing."

Wet heat took over, pooling between my thighs so fast I had to clench them together. Why had I thought one-time hookups were the way to go? This restrained foreplay was sexy as hell, and knowing I was guaranteed to spend the night with Noah, I was in a hurry to get out of there before one of us changed our minds or got too drunk to walk.

I reached behind me and squeezed the hard length straining behind his zipper, intending to respond with a sexy comeback, but my brain abdicated control to my nether regions.

"Now is good."

18

Chloe

I tossed the wet jeans into the dryer with the rest of my clothes and groaned. This was a punishment. Karma. Payment for the regular orgasms and new habit of lounging in Noah's room all day.

Noah did laundry regularly in their little stackable machines, and I'd started throwing some of my stuff in there. Why not? He was already running a load. Except today, Noah and the others had left for training early, and I'd slept in.

No one had switched the laundry.

I started the dryer and stretched my arms over my head, staring down at the bright teal panties and tank top I still wore. The only non-soaking-wet clothes I had in the apartment. After spending the last few weeks sleeping over at Noah's, I'd sort of stopped going home.

Unfortunately, home was where the rest of my clothes lived. I was supposed to meet Eva in ten minutes to go get coffee, and now I'd have to pray she wasn't around to see me come in pantsless.

It was a fifty-fifty chance since she expected me to be late.

With a sigh, I grabbed my bag, checked the landing to make sure it was empty, and scooted across to my door. At least the weather was cooperating with warm temperatures. The second I stepped inside, I saw my prayers were in vain.

Eva lounged on the couch with a thick book, and the gleam of joy when she spotted me said I'd made her day. Fantastic.

"I don't want to talk about it," I muttered as I crossed the living room.

Eva sat up from her sprawl and laughed. "Where are your pants?"

"I don't want to talk about it," I repeated through clenched teeth, heading for my room.

I shoved the door closed behind me, but instead of a satisfying slam, I heard soft footsteps on the carpet.

"Please tell me Noah stole all your pants so you couldn't leave, necessitating a daring escape on your part. I'm working on this theory where he keeps you chained to his bed so he can have his wicked way with you whenever he wants."

A blush warmed my cheeks. She wasn't far off. "I saw you a few days ago at lunch. This was a minor laundry mishap."

Her brows rose. "He purposely shrunk all your clothes so you'd have to walk around naked?"

I stopped rummaging through my dresser to turn and stare at her. "Why is Noah an evil genius in all of your fantasies?"

She crossed her arms and leaned against the doorframe. "He seems like the type. Quiet and unassuming on the outside, freaky when he lets loose. If you'd share any of the details you're hoarding, I wouldn't have to resort to my imagination."

The heat on my face spread to my ears. "The answer is still no." Though her imagination was disturbingly accurate. "Are we getting coffee or not?"

"I wasn't sure you'd be able to tear yourself away from Noah," she teased.

I flipped her off while yanking on a clean pair of leggings. I'd only cancelled on her twice, and I saw her regularly. Just not here. After the first night in my bed, Noah declared it unfit for a guy his size. I couldn't argue after I experienced the sheer breadth of his mattress. Four of me could fit on there—or one me and one Noah, which was all I needed.

His spring football practices stepped up, my classes got harder, and it was just easier to stay at his place. Was this what happened to normal girls when they started dating someone? They abandoned their friends for consistent—spectacular—dick?

I shook off the lingering concern I might be a bad friend and spread my arms. "There. Ready. I'm all yours for the rest of the day."

Eva grinned. "Until your date, you mean?"

"Why do you even talk to me when you already know everything?" I'd put off the date I'd promised Noah until he'd asked me again during a weak moment, one with his face between my legs.

Sex was easy, especially with him, but dates reminded me of all the ways I'd failed in my last relationship. We were supposed to go out tonight, so it was probably for the best I finally came back to grab some fresh clothes.

"What information you give me—and what you don't—tells me a lot. Anyway, I need a couple of minutes to do something first." She nodded her head toward her door, and I followed her, fully expecting some kind of ambush.

I wasn't wrong.

A brown-headed duck in a cloth diaper waddled around under Eva's desk. I pinched the bridge of my nose where I could feel a headache starting to form. "You stole Henry?"

Eva closed the door behind us. "I didn't steal him. Alexis needed someone to foster him while they fix the duck enclosure." She brushed past me to crouch by Henry who wiggled his butt happily.

I blinked a couple of times until my brain caught up. "Foster?"

"Yeah. It's temporary. They should be ready for him to go home this weekend."

"What happened to the rest of the ducks?"

Her lips twisted as she stood and sent me an exasperated look. "They were all adopted except for Henry. Apparently, he's been causing trouble—biting the volunteers—so no one wants him."

My gaze flicked to the bird, who gave me some intense side-eye while following Eva into the bathroom. I wasn't surprised Henry was acting up, but I also felt a bit of kinship with him. He didn't fit in with the other ducks, and everyone saw him as a trouble-maker when he was really just trying to live his best life.

Water started running, so I moved to the bathroom doorway. "Are we even allowed to have ducks in our apartment?"

Eva adjusted the flow into the tub and stripped the cloth off Henry before setting him in the water. "I'm not worried about the lease. He mostly lives in the bathroom, so he's not destroying anything. Alexis gave me these duck diapers to keep his mess to a minimum, and he's been happy to play in the bathtub." Henry let out a relatively quiet quack, then dunked his head.

"If he's living in your bathroom, where are you showering?"

She gave me a blank look. "*Your* bathroom. It's not like you're here to object. At this point, I might as well start billing myself as a halfway house to the apartment full of football players across the landing."

I squinted at her. "Are you upset?"

Eva sighed, shutting off the water. "Not about you and Noah. Come on." She led me back into her bedroom, closing the bathroom door behind us.

"Is he going to be okay in there alone?"

"Yeah, we have a system."

She and the duck had a system, but I couldn't scrape my life together enough to date someone I really liked.

Eva turned and speared me with her sharp gaze. "Okay, while Henry swims, tell me why you've gone off the grid."

My first instinct was to run. Eva in interrogation mode was scary, and I had a lot of mixed-up feelings I'd prefer to ignore. She stared at me, waiting, and the words built up behind my lips.

"I'm hiding from my brother." I blurted out. "He's called four times this week, and I've sent all of them to voicemail. Suuuper busy. Can't talk. I forgot how persistent he could be."

She tilted her head. "Why?"

I dragged my hands through my hair, then collapsed facedown onto her bed. "Can't you go back to harassing me for the size of Noah's dick?"

"I could, but I'd be derelict in my duties as your bestie. Plus, I already have that information."

I frowned at her. "How do you know Noah's dick size?"

"Mac likes to talk when we work on stunts." She sat on her desk chair and swiveled to face me. "Why are you hiding from your brother?"

"He doesn't know about Noah yet." That wasn't the whole reason, but it was the most prominent. I dropped my eyes just in case Mac's mind-reading theory was correct.

A bit of neon pink peeked out from under her bed. The color reminded me of something, but I wasn't sure I'd ever seen Eva wear something neon. She was more of a jewel tone girlie. Desperate for a change of subject, I grabbed the material.

"What's this?"

Eva didn't answer, but I didn't need her to since I had eyeballs. Running shorts. I pursed my lips and propped myself on my elbows. No wonder the color was familiar. Pretty sure the last time I'd seen these they were speeding past me at the 5K.

"Aren't these Mac's?" I held the shorts up so she could see them.

Eva shrugged and took them from me, tossing the shorts into her laundry basket. "He must have left them here at some point. Mac never met a piece of clothing he couldn't wait to take off."

I narrowed my eyes. "They were under your bed."

She raised a brow and crossed her arms. "Good try, but we're not talking about me."

"Maybe we should be," I muttered.

Eva snorted. "Nothing to talk about. Now explain to me why you haven't told your brother you're banging one of his former teammates and current best friends."

I sighed, rolling over to stare at her blank white ceiling. "When I'm with Noah, it's like no one else exists. I'm not D's little sister and he's not D's friend. We're just..."

She sighed and joined me on the bed as I trailed off. "What does your relationship have to do with D?"

"Nothing. For now. But the second he finds out, he'll get involved."

Eva chuckled quietly. "D is the farthest thing from disapproving. He'll be happy for you as long as you're happy."

I rolled my head to meet her eyes. "I know, but he'll *be* there. I wasn't even sure I wanted a relationship with Noah beyond a quick fuck."

"Girl, same." She held up her fist, and I reluctantly bumped it.

"But he wouldn't let me bang and bye—claimed he wasn't interested."

She scoffed. "Don't lie to me. I've seen the way he looks at you, not to mention Mac's aforementioned inability to stop talking and Noah's inability to keep his hands off you when you're together."

"Exactly. Plenty of banging, none of the bye."

Her face softened. "I get it. Noah's always been the burnt marshmallow of the group. Hard outside, squishy, delicious center. He wants more than banging." I shook my head at the weirdly accurate comparison, and she pointed a finger in my face. "You're happy though."

"I'm happy," I confirmed softly. "Noah makes me happy. Not that I can't get there on my own, but it's different. I want to spend all my time with him, even if we're not naked, which is why I wanted some time without D's interference. He'll get all invested. What if all this happiness fades? What if Noah gets tired of me or realizes I'm more trouble than I'm worth?"

Eva laughed in my face. "I have so many reasons why your fears are unfounded, but let's start with the fact that Noah calls you Trouble as an endearment. I don't think your wild side is going to scare him away. That said, it's not fair to Noah if you're going into a relationship with a bag packed waiting for it to fail."

"I know," I said again.

"Do you want it to succeed?"

"Yes." An immediate rush of certainty calmed some of my fears. I wanted to make the relationship with Noah work. Probably I always had, but the last few weeks had given me enough confidence to admit the truth to myself.

She leaned forward, clasping my hands. "Good, but have you considered how he feels about you wanting to keep him a secret?"

"It's not much of a secret. You guys all know. Honestly, it's a miracle Mac hasn't spilled to D already."

"You know what I mean. Call your brother. See what he wants, and if you're feeling it, tell him you're spending every night riding Noah's dick. Maybe go into excruciating detail. Actually, call Nadia first so she can film his reaction. I'm going to check on Henry while you do that, then we'll go get coffee."

I glared at her as she tossed my phone at me. "This is duress."

"I prefer to think of it as positive realignment." She pointed to the phone. "Call."

Henry quacked when she opened the door, but at least she closed it again behind her. I considered pretending he didn't answer, but she'd know. Somehow, Eva always knew.

I pulled up D's contact and took a deep breath before hitting call. Maybe he'd be at practice. In the off-season. An hour after he left a message saying he'd be free all day.

Hope springs eternal and all that. I deflated when he picked up.

"Hey Clo, finally. You're a hard lady to get ahold of."

As much as I'd been dreading talking to him, D's voice always made me feel like I was back home. Stupid insecurities aside, he was still my big brother.

I cleared my throat, trying to adopt my usual sarcastic tone. "Yeah, I've been busy horning in on your friends. They like me better by the way."

He scoffed. "Of course, they do. What's not to like?"

Warmth filled my chest at D's hype. He meant it. I had my issues with his fame and perfect...everything, but D never made me feel inferior. Another way I didn't live up. A nice sister would hype him right back instead of throwing sass.

I sucked at being a nice sister. "Right? Too bad you got stuck with all those attractive, athletic, charming genes. Everyone knows petty is where it's at. What did you need?"

"I'm flying down for the spring game next weekend, and I was hoping to see my favorite sister for more than the length of a stuffy alumni dinner. You're coming to the game, right?"

The spring game was the culmination of the spring season, basically a glorified practice with another team. The guys loved it because they got to show off. Their previous coach took the game seriously, but the current one seemed like he'd let them have some fun.

Of course, I was going. No way would I miss watching Noah play. I may pretend to not care, but I liked football. The challenge and skill involved always interested me, and I'd throw elbows to be front row for Noah.

I snorted. "Will your entourage be there? If so, I might sit somewhere else."

He chuckled. "No. I'm traveling under cover. Em knows, but the publicity people don't."

"Is Nadia not coming? What about Soren?"

"She's working that weekend, and Soren has a charity thing. I thought I'd stay the night on Mac's couch and head back the next day. No offense, but the idea of staying in Eva's apartment terrifies me. Other than sleeping, it's just you and me next weekend."

And Noah. And the rest of the crew. Honestly, I'd been sharing him with the others since he started college, but everything felt different now. Eva, Mac, Shaw, Noah—they'd all become *my* friends, and D never even met Riley. I was a little nervous that with D's return, I'd be dropped back down to Baby Asher status.

"Sounds good. Our couch isn't big enough for you anyway, and I'm not giving you my bed." Though, if I would just woman up and tell him the truth about Noah, he could stay in Noah's bed. "Was that all you wanted—to warn me you'd be in town taking all the attention away from me?"

"No, I had something else I wanted to talk to you about."

Sirens went off in my head, and my chest froze up. *He knows* repeated in my head over and over again, so loud I missed what D said.

"Sorry, what?"

He laughed. "Remember Harper, Soren's cousin? She had to fire her last assistant for a reason I can't remember, and she asked about you."

I let out the breath I'd been holding, and the lightheadedness added to my confusion. "Me?"

"Yeah, she remembered the party you pulled together after the draft. Apparently, you impressed her with your organization skills and your take no shit attitude."

I leaned back against Eva's pillows, trying to wrap my

mind around what he was telling me. "Wait, are you offering me a job?"

"Not me, dumbass. Harper needs an assistant, a virtual one so you could do it from there, and she wanted to know if you were interested."

"What the hell, D? Why didn't you just give her my number? Or my email?"

He cleared his throat, just like I'd done at the beginning of this fiasco of a conversation. "We thought you'd be more likely to say yes if your favorite brother asked. It doesn't pay well, and it's a lot of work, especially while you're still in school. Are you interested, or should I tell her to look elsewhere?"

Was I interested? Yes, but the prospect was terrifying. I wouldn't have the safety net of apathy if I crashed and burned as usual. Harper and the others would have front row seats to my ineptitude. The usual insecurities tried to get me to turn the opportunity down before I could fail, but dammit, I didn't want to spend the rest of my life drifting.

I was good at organization. Theoretically, I could do this job, but I wanted to get it on my own terms, without D's influence.

"Tell Harper to call me. If she's really interested, I'll discuss it with her." I patted myself on the back for the mature answer. Old me would have grabbed any excuse not to take the risk. "And tell Nadia she's my favorite."

D laughed. "Sure, brat. See you next weekend."

I stared down at my phone for a long moment after we hung up. The job offer scared the shit out of me, but so did D's visit. I still hadn't told him about Noah, but maybe that conversation would go over better in person.

The soft sound of dawning realization jerked my gaze to

the bathroom door, where Eva stood holding Henry in a new duck diaper.

A slow grin took over her face. "Harper wants to hire you as her new assistant. Smart. You'd be great at it, and she could pay you shit because you're still in school."

I frowned at her. "Excuse me, I'm worth slightly more than shit."

"You should put that on your resume," she deadpanned. "I assume D is coming to the spring game too?"

"You already knew that, just like you already knew Harper needed a new assistant."

She shrugged and carefully set Henry on the floor. "I know a lot of things. Makes life easier to predict."

I pursed my lips, debating if I wanted to try to out-Eva her to find out where she got her information. Not worth the trouble. I wouldn't be able to do anything with the knowledge, and Eva used her powers for good. Mostly.

The alarm on my phone buzzed, and I double checked the time. "How have we been in here for an hour already?"

She frowned. "Why do you have an alarm set?"

"Because I wanted to put some actual effort into my appearance tonight. I'd planned to beg you to help me get ready after the coffee. I haven't been on a real date since high school."

Eva held up a finger. "I'm going to need more details than that, but I'll let the comment pass for now since we've shifted into date preparation mode. Where are you going?"

"Noah won't tell me. When I asked, he said jeans were fine, but that man lives in sweats and workout gear. Not that I'm complaining about those gray sweats." I shared a look with Eva, and we both fanned ourselves.

"Knowing our silent giant, you're going to want sneakers and something you can move in."

I scrunched my nose. "He's not going to make me exercise, is he?"

Henry quacked in shared horror—or maybe because Eva was shooing me into the living room. She closed the door in his face, and I snickered. That's what he got for ruining my favorite green sweater.

Eva propped her hands on her hips. "Are you being mean to my duck?"

"*Your* duck?"

She waved her hand at the closed door. "*The* duck. Whatever. I'm officially kicking you out until Henry goes back to the rescue. I need your room to escape his unbridled love. Also your shower. Let's get you some new clothes for naughty time at Noah's."

"Please don't call it that," I muttered as I followed her into my room.

"Since I didn't hear you tell D about your extracurricular activities, I'm assuming you'll be back next weekend."

I snorted. "Unless Henry sticks around."

"We can share your shower until you grow a pair of lady balls and tell your brother you're getting naked with his friend."

"Keep it up and I won't tell you what Noah calls his penis."

She threw a balled-up sock at me, followed by a tote bag. "That's a false promise. He doesn't have a name for his junk."

I shoved the socks and a change of clothes into the tote bag. "How did you—" I sighed. "Mac."

"Mac," she confirmed.

"He's going to spill everything to D this weekend, isn't he?"

"Yep," Eva answered cheerfully. "Better figure out what you want to say before Mac paraphrases for you."

Fantastic. Now I really did have a deadline. My stomach cramped up at the thought, but I refused to let my own insecurities get in the way of spending time with Noah tonight. As long as he didn't make me go hiking or something. I couldn't be expected to accept a relationship *and* cardio.

19

Noah

"Johnny's tonight!" Mac whipped past me, slapping my stomach on the way.

I grunted and tried not to drop the weight bar on my face. "Can't."

Mac circled our section of the weight room in my peripheral vision while I finished my set. When he got back to me, I'd already re-racked.

He punched my shoulder. "Yes, you can, big poppa. I believe in you."

Sweat dripped down my face as I ignored him to strip the plates. "I have plans."

"Bring Chloe with you. She loves when I sing at her."

I swallowed a laugh. Chloe loved Mac, but the look on her face when he sang wasn't for his voice—it was for the hand I had down her pants under the table. She did a pretty good job of maintaining her composure, but she couldn't hide the flush on her neck or the hitch in her breath. Those were all me.

My favorite was when she tried to carry on a conversation on the phone with me buried inside her. Fighting the impending orgasm while trying to get her parents to stop talking always made her ravenous the second she hung up. My wild girl.

"No, I'm taking her out tonight. She finally agreed to a date."

Mac threw my sweat towel at my face. "About time. Is she going to tell D anytime soon? Keeping you two a secret is slowly killing me. It's filling up my insides with sadness. Do I look bloaty to you?"

He turned sideways and ran his hands down his abs with a pout. I threw my towel back at him.

"She's not ready yet."

"You better make her ready. D isn't stupid, and he'll be here this weekend. Her hangup isn't about you, it's about him. It's time to push, man."

I sometimes forgot how perceptive Mac was when I was faced with his ridiculous personality day in and day out.

"Thanks, Mac."

I thought he'd take off to do another lap of convincing people to come listen to him sing, but he followed me into the locker room.

"What's going on? You're crankier than usual," he asked.

I tossed my towels in the bin and debated showering there or just going home. "Nothing new."

Mac nodded, used to my succinct answers. Even if I wanted to talk, I wouldn't know where to begin. He knew I grew up with my uncle and I didn't go back to visit, but I'd only told Chloe about the rest of my history. I had the uncharacteristic urge to explain about Craig calling me multiple times this month.

He was close by at a convention in Dallas for the next few days, and he wanted me to come have dinner with his colleagues so he could pretend to be the doting uncle. I wanted to focus on convincing Chloe to stop holding back in our *situationship*—preferably while I had her naked and writhing underneath me.

Or over me. I wasn't picky.

Mac's hand came down on my shoulder, mercifully pulling me from my thoughts. "If you ever decide you want to talk, I'll listen."

"You?"

"I can listen. I'm listening right now. Ask Eva. My listening skills are top-notch." He looked vaguely offended at my disbelief, so I tried to take him seriously.

"Thanks. I appreciate you offering me your skills."

Mac grinned at me—crisis averted. "Remember, if you come to me first, I'll split the money with you from the pool."

I scowled, abandoning any effort to make him feel better. "You bet on me talking about my problems?"

"Not just me. Shaw, D, Soren, RJ, and Holbrook."

"Holbrook?" I yelped.

"He overheard Shaw setting up the take on speaker phone. We couldn't exactly tell him no. It would mess with morale."

"You guys are all assholes. RJ too."

Mac laughed as I gathered my stuff. I'd definitely be showering at home until I didn't feel the crawling sensation of my supposed friends watching to see when I'd finally break down.

"Don't worry. It's been weeks. At this point, I think only Holbrook remembers."

I eyed him as I slung my bag over my shoulder. "Better lock your door. I know a certain someone who isn't aware you're the one who drank all her Frappucinos in an attempt to stay up for a special midnight screening of Wonder Woman."

Fear passed across his face, but he recovered quickly, yelling at my retreating back. "Ha! Joke's on you. I told her that shit months ago."

I chuckled as he muttered to himself about Eva's sadistic vengeance streak.

———

CHLOE WASN'T in the apartment when I got home. Theoretically for the best if I wanted to actually go out with her, but my dick disagreed. When I got out of the shower, I had two missed calls from the same unknown number.

I frowned down at my phone as I counted the times they'd called without leaving a message. Seven. Seven times since the article. I should mark the number as spam, but a nagging sense of unease kept my thumb hovering over the button instead of pushing it.

Shaw pounded on my door, his usual way to get my attention, then yelled, "Package for you, man."

RJ snickered, and I rolled my eyes as Shaw made a joke about his package. I waited until I heard their door down the hall close to risk emerging. A few weeks ago, I'd mistimed it and gotten an eyeful of RJ's boobs. Not an image I wanted in my brain for one of my teammates.

A large brown envelope with my name on it sat on the kitchen counter. I picked it up, frowning at the return address. Why would the athletic department send me something?

I tore the envelope open and shook out two sheets of paper. The first one I recognized—a piece of stationery with the athletic department's letterhead. They politely asked me to refrain from having my mail sent to the main office. Weird.

The second was a sheet of lined notebook paper covered in a messy scrawl, with my name at the top. The page crumpled in my hands as I scanned it, until I got to the signature at the bottom. Micah Olsen—my father.

I hadn't heard from him in fifteen years. Blood pounded in my ears, and I sank down onto the couch. My first reaction was to chuck it in the trash, maybe burn it. The thought reminded me of Chloe, so I forced myself to forego starting a fire in favor of actually reading the words.

He was out of prison, and he wanted to see me. Apparently, he'd found me through the damn article.

I stopped at the word *found*. He hadn't known where I was? A little voice that sounded annoyingly like Craig whispered he hadn't cared where I was, why would he keep tabs? I mentally junk-punched the voice and read the rest of the message.

He was in town, doing some part-time work at a car shop, and he'd stay around until I met with him or told him to get lost. A phone number was written across the bottom —one I recognized since it had been calling me on and off all semester. Guess that answered the question of whether it was spam.

Fuck. I ran a hand through my hair and considered blocking the number anyway. I had a plan for my life, and it didn't include my asshole father showing up again after dumping me with his unwilling brother. I knew intellectually it hadn't been his choice to go to prison, but it had been his choice to beat someone nearly to death.

It had been his choice to ignore my letters and emails. He clearly hadn't wanted to be a father, so what had changed?

Did I really want to find out?

I sighed and stuffed the letter into the pocket of my jeans. Not right now, I didn't. I wanted to take Chloe out for a date, then bring her back here and tease her with my tongue until she surrendered, soft and pliant.

Soft Chloe hit me every time. She worked so hard to convince the world she was tough and untouchable, but with me, she dropped her armor—and I didn't want her anywhere near my father.

I still had fifteen minutes before I was supposed to pick her up, but I didn't want to sit there stewing about all the ways that letter could fuck up my life. Shaw and RJ were busy in their room, and Mac hadn't shown up yet, which meant he'd probably gone straight to Johnny's.

Chloe would make a great distraction, especially since she wasn't expecting me yet. Maybe I'd catch her naked. The thought was enough to get me moving.

The second I let myself into her apartment, my phone vibrated with a message. I checked the screen to see it was from Craig, not Chloe as I hoped.

I need you to make an appearance at the conference reception tonight.

A stupid part of me still held on to the hope he'd come to one of my games—or do *anything* that showed he cared, even a little bit. When I'd told him about the spring game, the same as every year, he'd said he'd be too busy at this medical conference.

Apparently, he was too busy for me, but I was supposed to drop everything and drive to Dallas. Typical.

This wasn't the first time he'd trotted me out to impress one of his colleagues, but it might be the first time I was willing to go. I had questions about the letter from my dad, and short of calling the man I hadn't seen in fifteen years, Craig was the only other person who could answer them.

Another message from Craig followed the first without me responding. *Preston Hotel 7 p.m.*

I'd worked my ass off to get Chloe to agree to a date. As much as I wanted those answers, Craig would have to wait. Chloe came first.

"Where are we going?" she asked from her bedroom doorway.

I looked up from my phone and completely lost my train of thought. She was wearing a dark green dress that made me reconsider my plan to leave the apartment. With a knowing grin, she spun in a circle, and I swallowed hard at the expanse of smooth skin exposed by the plunging back of her dress. Thin straps criss-crossed down to her waist with nothing in between.

She wasn't wearing a bra, and I desperately wanted to know if she'd chosen panties to match. Knowing Chloe, she was one hundred percent naked for me under there.

"Well?" she asked.

"Dinner." I cleared the huskiness from my voice and tried again. "Dinner at San Miguels, then a surprise in the woods."

Her eyes lit up. "I love San Miguels. I'm not as excited for anything in the woods, but if the surprise involves your dick I'm all in."

Suddenly, standing in the woods with Chloe on her knees in front of me, my fingers in her hair and my cock down her throat, was the number one fantasy on my list. The little known miniature golf course I'd intended to take her to paled in comparison.

As if she knew I was rapidly rearranging my plans for

the evening, she waltzed past me and out the door. "Come on, big guy. I'm starving."

Me too, but food was the last thing on my mind.

I managed to make it to the restaurant without pulling over to feast on her instead, and we finished an entire meal without me slipping my hands under her dress at the table. By the time Chloe ordered dessert and I'd paid, we'd talked enough I was confident I could make it through mini golf without finding a secluded tree to fuck her against.

After all the fuss, I couldn't remember why I'd insisted we needed to go on a date. Being in public with her didn't prove anything about her feelings for me, and I'd spent the entire time telling my dick to stand down while wishing we'd stayed home.

Not that I wasn't enjoying myself. Chloe told me about the job offer from Harper, and I couldn't be happier for her. The opportunity sounded perfect, but she still had shadows of doubt in her eyes.

If she couldn't see how good she'd be as Harper's assistant, I'd help her. "Why are you hesitating?"

Chloe pressed her lips together for a second and stared over my shoulder. "I'm going to fuck it up." I laughed, and her offended gaze darted back to me. "What the hell, Noah."

"So what if you do? It's a new job, and no one is perfect right from the beginning. Harper knows that. I've seen you reorganize our fridge for maximum efficiency, and I *know* you already started a spreadsheet of pros and cons."

A blush crept up her cheeks. "Your fridge was a disaster of rotting leftovers, and anyone who's not an idiot would make a list before accepting a job in a field they haven't worked in before."

I made a noise of assent, and Chloe's eyes narrowed. "What?"

"Is your spreadsheet color coded with references?"

A smile tilted the edges of her lips up. "Yes."

"Chloe, I think you're going to be fantastic, but even if you aren't, you learn from your mistakes and move on. You can't go into it expecting to fail. You have to try."

She looked down at her hands, clasped on the table, and I didn't understand the flash of guilt. When she met my gaze again, her usual confidence had returned.

"Thanks, Noah," she said softly as the server dropped off a slice of cheesecake covered in strawberry sauce.

"Anytime, Trouble."

I meant it. I'd spend the rest of my life building her up if she let me. As a bonus, for a few hours, I was able to put all the bullshit between Craig and my dad out of my mind. I should have known better than to think it would last.

Chloe licked cheesecake off her spoon and studied me. "What's wrong?"

My shoulders tensed, but I tried to play it off anyway. "Nothing."

She shook her head. "Nope. Not doing that. We're on a real date, and I'm pretty sure people in a situationship are supposed to share the things bothering them. You've been supportive and amazing while I talked, now it's my turn. Give me the chance to be supportive and amazing too, Noah."

Chloe stared up at me, beautiful and demanding, and I couldn't deny her. I never could.

"Craig wants to show me off tonight at a conference he's attending in Dallas, and I got a letter from my dad. He's out of prison. Sounds like he has been for a while."

Her brows shot up, and she grabbed my hand. "Tell me everything."

I found myself blurting out the details of the letter and

Craig's disinterest until I became useful. My dad's phone calls and the weirdness with him "finding" me.

Chloe's nose wrinkled, and she made a noise of disgust.

I knew that look. She was about to jump headlong into trouble.

"You know, I always wanted to go to the reception for a medical conference at a swanky hotel. Sounds like the perfect first date." She pulled me from my seat and out of the restaurant, looking over her shoulder with mischief in her eyes. "Want me to drive?"

Fuck. I might love her.

20

Noah

The Preston Hotel was as pretentious as my uncle, which was an impressive feat. I should have known any conference he deigned to attend would appeal to his inflated sense of worth. The valet helped Chloe out of the car, and I had a moment of déjà vu back to the alumni dinner.

Her dress was shorter, but my blood still burned to touch her. This time, I didn't hold myself back, curling my arm around her waist and holding her against me as we found the correct ballroom hosting the conference reception.

It didn't take long for Craig to notice us, considering everyone else in the room wore cocktail attire. Chloe's dress could pass, but my jeans stuck out.

The man himself wore a navy suit with a subtle pinstripe. He stood several inches shorter than me, with a slim build and long graceful hands. At first glance, we looked nothing alike. His wavy brown hair only showed hints of a red undertone, but his green eyes matched mine.

"Noah?" Craig offered me a pleased smile, but I could

see the edge to it. He didn't like surprises, and despite asking me several times to make an appearance, he wanted me to do it on *his* schedule.

A small, petty part of me took joy in unsettling him, especially since he couldn't voice the frustration I saw in his eyes. Probably not a healthy reaction to the man who'd raised me.

His gaze darted to my arm wrapped around Chloe, then back to me. I had to give him credit for retaining his polite smile.

I tugged her forward, letting go of her waist to slip my hand into hers. "Uncle Craig, this is Chloe Asher, my girl-friend. Chloe, this is Dr. Craig Olsen."

The lines around his mouth tightened when I left off the rest of the qualifications he insisted I use when introducing him, but he extended his hand to shake Chloe's.

"What a wonderful surprise. I wasn't aware Noah was seeing anyone." The jovial welcome sounded false to me, and judging by Chloe's half-smile, she'd picked up on the insincerity.

"It's nice to finally meet you." The feral grin she offered him confirmed I hadn't imagined the threatening undertone of her words.

I freely admitted I usually enjoyed Chloe's brand of trou-ble, but I'd been conditioned my whole life to present a certain image to the world at large. Despite the clear evidence of my dad's letter, I wasn't ready to set fire to my relationship with my uncle just yet.

"If you have a minute, I'd like to speak to you in private," I told him.

"Of course, but first, let me introduce you to Dr. Allen Hastings. He's a fan of college football." Craig waved over an older guy with a head of fuzzy white hair that made him look like he'd electrocuted himself at some point in the evening.

"Allen, this is my nephew, Noah. He plays football for Teagan University." Craig ignored Chloe standing next to me. When I chanced a peek at her, she squeezed my hand and her sharp smile softened.

Allen came over to ask me about the off season so far. I wasn't used to talking about my football career, despite the press conferences we were sometimes forced to attend. I usually just let the other guys talk while I stood there looking intimidating. Reporters were surprisingly unwilling to approach a human wall with a scowl.

Craig sipped his drink, probably expensive whiskey, and appeared pleased with himself. I did my duty and asked Allen about his work, sounding appropriately impressed with the medical jargon he spewed off. After a few minutes, someone else called Allen away, and we were finally left alone with Craig at the edge of the crowd.

Before he could show me off to anyone else, I stepped into his line of sight, blocking his view of the room. "We need to talk."

Craig stilled, and he frowned with a pinched expression. "What's this about, Noah?"

"I got this in the mail today." I pulled the crumpled letter from my pocket and held it up.

Craig snatched it from me and gripped it with two fingers as if the paper would contaminate him. "What's this—"

I could see the moment he realized it was from my dad. His head snapped up, and he scanned the immediate area. I thought for a second he might tear the page to shreds, but instead, he carefully folded the letter and handed it back to me.

"You should throw his number away and forget he ever contacted you."

My brows rose, and I ignored his comment. "Did you know he was out?"

Craig hesitated. "Yes, but I didn't know he was living near you. He hasn't kept in regular contact. It's for the best if you don't get attached. Give it time and he'll be right back inside. It's who he is now."

"Why wouldn't he have known where I was until the article?"

He smoothed a hand over his hair without mussing a single strand. "Who knows? Micah was a liar, and a violent one. We've discussed his shortcomings before." Craig's tone dismissed the topic, and his eyes landed on Chloe for only the second time that night. "I'm much more interested in learning about your girlfriend."

Chloe tilted her head. "That's funny, I'm much more interested in learning about why you *needed* Noah's attendance tonight."

"It's in his best interest to learn how to network. If he wants to maximize his endorsements, he needs to be a fan favorite. But I'm sure I don't have to tell you about his future career."

Frustration crashed into the wall I'd erected to prevent this exact conversation. Craig didn't care what I wanted—he only cared about the potential money and fame in my future. As long as he believed I was at TU playing football with the intention of entering the draft, he left me alone to live my life with only the monthly phone calls to check up on his investment.

As soon as I'd picked TU, Craig had become friends with the dean, and he was petty. He'd have no problem destroying my academic career to punish me. I knew from experience when I'd wanted to try wrestling after my freshman year of high school. He'd insisted to the school I needed summer classes to keep up, and I'd missed the try-outs. Bonus for him, he convinced the administration I was quiet because I was stupid. Thank god my actual teachers didn't believe his shit.

I had one more year to my degree, and then Craig lost all his power.

Chloe smirked at him, undeterred. "Don't worry, I'm well acquainted with what Noah wants in the future."

Craig narrowed his eyes and took a sip of his drink. "I can see why he'd be enamored by you, but you won't get anything from him. Noah knows better. You'd have more luck with a different target. I'm sure it wouldn't be hard for you to find a suitable substitute with your... charms."

His clear disdain grated on my nerves, but I could have ignored his opinion if he hadn't let his gaze linger on Chloe's curves. The way he looked at her—as if she were a posses-sion he'd enjoy owning—ignited my fury. I'd avoided the conversation for three years, and in one fleeting glance, I broke through that wall because I wasn't going to let anyone treat Chloe like that. Not even the man who could destroy my future.

"I'm not going into the NFL, and Chloe isn't a ball bunny. You need to apologize."

Annoyance darkened Craig's eyes. "Of course, you're going into the NFL. Chloe, would you excuse us for a moment?"

I crossed my arms. "Apologize first."

Craig sighed. "You're acting like a recalcitrant child. I'd thought you were past this." With obvious reluctance, he faced Chloe. "I'm sorry if my advice offended you. Now if you'd be so kind, perhaps a drink at the bar?"

"She's not going anywhere," I told him calmly, belying the anger pulsing inside me.

Chloe laid a hand on my arm. "It's okay. I have to take a leak anyway. Craig, I'm sure we'll meet again since I plan to be around for a long, long time. Seeing as how Noah can make his own decisions." Chloe flashed me a smile, and I knew she'd purposely phrased her exit to antagonize Craig. A bit of rebellion in my defense without forcing me to intervene.

I definitely loved her.

Craig watched her thread the groups of people on her way out of the reception area, then checked to be sure none of those people had crept close enough to overhear our conversation.

"You'll need to break up with her."

I frowned and managed to muzzle my first reaction of *hell, no*. Craig didn't react well to displays of emotion, and I'd already lost my temper once. "I disagree."

"She's completely inappropriate, and I can only imagine your change of heart about professional football came at her behest."

"Chloe encouraged me, yes, but she supports whatever I decide."

He took a sip of his drink and scoffed. "She's hoping you'll prove an easy road to a life of luxury. You need to be aware of the dangers inherent in letting your baser instincts run amok. Look at your father."

My frown deepened. "What does that mean?"

Craig shook his head and lowered his voice. "He had a solid future set out for him until he met your mother."

I'd heard the second part before, but the first part was new. Craig didn't often speak well of his brother, but he regularly blamed my mother and her unexpected pregnancy for ruining my dad's life. If not for my dad's abandonment, I might have been tempted to think Craig's opinion was skewed by his own feelings.

"Did he ever try to contact me?" I'd never asked the direct question before. Craig had always been quick to point out how easily my dad had forgotten me when he was trying to excuse his own shitty parenting, and I'd believed him.

Craig shifted his gaze off to the distance with a frown. "No. Micah may be out of prison, but he has no place in your life. Just like Chloe. Break up with her. End of discussion."

My jaw ticked at his obvious lie and attempt at misdirection. I couldn't tell the extent of his interference, but I was pretty sure now there was more to the story of my father's imprisonment. We'd moved shortly after for Craig's job, and I'd never considered that he wouldn't keep my dad updated.

I'd written Micah letters, so many letters, until the utter lack of response convinced me Craig was right. My dad had left me behind along with the rest of his life. If Craig had sent the letters, Micah would have known where to find me.

"What did you do, Craig?"

He leaned closer, his voice tight with anger, "Quiet down please. These are my colleagues, and you're here representing my name. Micah is only going to distract you from achieving the goals you've worked so hard for. He's a bad influence, and I'd hate to see you follow in his footsteps."

I shook my head as my world shifted. Craig was still trying to control me, but his hold was broken. Had he *ever* told me the truth? My father had gone to jail for aggravated assault, that much was confirmed from the letter, but what had Craig left out for his own benefit?

My temper rose up like a wave, pushing me to use my strength to find the answers. I could make Craig fear me.

The temptation was strong, especially after the way he'd treated Chloe, but I wasn't willing to live up to his worst opinion of me.

Craig could have his secrets. I didn't need his half-truths and manipulations—I had Micah's number. Assuming I could trust a man I hadn't seen since I was six. If Craig wanted to retaliate, let him. I'd find a way around him.

A sense of freedom spread in my chest, and I took a full breath for the first time in maybe forever. Fuck Craig. He didn't deserve my loyalty.

"You don't get a say anymore. I don't want to hear from you or see you. Use my name all you want to make yourself look better, but if anyone asks me, I'll deny a relationship with you. Have a good night."

"I didn't raise you to be so disrespectful," he hissed, but I'd already dismissed him to look for Chloe.

I strode away from Craig with my pulse pounding in my ears. I'd just detonated my past and possibly my best chance at a future, but he couldn't take the people I loved. Mac, Shaw, RJ, Eva, D, Soren—those guys were all the family I needed.

And Chloe. Always Chloe. She wouldn't mind one bit if we left all this bullshit behind and finished our date.

I followed the signs toward the bathroom down a side hallway, and for the second time, I found another guy with his hands on her. Chloe stood stiffly by the ladies' room entrance while he held onto her arm and leaned toward her.

Rage blocked out any conscious thought. In the back of my mind, I registered the paunch under an ill-fitting suit, the receding hairline, and the red lanyard around his neck indicating he was one of the medical people there for Craig's conference.

I didn't care.

Chloe stepped back before I could reach them. He swayed slightly, and his hand fell from her arm. Probably the only thing that kept me from coming in swinging. I grabbed a handful of his wrinkled jacket and shoved myself between him and Chloe.

The guy let out a surprised grunt, and I had to blink tears away from the sour smell of tequila. He squinted, trying to focus on my face, but the sharp edge of my fury didn't dull a bit.

"Touch her again and I'll rip your arms off." I tossed the guy toward the elevator doors with a growl.

He stumbled and regained his balance with a confused frown at Chloe. "Angel?"

Chloe stepped in front of me before I could go in for a second round, flattening a hand on my chest. "Stop, Noah. It's not what it looks like."

My rage itched under my skin, searching for an outlet, but I tore my gaze away from the drunk guy swaying in the hallway to Chloe's pale face. Fear edged into her eyes, and my stomach turned.

I took a step back, giving her plenty of space, but she shook her head.

"You idiot," she muttered under her breath. "Stay here for a second."

Chloe approached the drunk guy, and his face split into a sloppy smile. She gingerly took his arm and steered him toward the elevator.

"Your wife is at home, remember? Do you need me to have someone help you to your room?"

He squinted at her then patted her hand. "No, thank you, darling. You're beautiful, just like my angel. She's at home keeping the dogs company while I'm here."

Chloe smiled at him. "You told me. Why don't you go on upstairs and get a good night's sleep?"

"Yes. Sleep. Big day tomorrow. G'night, Angel." He stumbled away toward the open elevator, and Chloe's shoulders relaxed as soon as the doors closed behind him.

I approached her tentatively, her fear fresh in my mind. "Chloe?"

She let out a huff and turned toward me, propping her hands on her hips. "I'm not afraid of you, Noah, so stop acting like I should be running the other way."

I tilted her chin up, searching her face, and she met me with a patient smile. "You sure I didn't scare you?"

She moved closer, pressing her body against mine to kiss my jaw. "No. I know you'd never hurt me. I was worried you might hurt him to keep me safe. Your protection is sexy, but not needed at the moment. Let's go home, and you can take advantage of all the tingly feelings you caused."

Her complete faith shattered me, especially after my less than stellar reaction a moment ago. I wrapped an arm around her, resisting the urge to find a nice shadowy corner to explore those tingly feelings.

We moved toward the main reception area, and I leaned down close to her ear. "Next time we're in a hotel, I'm not leaving your side."

She peeked up at me. "Are you mad?"

"Not at you. That guy was easily twice your age and wearing a wedding ring."

"He was drunk and thought I was his wife." She held up her hands when I frowned down at her. "He didn't do anything except lean on me and call me beautiful."

With her under my arm, my temper finally fizzled out. "So you didn't need my help this time?"

She raised a brow. "If he'd actually passed out, I might

have recruited you to carry him upstairs, but no. I had that one handled."

Of course, she did. I'd let my anger at Craig get the best of me and assumed the worst. A chill went down my spine at the violence I might have caused had she not stopped me. Craig might be a lying asshole, but he wasn't wrong about everything.

I could be dangerous, just like my dad. Instead of me saving Chloe, she'd saved me.

"I'm sorry for overreacting," I said quietly.

She tightened her arm around my waist and smiled up at me, full of sunshine despite the disastrous evening. "It happens. Don't worry, I'll make sure you only beat the people who deserve it."

I pulled her close and kissed her head. "Life is never boring with you, Trouble."

Despite the exhaustion that came with my adrenaline fading, a smile pulled at my lips. I didn't know what I'd expected from a date with Chloe. Nothing in our relationship had taken a normal route. Our first date was destined to be a disaster. She laid her head on my shoulder for a second, wrapping her arm around my waist, and I met Craig's gaze as we made a direct path to the door.

His eyes narrowed on Chloe, and my grip tightened. He probably blamed her for my outburst since as far as he was concerned, nothing was ever his fault. If he tried to touch her, I'd end him.

No history, no blood relation, would stop me. Nothing was as important as the woman cuddled against my side.

21

Chloe

After the debacle of a first date where Noah cut ties with his uncle, the rest of the week passed by with surprisingly little drama—and surprisingly little time to spend with Noah. I had major projects due in two of my classes plus learning the ropes with Harper, and Noah was busy as hell leading up to the spring game with practices and training and film time.

Add in my stomach had been upset on and off all week, and I was spent. At the end of each day, we were both too tired to do more than fall asleep wrapped around each other. By the time Friday rolled around, I'd had enough.

When Noah came home from practice, I was waiting for him. Naked. Sprawled across his bed in the soft twilight.

He stopped short, then shoved the door closed. "My favorite way to find trouble."

I drew a finger between my breasts and down my stomach. "Welcome home."

He grinned at the sight and stripped down, stalking toward the bed. I licked my lips at the sight of his dick bobbing against his stomach, already hard.

"What's the occasion?" he asked.

"No occasion, but I *did* say I'm your girl if you need help in the bedroom department."

He gripped the base of his cock and gave it a long, slow stroke as I watched. "You're my girl in every way, not just the bedroom."

"Then come over here and prove it."

The words were barely out of my mouth when Noah knelt on the bed and pulled me to my knees, roughly turning me to face the headboard. He loosely circled my wrists, placing my hands on the padded headboard.

"Don't let go," he murmured, trailing his lips over my shoulder.

I heard the crinkle of a condom wrapper, and then his hands were on me. Everywhere. Noah knelt behind me, pressing his big body against my back, and teased my nipples, my clit, my pussy. My head fell back onto his shoulder, but I didn't let go of the fabric covered wood.

He nudged my legs farther apart, and slowly pushed two fingers inside me. My legs trembled, and amid the tight waves of pleasure, I wasn't sure I'd be able to keep holding myself up.

It didn't matter though, Noah would catch me if I fell.

His other hand spanned the base of my throat as he held me in place. "Okay?" he whispered silkily into my ear.

I gave a sharp nod, willing to let him do just about anything to my body. The delicious loss of control ignited me like nothing else ever had. I whimpered when his fingers retreated, and moaned low when he replaced them with his cock. *Yessss.*

Wetness smeared across my skin as he splayed his hand on my stomach. Noah knew exactly how to make me burn.

Hard, deep thrusts that seemed to hit every nerve ending in my body.

My nails dug into the headboard, and I couldn't stop the delicate shivers running through me, from where we met up to the top of my head and down to the tips of my toes.

The light pressure of his fingers on my neck never let up, but Noah groaned into my hair. "Fuck, Chloe."

I was close, *so close*, when I heard the apartment door shut, but it didn't register as important until D's voice reached me.

"Surprise, assholes. I'm here early."

Mac laughed, sounding way closer than he should have been. I glanced over my shoulder and sucked in air. A thin bar of light from the hallway lit up the growing darkness.

We'd accidentally left Noah's door cracked. Alarm tightened my chest even as I clamped down on Noah inside me, balanced on the brink of an orgasm.

"Door's open," I managed without letting out a moan.

Noah tensed for a second, then instead of stopping, he rolled us over without missing a beat. He braced himself on one forearm and slid his hand over my mouth, pressing his lips to my ear.

"Hold on tight and don't make a sound," he whispered.

I arched up, too far along to stop and too turned on by the chance we might get caught. My legs curled around his hips, and he reached between us for my clit. My inner muscles clenched as the added stimulation threw me over the edge.

"Yes, Chloe," he whispered in my ear.

Noah pressed his mouth to my shoulder, muffling the groan as he came. Both of us silently gasped for air, and my heart beat like a thousand butterflies in my throat. His head raised enough to meet my gaze, and I saw the same illicit pleasure in his eyes. He'd liked the danger of getting caught as much as I had.

Hell, we might still get caught.

Mac's voice came from the living room, and I tensed. "Hey, man, good to see you. Shaw and Noah are out, but I'm free for some shenanigans. Just gotta grab something from my room real quick."

He got louder as he came down the hallway toward us. Instead of turning into his room, the crack in our door disappeared with a quiet snick. Their muffled voices faded until the front door slammed shut.

I collapsed back with a deep exhale. Noah rolled away, disappeared into the bathroom for a moment, then sat on the bed next to me, bare ass naked. My pulse hadn't settled yet, and judging from the churning in my stomach, it wouldn't as long as I was naked in here with Noah where D could spot us.

"Did Mac just cover for us?" I asked.

Noah let out a short laugh. "Yeah, I think he did. Good to know Mac is still capable of surprising me." He tilted his head when I scooted past him. "Going somewhere?"

My legs were still jelly, but I took my chances standing. When I didn't immediately sink to the floor, I dropped a hard kiss on his mouth and started searching for the clothes I'd discarded earlier. "That was hot, but I should head home before D checks my place."

Noah jerked his chin toward the living room. "D is probably standing outside the front door with Mac right now."

"I'll go out the window." I grabbed my leggings and shoved one leg in before realizing they were backward.

"You're going to climb out the window?" he asked, scrubbing a hand down his face. "Come on, Chloe. Isn't this a little dramatic, even for you?"

I tried not to be hurt by the last sentence, but it took work. My toe got stuck on my pants, and I nearly sent myself catapulting back onto the bed. When I overcorrected, Noah caught me before I could faceplant into the ground. My hero, as usual.

Instead of setting me on my feet, he hauled me back onto the bed with him. "Take a breath. Mac will keep D busy."

I relaxed with my cheek against his chest. He was right. Going out the window was crazy. None of the guys dared to burst into Noah's room, not even Mac. As long as I stayed here with him until the others left, we'd be fine.

Noah ran his fingers through my hair, and the repetitive tugging lulled me out of my panic. Of course, we could always stay here until he had to leave for the game tomorrow instead.

"I want to tell D," he said quietly.

"Tell him what?" I mumbled.

Noah chuckled. "About us."

My eyes flew open, and I was suddenly wide awake. "No."

He tipped my chin up until I met his gaze. "Why not?"

I opened my mouth to spew the usual reasons—D was overprotective of me, and I didn't want Noah to see me as D's little sister—but they weren't really true. My teeth snapped shut, and I groaned.

"It's complicated," I whined.

"Take your time. I'm not going anywhere." His thumb stroked down my throat, a visceral reminder of what I'd let him do to me earlier.

My body heated, but he wasn't touching me to elicit a response. He wasn't hoping for another round, though I was one hundred percent on board. Noah simply liked to touch me. He liked me, protected me, took care of me—even when I didn't need it—and he deserved better than a half-assed response.

I sucked in a deep breath and held it for a second, pushing past the ever-present fear. "I like being just you and me. You're mine, only mine, and as long as D doesn't know about us, I don't have to share you—or hear about how this is probably another one of my mistakes."

He threaded our fingers together and lifted my hand to kiss it. "Nothing about this is a mistake, and you never have to share me. I'm yours, all the time."

I nodded, a tiny movement that didn't accurately reflect the massive leap I was about to take. "I'll tell him tomorrow at the game. I promise."

———

"Nachos or hot dog?" D shoved both in front of my face as he took his seat next to me.

My stomach lurched at the smell, and I pressed a hand to my abdomen. "Ugh, don't talk about food. I've been fighting off nausea the last couple of days."

He sent me a worried glance. "Eat something bad?"

"Hell if I know. I haven't actually puked anything up, but the thought of food makes me queasy. I've been living off of chicken noodle soup and crackers."

D wrapped an arm around my shoulders, pulling me into his side. "Sorry, Clo. If you do decide to hurl, point it the other direction, okay? My delicate sensibilities can't handle you spewing."

"Thanks, asshole. I can feel the love."

"Hey, I love you. Look on the bright side, at least you're not pregnant, right?"

D laughed at his own joke, but the world around me shrank to a pinpoint. I'd been so preoccupied with Noah and school I hadn't been paying attention to my cycle. My last period was the week before the alumni dinner. I counted back, then squeezed my eyes shut. *Fuuuck.*

My periods were usually pretty regular, and I'd never gone this long before between cycles. How dumb did I have to be to not notice?

For the rest of the game, I was two people. On the outside, I cheered and joked with my brother, but on the inside, I was berating myself for making the stupidest of stupid mistakes. Noah and I had used protection, every time, but I wasn't on the pill. The hormones fucked with my body too much for it to be worth the trouble.

Suddenly, mood swings and fatigue felt like the better option.

I breathed a sigh of relief when the game ended, but I'd paid such little attention I couldn't even say which team won. As planned, D and I went down to the tunnel to meet Noah and the others. Going down the steps, I realized I hadn't had *the talk* with D. I couldn't do it now, not until I knew for sure.

Eva was waiting in the tunnel when we got there. I hung back while they jumped all over D. Normally, being ignored in favor of my brother would trigger my insecurities, but my world had shifted over the last few hours. Or maybe it had been shifting for longer than that and I hadn't realized.

With my head pulled firmly out of my ass, I saw things I'd maybe missed before. Eva's eyes flicked to me while she talked to D, and Mac rubbed my arm as he danced past to leap onto D's back. Riley shook her head and sent me a smile. Even Shaw showed he hadn't forgotten me by catching Mac's flailing arm before it smacked me in the face.

The prickly version of me convinced she'd never be good enough finally settled down. She wasn't gone, but she'd lost some of her control. At least for now.

Apparently, I only needed a bigger fuck up to put the rest of my life into proper focus. My timing could have been better.

When Noah emerged from the locker room, he made a beeline for me. Shit, he thought I'd told D. I sidestepped him and gave a subtle shake of my head. Disappointment flashed across his face for a split second before the emotion disappeared behind his usual mask.

D clapped Noah on the back, congratulating him for the win, but Noah's eyes never left me. My stomach turned again. I needed to tell him—about breaking my promise. The baby talk could wait.

———

Hours later, I'd managed to sneak Noah away from the crew to steal some alone time in his room. He hadn't brought up my promise, or my utter failure to keep it, and I'd managed not to throw up on anything despite the nausea that could be from food poisoning, nerves, or a baby.

Noah stripped his TU shirt off and did a graceful flop back onto the bed, then beckoned me to join him with a wave of his hand. I chewed on my lip, but even secrets and possible babies couldn't keep me away from him.

As I cuddled next to him, Noah pulled my shirt over my head, but I flattened his hand on my stomach to stop him from unbuttoning my pants. He linked his fingers with mine, content to simply lay with me.

"You okay?"

I winced, drowning in guilt. "I didn't tell D. I'm sorry."

Noah sighed. "It's fine, Chloe. I'm not going to push you when you're not ready."

"I *am* ready, and it's not fine. Broken promises are not fine. I saw your face when you realized. Not. Fine."

"I was disappointed, yeah, but only because I missed you. This was the first time you'd come to one of our games to see *me*, and I spent the entire time with you on my mind. After it was over, all I wanted to do was kiss you. Instead, I got your brother." He kissed my temple. "I wanted *you*. First. Always."

"You have me," I whispered, but I couldn't convince myself he'd want to keep me in the end.

His brows drew together. "Something else is bothering you."

I drew in a shaky breath. Yeah. A potential baby. "I don't want to talk about it yet."

"Okay, what do you want to talk about?" he asked, stroking my back.

I didn't have another topic—my mind was helpfully blank—but one gorgeous phoenix wing was spread out under me. "Why did you pick a phoenix?"

Noah let out a single dry laugh. "Because meeting your brother and the others, forming friendships with them, helped me rise from the ashes of my previous life."

I smiled, amused despite myself. "And now you're a beautiful flaming bird?"

"The phoenix isn't me—it's them. A reminder of the strength we achieve together, on the field and off. It's protection and encouragement and... brotherhood. Like you said before, they're my chosen family. Like you."

"Chosen family," I murmured, tracing from the tip of the

wing around to his back. "They're behind you, supporting you, but they still guard your heart."

Noah rolled over, splaying me across his chest. "Like you."

"Like me," I agreed softly.

He watched me with quiet amusement, and I lived for the happiness in his eyes. I did that, and I'd never do anything to hurt him. Except I wasn't telling him the whole truth.

I tilted my head up to meet his gaze, and the emotions inside me ballooned up, pushing against my heart and my head until I thought I would burst. If I was really pregnant, it would change everything.

How was I supposed to protect his heart and help him fly when I was the thing tying him down?

Talk about a major fuck up. My parents were going to freak, D was going to freak, Noah *should* freak. Wasn't this exactly what his uncle had warned him about last week? Trapping him in a relationship with a pregnancy, without all the money and fame though.

What if he decided Craig was right? What if he finally had enough and wanted nothing to do with me?

Deep down, I knew Noah would never abandon his child, but I couldn't stop my mind from conjuring up every horrible what-if that had haunted me since I'd agreed to date him. The phantom pain of losing him sliced through me, but I couldn't keep this secret from him.

When had he become so important to me?

My heart raced, and I hoped Noah wouldn't notice. A tiny voice whispered the feelings had always been there, I was just too stubborn to see them. Another asshole voice insisted Noah would be better off without me.

He traced my jaw. "What's going on in that mind of yours, Trouble?"

"Noah, I have something to tell you."

His expression didn't change, and I felt a flare of hope. Noah knew me, better than anyone else, and he still chose to be with me every day. Maybe I wouldn't ruin us after all.

Before I could gather the words to tell him I thought I might be pregnant, his door flew open and in tumbled my brother.

22

Noah

All three of us froze.

Chloe cursed under her breath, breaking the moment and spurring me off the bed. I'd wanted D to know about me and his sister—to know how much I loved her—but not this way. D's face closed down, and he turned without a word.

Shit. We needed to do damage control. Chloe scrambled after me, and I barely beat her into the hallway.

"D, wait," I said.

He spun at the entrance to the living room. "What the fuck, Noah?"

I held up one hand, clamping the other on Chloe to keep her behind me. "It's not what it looks like."

His jaw ticked. "It looks like you had my sister in your bed, half-naked."

She popped her head around my shoulder. "Alright so that part *is* what it looks like, but you need to calm your ass down."

I squeezed her hip, hoping she'd get the message and stay quiet for once. "I'm not fucking around with her."

D whipped out an arm in her direction. "Is she fucking around with you?"

An angry noise behind me gave me half a second of warning before Chloe came out swinging. I caught her around the waist as she lunged for D's face.

"You sanctimonious ass. Noah is one of your best friends, and you're giving him shit? He treats me with respect and care and actually listens when I talk."

D glared right back. "I'm not mad at Noah, I'm mad at you."

"I'm a grown ass adult who can make my own choices, and I choose Noah. Deal with it."

At Chloe's shout, Mac's door opened, and Eva's head popped out, her hair wild. Her gaze flitted over Chloe's bra and my naked chest, then stopped on D's flushed face. For once, she chose to stay out of the situation and simply leaned against the doorframe.

D threw his hands in the air and paced away. "Deal with it? I spent *all afternoon* with you, and nothing. You lied to my face. What did I do to deserve that? Why didn't you trust me?"

I rubbed my chest where his words sliced open a wound. He was right—we should have trusted him. Still, Chloe looked like he'd slapped her, face pale and drawn, and I wouldn't let her take the brunt of his anger.

My chin went up. "It was my idea."

Chloe's head swiveled toward me, and I met her eyes.

"We wanted to see how things went before we told everyone," I continued.

D snorted. "By everyone, you mean me, specifically. No way you kept it a secret from Eva and the others." His nose flared, and he leveled Chloe with a hurt look. "I expected better from you."

Chloe clutched her stomach, and I wondered if the stress of the situation was making her feel sick again. It would serve D right if she puked on him since he still hadn't learned to respect the privacy of someone's bedroom.

D studied my arm around Chloe for a long moment, then pressed his lips together and walked away. Chloe tried to pull free so she could chase after him, but I didn't release her.

"No, I'll go," I said. "He and I need to get a few things clear. Eva?"

She straightened from her silent perch to pull Chloe away from me with an arm around her shoulders. "Yep. I've got her. Come on, Chloe. You look like you need to sit down, and maybe we should find your top."

Chloe shrugged off Eva's arm. "I'm not an invalid." She glanced back at me. "We still need to talk."

Despite her ominous tone, a smile tried to escape. Whatever trouble she'd gotten into, I was there for it. "Do you need me right now?" If she said yes, I'd stay. No questions asked. D was like a brother to me, but his sister was everything.

She hesitated, then shook her head. "No, it can wait. You better hurry or D will get halfway to campus before you can catch him."

I hooked the back of her neck and dropped a kiss on her lips. "I'll be back soon."

Eva fanned herself as I sprinted out of the apartment. Bare-chested. At least the temperature was warm enough I wouldn't freeze my nipples off. My feet were a whole different story as I found every sharp rock between our apartment and the parking lot.

I'd intended to check for D's car, but that plan of action proved unnecessary. Contrary to Chloe's concern, D hadn't gone far. I found him on a bench near the walking path around our complex. Night had fallen while our secrets came to light, so I couldn't see his face. His relaxed stance said I probably wouldn't get punched if I approached, but I was prepared anyway.

He didn't say anything as I sat down, mirroring his position of staring straight ahead. The trees were just starting to bud, so they didn't block much of the view. We looked out over the dark parking lot, avoiding each other because guy code dictated absolutely no eye contact while discussing my relationship with his sister.

The silence lasted a few minutes, but I was used to not talking. Keeping my mouth shut was easy. Finding a way to bring up Chloe without apologizing proved harder. I wasn't sorry for what we'd done. Hell, I'd do it again in a heartbeat if it meant I got to have Chloe.

D was pissed we'd kept it from him, but in the end, what we did together was none of his business. He had no right to information about Chloe and who she chose to date unless she decided to share it.

Better not to start that way, though.

"I never wanted you to get hurt." My voice sounded loud in the still air, but at least D didn't immediately head for his rental.

He stretched his arm along the back of the bench and dropped his head to watch the sky. "I know it wasn't your idea."

I grunted, unwilling to confirm the truth.

"This isn't what I meant when I asked you to take care of her," he gritted out.

"It doesn't matter what you meant, just like it doesn't matter that you asked. With or without you, I'd have helped Chloe any time she needed it. In the end though, she doesn't *need* any of us. She's strong and capable and such a badass."

D sighed. "You think I don't know that?"

"I'm glad you do, but your opinion matters to her. She's back there hurting because she thinks she disappointed you. It's one of her biggest fears. To be clear, I didn't come out here to beg for forgiveness. I came out here to make sure you understood the effect you have on Chloe... and to make sure you apologize."

He frowned at the stars. "Me? I'm the one traumatized by seeing her in bed with you."

The prospect of losing D's friendship, losing every connection I cherished, sent bolts of panic through my system, but I wouldn't lie to him. Either he learned to accept my feelings for Chloe, or he didn't. The most I could do was be upfront with him now.

"I'm sorry you found out the way you did, but I don't regret a single moment I spent with her."

D scoffed. "Do you regret lying to me? Did you even wait a day after she moved in, or did you hang up with me and immediately invite her into your bed?"

His accusation hurt, but unlike with Craig, I didn't feel the telltale prickle of my temper. D was speaking out of anger, and I hoped we could come through the night without fracturing any relationships.

I blew out a breath, choosing my words carefully. "That's not me and you know it."

"I *thought* I knew it," he muttered. "Turns out I don't know nearly as much as I think I do. I expected you to come out here apologizing and begging me for approval."

"I don't need your approval. Your opinion, your friendship, matter to me, and I stayed away for *years* out of respect for you. That time is over. I don't want to have to choose between the two of you, but if you make me, I'm choosing her. I'll always choose her."

D turned to stare at my expression, and I let him see the truth on my face. I'd mourn the crew we'd built, but I would sacrifice everything for Chloe. Burn it to the ground and dance on the ashes with her.

He cursed quietly under his breath, and his jaw ticked. "I'm pissed you guys lied to me, and I'm hurt you thought you needed to hide. It might take me a little bit to get past that, but I'd never make you choose. I might pay some of the defense to beat your ass though—to make up for the image of you and Chloe I'll never be able to erase."

I hated the lingering resentment between us, but D hadn't turned his back on me like I'd feared. "Your cock-blocking ass barged into *my* room. Deal with the aftermath like a big boy. Are you going to set things straight with Chloe on your own or do I need to drag you back in there?"

"Look, tonight was kind of a shock, but I'll make things right with Chloe. I overreacted because I thought she felt comfortable telling me anything. It's a nasty surprise to learn we have boundaries after all. Despite my stupid big mouth, she could never disappoint me. I'll make sure she knows that." He clapped me on the shoulder. "I'm still salty about the secrets, but I'll work on that myself. Honestly, I'm glad she finally broke down for someone. Chloe is at her happiest when she's taking care of other people. I feel better knowing she has someone to take care of her now. She's shit at picking guys for herself though, so don't let her fuck this up."

The tight band around my chest released, and I took a full breath for the first time since he'd busted into my room. "I love her. Nothing could drag me away from Chloe. Not even her."

D laughed, and the last of my tension drained away. "Good luck, man, and sorry for barging in. *So* sorry."

"Maybe knock next time if you don't want to see your sister naked."

"Maybe lock the door," he countered.

"Maybe stay out of my room."

He scoffed. "Like that's going to help."

"It should. We're not in the habit of running around without clothes anywhere else."

He nodded at my chest. "Your nipples say otherwise."

"Leave my nipples out of this."

D stood and grumbled, "I'm going to borrow Chloe. You can have her back later."

I grunted. Damn right I'd have her back later. Now that our secret was out, I wasn't letting her go again.

———

Chloe

"It wasn't Noah's idea—it was mine." The truth blurted out of me approximately two seconds after D walked into my apartment.

I stood in the living room with my fingers tangled together in front of me, fighting the urge to throw up. By this point, I didn't care what was messing with my stomach, I just wished it would stop. I'd been holding it together for

Eva's sake, but she'd disappeared into her room as soon as we heard the door.

D nodded and pulled me down on the couch with him. "I know, but why? And no bullshitting me. I can tell."

I toyed with the idea anyway, simply out of habit, but this wasn't the time. "At first, I thought I didn't want anyone to see the relationship go up in flames. Dating has never worked for me, you know that. If we kept it quiet, I could pretend it wasn't serious, that I wasn't risking my heart. I can't fail if I'm not trying. Telling you would have made it real. Now, though, now I didn't want to risk anything ruining it."

D covered my hand with his. "Only *you* think you're a failure. I'm sorry for what I said earlier. I was hurt because I wanted you to share your important things with me, but I shouldn't have tried to put my expectations on you. Unlike most people I know, you're not afraid to dive into something new. Sometimes it doesn't work out, but you immediately get up and try something else. All those times you failed were just steps toward the life you want. I'm proud of your resilience."

I rolled my eyes. "Sure, except I was so terrified of a relationship I made Noah promise not to talk to you even though it was literally the first thing he brought up after we kissed at the alumni dinner."

D's hand tightened on mine. "You guys hooked up at the alumni dinner?" He opened his mouth like he was going to ask another question, then snapped it shut and shook his head. "Nope. I don't want the details. I'm already going to have a hard time erasing the image of you and Noah on his bed. I don't need to add my imagination into the mix. As long as you're happy, I'm happy, even if you don't tell me about it. But maybe convince your boyfriend to start locking his door."

I grinned, tempted to provide details anyway, but I remembered the little problem of my missed period. Another secret I wasn't going to share with him right away. No matter what, Noah deserved to know first.

"Or you could knock," I answered him.

"That's what he said," D muttered as he stood. "You've always been the stronger one between us, but I'm glad you have Noah to lean on now too. Are we good?"

"Yeah." I jumped up and wrapped my arms around his waist, fighting back tears as I clung to him.

He let me squeeze him as hard as I could just like when we were little. It was like hugging a brick wall. I'd never known he thought I was the strong one, and I'd never considered my failures to be stepping stones to the next thing. His perspective didn't suddenly banish years' worth of self-confidence issues, but it made me think about my choices in a different light. A kinder one.

"I love you, brat," he said quietly. "Don't break Noah. I'd hate to see what happens when he loses his shit."

I let out a wet laugh and pulled back. "It's a sight to behold."

The moment the door closed behind D, Eva pounced. Literally. She bolted from her room, used the couch as leverage, and nearly tackled me in a flying hug. Miraculously, we stayed upright, but my happy glow from all the hugging disappeared when both her hands landed on my belly.

A horrible feeling crawled up my spine, and Eva confirmed it when she looked up at me with wide eyes.

"Are you pregnant?"

23

Chloe

What the actual shit? I gaped at Eva, and my shock must have been answer enough because she squealed and danced around the living room.

That was *not* the reaction I was expecting. Damn her and her psychic abilities.

I caught her arm on the next pass. "Slow down, you're making me dizzy."

"Sorry." She reached out to touch my stomach again, and I swatted her away.

"Would you stop that? I don't know if I'm pregnant. I missed my last period, and I've been nauseous a lot. And tired. And my nipples are sore, but that might be Noah's fault."

Eva's smile got bigger the longer I talked, so I forced myself to stop with the verbal diarrhea. "Did you take a test?"

"Not yet. I only realized today at the game."

She pushed me back to the couch just like D had. No wonder they were friends. "What did Noah say?"

My gaze dropped down to my toes as I sat. "I haven't told him. We were interrupted by D's spectacular timing."

"Okay, well walk across the landing and tell that man he's going to be your baby daddy. Or we can go get a test to confirm first. I'm fine with either course of action."

I pulled my hair away from my face into a tight ponytail, then remembered I didn't have any elastics on me. When I let it go, the strands fell around me, hiding my face. "Do we have to do this tonight?"

Eva tilted to look through my hair. "Why would you wait?"

Might as well tell her the truth, I'd already bared myself once in the last hour to D. "Because I'm afraid Noah will be done with me if he finds out. I'm the queen of fuckups, and so far, he's been into it. But this isn't a runaway duck or a little fire. This is a baby—a lifetime commitment."

She opened her mouth, but I held up a hand. "Not done. We both still have a year of college, and Noah knows exactly what he wants to do when he graduates. How am I supposed to tell him there's been a change of plans? And how am I supposed to keep him from resenting me if he *does* stay?"

She laughed so hard she nearly fell off the couch. Rude. "Oh, honey. No. First of all, it takes two people to make a baby. This fuckup, and I'm going on record to state I disagree with the assessment that any child is a mistake, is shared equally by both of you. Noah knew what he was getting into, literally. He stuck his dick in you—he needs to be ready for the consequences."

The low-level panic I'd been living with all day abated slightly with her logic. "I agree with you, but—"

"No buts. Noah has his hang-ups, but being with you isn't one of them. He's not built for casual, remember."

Strangely, I didn't doubt Noah's feelings for me. He'd shown me in a million ways he cared—maybe more than cared—but Eva didn't have all the information for once.

She didn't know about his uncle's insistence that having Noah had ruined his dad's life or Noah's determination to prove he was better than his father. Out of all the things I could do to drive him away from me, an unplanned baby felt like it would be at the top of the list.

Eva tapped my arm. "Stop whatever disastrous thing you're thinking. I have more. Second of all, waiting wouldn't solve any of those problems anyway. If Noah leaves you for this, which he won't, he was never worthy of you in the first place."

"What if I'm not worthy of him?" I asked in a small voice.

She pointed at me. "No. I know you've crowned yourself the queen of fuckups, but you're not. Everyone makes mistakes, everyone makes bad choices sometimes, you are not unworthy of love because of that or any other reason that has to do with D. You need to say it until you believe it. Say 'I'm worthy of love'."

Eva stared at me until I mumbled out, "I'm worthy of love."

"Louder," she demanded. "With confidence."

"I'm worthy of love." Something eased in my chest, so I said it again.

Eva grinned. "Yes girl. Now we have to make sure the neighbors hear us."

I repeated the phrase with her, increasing in volume until we shouted it to the universe and collapsed laughing next to each other.

Eva wrapped an arm around me, squeezing me hard against her side. "Better?"

I rubbed my temple. "Yeah. Not sure if it'll stick, but I'm

spent. I don't think I can handle another emotional conversation tonight. Can we put on a movie or something? I miss spending time with only the two of us." Eva glanced at the door, and I narrowed my eyes. "Unless you have something pressing to do at the other apartment?"

She gave me a tight smile. "Nope. Nothing pressing."

In a flash of insight worthy of Eva, I realized she'd come out of Mac's room without him. With sex hair. Mac never missed a chance to get involved in drama. Either he wasn't home, unlikely since Eva had no reason to spend time in his room alone, or he was indisposed for the couple of minutes we spent yelling at each other in the hallway.

I gasped. "You and Mac—"

She didn't let me get any farther, clapping a hand over my mouth. "We're not talking about me."

I tried to pull her hand away, but Eva was freakishly strong. "We are now," I mumbled.

Her face fell, and she backed off to curl into a ball on the other end of the couch. "It's nothing I can't handle."

I pointed at her. "Then why are you making that face instead of dancing around the room like you did when I told you I might be *pregnant*?"

She slapped my finger away. "I might have fucked up."

"Crap, it's contagious," I whispered, garnering a dry laugh from her.

"Not that kind of fucked up. Mac and I have had a... thing for a while now."

She watched me, cataloguing my reaction, and I couldn't honestly say what I was feeling. Not surprise, not really. I kind of wanted to yell *I knew it!* but I hadn't truly considered it a possibility. Eva and Mac had been friends for a lot longer than I'd known them. Wouldn't they have tried hooking up before now?

I was dying to know how them getting together qualified as a fuckup, but I should probably ease into it. "How long?"

Eva grimaced and dropped her head onto her knees. "Since before you moved in. It was great at first. This fun little secret we had—friends with benefits—and I thought, why didn't we do this years ago?"

I scooted closer, rubbing her back. "I can safely say we've all wondered that."

"Didn't seem like a good idea. His parents are hardcore married, like so happy you can't believe it's real, and Mac always wanted what they have. I'm a poor little rich girl with absentee parents and no inclination to get married. Ever. I'd destroy him."

I had so many questions. Did anyone else know? Who started it? What the hell had she been thinking? None of those seemed particularly helpful though. She seemed genuinely upset, or as upset as Eva ever let anyone see.

"What changed?" I asked.

Eva lifted her head and scrunched her nose. "He's been fucking his way through his junior year, so I thought, maybe he's let go of the ideal. Maybe we can have some fun without getting caught up."

"And then you got caught up?"

"Worse. He did."

I hissed at the implication. Eva wasn't upset because Mac had broken her heart—she was upset because she was going to break his. Or she already had.

"Why didn't Mac come out into the hallway earlier?"

My tentative question made her shudder, and I wondered if I should get Noah to check on Mac. Better yet, Noah could handle emotional Eva with his steady presence. I belonged to the get drunk and do something stupid style of working through emotions.

"We had a fight," she admitted.

Shock dropped my mouth open. I couldn't imagine Mac fighting with anyone, let alone Eva. Every time I'd seen them disagree, Eva told him how he was supposed to respond, and he fell in line.

As if she could sense my disbelief, she tilted her head to flash me a sad smile. "I know. Mac doesn't fight—he lives to make people happy—but lately, he's... not."

"Happy?"

"I don't think so. He has emotional needs, and no matter how hard I try, I can't meet them. Mac is fun, he's hot, he's talented, he's one of my best friends, and the thought of dating him freaks me out so badly I had to borrow my mom's anxiety medication."

"Thursday?" She'd cleaned the baseboards then passed out on the couch for ten hours.

"Thursday," she answered grimly. "Today, he gave me an ultimatum after the game, if you can believe it. Date me or lose the dick. That's a direct quote, by the way."

I pressed my lips together until I could control the snicker tickling my throat. The situation really wasn't funny. "I take it you didn't agree."

Eva deflated a little more. "No, and he really thought I would. I could see it in his eyes—the way some of that manic happiness faded when he realized I wasn't kidding."

My heart hurt for her, and for him, but right now Eva was my priority. I wasn't great with heartbreak, and I definitely didn't know how to deal with someone being the cause instead of the recipient. "Love is complicated. Normally, I'd offer to light his shorts on fire, but that doesn't seem like the right response here."

She tilted her head to smile at me, tears glimmering in her eyes. "It's definitely not, but I appreciate your willingness to jump straight to arson. I do love him, just not the way he deserves to be loved. He deserves all-consuming, uncontrollable love where everything else falls away."

I stroked her hair away from her wet face. "And that's not you?"

"That's not me," she whispered. "I'm not sure that will ever be me."

My throat got tight from the similarity to my own experience with Noah, except I'd *wanted* to date him deep down. Fear had held me back—was still holding me back. The love she described sounded a lot like the flutters in my chest and the heat in my belly, the burgeoning happiness so big I couldn't contain it in my body. When I was with Noah, the rest of the world disappeared.

With surprisingly little difficulty, the knowledge slid into me. I loved Noah. Every aspect of my life was better with him in it, which made the baby revelation all that much scarier. Like I'd told D, failure didn't matter when I had nothing to lose. Suddenly, I could lose everything.

A quiet voice in the back of my mind suggested I could also gain everything I ever wanted if I just talked to him. Unfortunately, that voice wasn't loud enough to drown out the fear completely.

Despite the shitty circumstances, Eva had given me a gift. A valid reason to put off talking to Noah until tomorrow.

I laid my head on her shoulder. "Okay, we're having a girls' night. No penises allowed. Only superhero movies and ice cream until we pass out."

Eva wrapped her arm around me. "Fine, but you have to promise me to talk to Noah in the morning and take a test either way."

My stomach pinched, but there might have been some

excitement mixed in with the nervousness. "Okay. Distraction tonight in the form of Chris Evans' ass, then real life tomorrow."

One way or another, things were about to change.

24

Noah

C hloe never came back to my apartment. I noticed, but Mac distracted me, bouncing off the walls like a toddler who'd downed several Red Bulls and a bowl of Skittles. A shadow in his eyes made me go along with him, but it wasn't until Eva texted me that I accepted I wouldn't see Chloe until morning.

Come get her tomorrow.

No context or explanation, but Eva believed in getting right to the point. She also believed in communication. If Chloe had a problem, Eva wouldn't let her sit on it, so I gave in to Mac's insistence we play an epic Madden tournament with D before he had to leave.

Shaw and RJ folded first, heading to their room around midnight, and I left Mac and D battling it out sometime around two. I crawled into bed alone, but despite the real-life football game I'd played earlier and all the shit that went down after, I wasn't tired. My mind kept returning to the discussion with Chloe her brother had interrupted.

I don't want to talk about it yet.

Something had spooked her—before D stuck his foot in his mouth. I crossed my arms behind my head and ran through the events of the day. Nothing stood out to me, but it didn't matter in the end anyway. Whatever had scared her, we'd deal with it together.

I watched the shadows play across my ceiling and waited for the doubts to creep in, but they never came. D knew about us, and I'd burned my bridges with Craig. I needed to decide if I wanted to contact my father, but deep down, I already knew I'd be calling him. There were too many unanswered questions to leave him in my past.

I smiled into the darkness. Chloe would approve. She'd probably be right there holding my hand. I hoped she knew I'd do the same—whatever she needed, I'd support her. Maybe it was time I told her that, along with the fact that I was hopelessly in love with her.

If dating freaked her out, she'd probably try to dump my ass when I started talking about forever. Good thing I wasn't easy to push away.

Unless Eva got involved, apparently. I rolled over and shoved my face into my pillow. It was going to be a long night without Chloe curled up next to me.

———

THE NEXT MORNING, I squatted next to a tangle of female limbs on the sofa. Three pints of melted ice cream sat on the coffee table behind me next to Eva's open laptop. Chloe slept face down on the couch with one arm hanging off, fingers touching the floor, legs intertwined with Eva's.

I brushed a loose curl of dark hair away from her face and ran my thumb along her jaw. She nuzzled into my hand,

and the lines on her forehead smoothed. My wild girl wasn't a morning person on the best of days. Didn't stop me from wanting to wake up next to her for the rest of my life.

She murmured my name, and my heart took off. I'd wait as long as she needed, do whatever it took to convince her we were end game. Chloe was it for me, always had been. From the first time her eyes had locked on mine and she'd grinned like we shared a secret.

I'd thought getting involved would be a mistake because of D and my past. Maybe it would have been, or maybe the mistake was pushing her away for so long.

Just as I was considering letting her sleep, she blinked sleepy green eyes at me and groaned. "So bright."

I smiled at her. "Morning, Trouble."

Chloe's face paled, and her eyes widened. "I have to throw up."

She shoved at my hand and Eva's legs, then bolted for her bathroom. Eva grumbled, curling around a couch pillow, and I frowned at the lack of alcohol present for this kind of morning. Chloe had been sick on and off for more than a week, but she'd said it was a food thing.

I followed on her heels, grabbing the water bottle from her bedside table and setting it on her bathroom counter. She'd hit her knees on the fuzzy purple rug and draped her upper half over the toilet seat. I squeezed in next to her and laid my hand on the back of her head. Worry snaked through me as her moan echoed off the water.

"Why can't I just throw up and feel better?"

She wasn't talking to me, clearly, but nothing about this seemed normal. "Chloe, are you okay?"

Her body relaxed, and she leaned her cheek against her arm on the seat. "Yeah, just my usual morning routine."

As I crouched next to her in the small bathroom, a niggling thought tried to break through. "The thing you needed to tell me..."

Her gaze shot to mine, full of fear I never wanted to see associated with me.

"Are you pregnant?"

She squeezed her eyes closed for a second, and when she opened them again, they glistened with unshed tears. "Maybe? I don't know. Yesterday, I realized I'd missed my last period, and I've been sick. I know we used condoms, but they're not one hundred percent effective. I haven't taken a test."

I sat back on my heels, but I didn't take my hand off her head. Fuck. How was this possible? We'd been careful. I frantically searched for alternate explanations, but Chloe knew her body. If she thought she might be pregnant, I believed her. It never crossed my mind the kid wouldn't be mine.

An influx of considerations crashed through my head one after the other—classes, next football season, doctor appointments, Craig's reaction, marriage. The weight of another human being sat on my chest and made it impossible to breathe. Chloe looked away, blinking quickly, and everything came sharply into focus. How long had she been worried about this on her own?

Under the shock and anxiety lived a tiny pocket of satisfaction. She wasn't on her own. A baby had definitely not been in the plans, but I knew absolutely that if I was going to have kids, I wanted them with Chloe. We'd done this together, and I'd do whatever I could to shield her from any negative fallout.

She dry heaved one more time, then wiped her mouth with her wrist. "I'm sorry. It wasn't supposed to go like this. I was supposed to leave old me behind and start making better choices with my life. I thought I had, but then I dragged you down with me."

I gathered her hair and held it away from the edges of the toilet. "There was nothing wrong with old you."

"Then why did you turn me down the first time?"

I tugged gently on her curls. "Because I wasn't ready. My feelings for you scared me. *You* scared me. I'd spent my life trying my best to fade into the background, and you lived unapologetically at the forefront. I couldn't look away."

"Yeah, like a train wreck," she muttered.

"No, like a beautiful display in a store window that I wanted but couldn't have. I'd just met D, just realized what it felt like to have people really care about me. I was terrified I'd make a wrong step and ruin everything."

Her shoulders rose and fell with a deep breath. "And then I went ahead and ruined everything for you. I understand if you want out—I have a habit of driving people away —but I'm keeping the baby. If there is one."

I wound her hair around my fist and pulled until she lifted her face to me. "I'm not going anywhere. Why are you so certain you're going to drive me away?"

"Because it happened before." She jerked her head, making me let go. I rolled to my feet, getting out of her way as she stood, then slammed the toilet shut and flushed with more force than necessary.

"I dated the same guy for most of my senior year of high school. For once, he didn't seem the least interested in D or his influence. Vince and I even applied to all the same colleges. I thought I loved him."

"What happened?" My voice was calm, but Chloe must have sensed my roiling anger.

She studied me out of the corner of her eye as she

yanked open a drawer and pulled out a new toothbrush. "My parents went out of town for a weekend and accidentally took my car keys. I had a brunch date with some friends, so Vince let me borrow his car. I got into an accident. It was my fault. I was messing with the radio and ran a stop sign. The other guy was apparently driving a tank because the collision totaled Vince's car."

My jaw ticked as I guessed where this was going. "Were you okay?"

"Yeah, just some bruising from the airbag and the seatbelt. Vince lost it. Claimed he was done with me being selfish and reckless. The last thing he said to me was I wasn't worth the trouble."

Even knowing the story didn't end in Vince's favor, I wanted to find this asshole and introduce him to my temper. He'd affected Chloe so deeply she'd decided she wasn't worthy enough to be loved. Fuck that. I'd spend every day proving him wrong until Chloe believed me.

I circled her waist from behind and met her eyes in the mirror. "I love your trouble. I love your sharp tongue and your fierce tenacity. Your unbreakable spirit and soft heart. I love you, and you are everything I ever wanted. With or without a baby."

Chloe sniffled, and she laid her hands over mine on her stomach. "Did D help you come up with that when he finally accepted things had changed between us?"

"Nothing has changed, Trouble. It's always been you. I just didn't have the words until now."

"So not D then?"

I'd missed the teasing sparkle in her eyes, but I still had to retaliate. My fingers dug into her side, making her squeal with laughter until she cried for me to stop. She yanked at my wrist, trying to free herself, but I was happy with her current position. I shifted my hips forward, pinning her against the counter, and she stilled immediately.

The air between us heated, but she wasn't done. "One benefit of this disaster is we won't need condoms anymore. It's not like you can get me *more* pregnant."

I growled out an agreement. "That *is* a benefit. I'd love to be inside you with nothing between us."

Chloe smiled. "We can make that happen."

"Are you sure—"

She reached up to cover my mouth with her hand. "I love you too, you know, with everything in me—especially when *you're* in me. You've always made me feel like I was more than enough, even before I let you into my pants. Also, I'm fairly new to this adult relationship thing, but I'm pretty sure this is when you're supposed to tattoo my name on your ass."

I ran my tongue along her palm, and she shivered against me. "Trying to mark your territory?"

Chloe dropped her hand back to the counter with a slap. "Hell yes. If anyone else touches you, I'm throwing hands."

"No going back now," I warned.

"I have no intention of going back. New me is ready and willing to face up to the challenges as long as I get you." Chloe sighed and dropped her head back on my chest to peer up at me. "I need to brush my teeth first, but will you come with me to get the test?"

I slid my hands down the curves of her hips, bending her forward over the sink until my cock settled between her ass cheeks. "I'm driving, then we're celebrating. Either way."

Heat clouded her gaze, and she nodded.

FIFTEEN MINUTES LATER, I'd talked my dick into submission, at least until we had answers, and Chloe clutched a tiny plastic bag with a pregnancy test inside. I still couldn't fully wrap my mind around the reality of a kid, but I was ecstatic we were committed to dealing with the results together.

She popped another gummy bear in her mouth, a hazard of taking Chloe anywhere near the candy aisle, and continued the conversation we'd started in the car. "I realize I kind of stole the show with my spectacular fertility, but what about Craig and the letter from your dad?"

"I'll handle them."

Chloe narrowed her eyes at me. "The fuck you will. If we're doing this together, we're doing it *all* together."

I chuckled and kissed the side of her neck. "Okay. One crisis at a time. Let's find out if I have super swimmers, then we'll deal with my shit."

We reached the sidewalk leading to our landing, and I jolted to a stop. Distantly, I heard the rustle and thud of something hitting the concrete by our feet, but my gaze was locked on the man standing next to my apartment door.

He was tall and broad, built like a linebacker, with shoulder-length dark red hair. Tattoos wound up his arms and under the sleeves of his T-shirt. When he turned, the familiar scar marred his chin from when he'd snatched five-year-old me off my bike, before I smashed into a tree at what seemed like a million miles an hour.

We'd rolled across the sidewalk, and he scraped his chin to the bone. Green eyes just like mine landed on me, and the frown smoothed away from his face, replaced with a guarded expression I'd seen in the mirror for years.

"Noah," he said.

Not a question, a statement of fact, because he'd recognized me as surely as I'd recognized him. Chloe let out a soft gasp next to me, but I couldn't tear my eyes away from my father.

"Micah, what are you doing here?"

25

Chloe

Micah didn't answer his question, and my gaze pinballed back and forth between them as the three of us stood there in the bright morning sun. They wore matching impassive expressions, like each of them was trying to prove who cared the least.

The man standing in front of us looked like a slightly older version of Noah, except with tattoos covering his arms and a dangerous glint in his eyes. I'd seen the same look both times I'd been cornered by assholes, but where Noah worked to keep it hidden, Micah wore it like a badge of honor.

Noah hadn't seen his dad in fifteen years, and stupidly, I cared a whole lot about making a good first impression. Sweat gathered at the small of my back as I desperately tried not to draw attention to the useless plastic bag I'd dropped. The pregnancy test peeking out would make an impression all right.

It wasn't in me to cower though. I may have had a history of monumental mistakes, but I owned all of them. I'd own this one too.

"Hi, I'm Chloe." I shifted to extend my hand, but Noah's arm tightened around me, holding me in place. "Noah's girlfriend."

The words hit me sideways as soon as I said them. After all we'd been through, girlfriend felt like such a weak way to describe my relationship to him.

Micah's eyes flitted to me, seeming to take me in with a single glance, and his mouth relaxed into a half-smile. "It's nice to meet you, Chloe. I'm Micah, Noah's dad."

Noah wasn't amused. He moved forward a step, tucking me behind him. "I didn't call you."

"Craig did—so he could warn me away. I've never been big on taking orders, and his insistence made me wonder what he was trying to hide." Without missing a beat, Micah bent and picked up the pregnancy test, leaving the plastic bag on the concrete. He raised a brow and held it out for me. So much for good first impressions.

My face flamed immediately, but I raised my chin as I took the box from him. "Craig is kind of a dick. Jury's still out on you."

Noah coughed out a laugh, and I flattened my palm against his back, over the phoenix hidden by his TU football shirt. This whole encounter was beyond awkward, but hell if I'd let the dad who'd disappeared for fifteen years judge the son he'd only just met.

With spectacular timing, Eva barged out of the apartment, nearly colliding with Micah. Her eyes widened as she looked way up at him, and she quickly backpedaled to the relative safety of the doorway.

She took in our positions, with Noah playing human shield in case his dad turned out to be a psycho, and shook her head. "I don't know what's going on out here, but I don't care at the moment. Chloe, your brother hasn't left yet." Her gaze dropped to the stupid test in my hand, and she tilted her head toward our apartment.

"Shit," I whispered, glancing at the other door on the landing.

I'd made my peace with D, mostly, but I wasn't ready for my entire family to know about a potential pregnancy. The smothering would never end, and I hadn't even used the damn test yet.

Noah pressed his lips to my hair and urged me toward Eva. "Go on. I'll be in as soon as I can."

My insides melted at how easily he figured out what I needed then gave it to me. If I asked, I had zero doubts Noah would blow off a showdown with his dad to come hold my hand while I took this test.

I wouldn't ask. He needed to see this through—without worrying about me. That didn't stop me from worrying about him.

"Are you sure you'll be okay? If you need me, I'm here."

Noah's lips tilted up in the little smile he often wore for me. "I'll be fine. I'd rather not give D a reason to take a swing at me this morning."

Micah chimed in. "I have a feeling Craig is going to show up sooner rather than later. Unless you want to deal with his head exploding, you might want to take care of your business in private."

Noah frowned at him. "Why do you think that?"

The older man shrugged. "He's my brother."

Eva propped her hands on her hips. "You heard Prison Daddy. Let's go take care of business."

Micah laughed, but Noah winced.

"How did you know about that?" he asked.

Eva sent him a pitying look. "If you don't want people to read your private letters, don't leave them on the coffee table." She hooked her arm through mine. "I'm stealing your girl for bathroom fun times."

Noah glowered. "It was in my pants *next* to the coffee table."

"Close enough." Eva chirped as she dragged me away, huddling her head close to mine to whisper. "Sorry I missed all the fun earlier."

"Where were you this morning when we left?" I hissed at her.

"Something came up. Noah's dad is hot. The bad boy vibe is doing it for me. Kinda makes me wish I was into older guys."

"Why? Why would you put that in my brain?"

She scoffed. "Like you weren't thinking it."

At the door, we both glanced back at the men watching us. "If that thirst trap is my future, I have zero complaints."

Eva snickered and closed us in the quiet apartment. "Come on. You can play with Henry while we wait for Noah."

This woman got me. I wouldn't take the test without him, and I didn't want to be alone. Lighting my dorm on fire may have been the best thing to ever happen to me. As much as I'd dreaded transferring to TU, I'd found the connections I'd always craved in the last place I'd expected.

I WATCHED Micah out of the corner of my eye as Chloe and
Eva retreated into their apartment. Craig had spent the last
fifteen years convincing me my father was dangerous, and I
wouldn't take a chance with Chloe, especially now.

As soon as the door closed, I faced him. "Say what you
have to say."

He spread his hands. "Is that any way to greet your dad?"

I couldn't call him dad. I just couldn't. The man I'd
known as dad disappeared a long time ago.

"I wouldn't know, Micah," I said, crossing my arms.

The way Craig described him, I expected Micah to want
something from me, but Craig's information wasn't exactly
unbiased. I waited for my father to say something, but all he
did was stare at me.

Was this some kind of intimidation thing? Joke's on
him. I lived most days in my head. Silence didn't
bother me.

"You played well yesterday," he finally ground out.

I drew back with a frown. "You came to the game?"

"Yeah. You had a good block in the third quarter. That
Mac kid is fast."

"Don't let him hear you say that," I muttered. "His ego's
already big enough."

Micah chuckled, and his shoulders relaxed a little. "The
girl is faster. RJ." He looked away and ran his hand through
his hair. "Look, I was hoping we could talk, without Craig as
an intermediary."

I wasn't against the idea considering the amount of
questions I had about our past now, but Chloe was waiting
for me to take a damn pregnancy test.

"We can talk, but now's not really—"

As if we'd summoned him, Craig came striding up the
walkway wearing a polo shirt and khakis, with a curl of

disdain on his lips. "Micah. I should have realized you'd run straight here."

Micah's body language changed from nervous hope to lazy contempt. "Yeah, calling me was probably a poor decision. Your first mistake was assuming you had any control over my actions."

"That's rich coming from someone who does nothing but make mistakes. How does it feel to know *your* poor decisions cost you a son?" Craig's dart hit its target, and Micah flinched. I'd heard the refrain enough it no longer affected me.

"I trusted you with Noah, and you turned him against me," Micah fired back.

I stepped between the two of them before someone threw a punch. "What are you doing here, Craig?"

His lips pinched together at my use of his first name without the uncle title, but he didn't comment on it. "I stayed an extra day after the conference to attend your game. After our last meeting, I thought it prudent to see for myself the kind of life you've been leading."

There was a time when I would have given anything for Craig to come to one of my games—to care at all about me without using it as a chance to malign his brother. All of a sudden it hit me, Craig was jealous of Micah. My affluent doctor uncle was jealous of my ex-con father, maybe always had been. The realization didn't change anything.

"You're not welcome here," I told him. "Not after what you said about Chloe."

Craig scowled at Micah and edged closer to me. "I stand by my point, and you need to come to your senses before you're faced with dire consequences."

"You mean like you using your influence to fuck with my classes unless I declare for the draft?"

His brow furrowed. "I admit, playing in the NFL would be quite the accomplishment, but I wouldn't do anything to interfere with your education. I was referring to letting those around you drag you down into their problems."

"As you can see, I haven't been dragged anywhere. You need to leave now."

Craig threw a hand toward Micah. "I'm not leaving unless he does."

My ire started to rise at Craig's insistence on ignoring me. "He's here at my request. You're not."

Micah's brow twitched, but he showed no other sign of surprise.

"He just wants the money," Craig sneered.

I turned to stare at my uncle. "What money?"

His eyes flared briefly with panic before they narrowed, and I knew—I *knew*—whatever he was about to say was a lie.

"He's hoping to use you to cash in on my bank account."

I swung back around to Micah and lifted a brow. "Well?"

Micah's face closed down, and he shrugged. "Always an asshole, big brother. Mind if I talk to my kid alone?"

"I do. He's not your child anymore. *I* raised him, and I won't have a degenerate, violent, ex-con making trouble for him. You should go before I call the police."

Micah took a step closer, invading Craig's space. "No."

I'd never used my size against Craig, but I had six inches and at least a hundred pounds of muscle on him. Micah was bigger than me. Tatted and dangerous, though I didn't fear him. To make the whole ridiculous scene truly over the top, D, Mac and Shaw came out of the apartment to stand at my back. A second later, RJ joined them, giving Shaw an evil look when he tried to edge her behind him.

These idiots. They had no idea what was going down,

but they had my back anyway. My chest tightened with the things I wanted to say to them—how much their support meant to me. All I needed was Eva and Chloe boxing Craig in to make this clusterfuck complete. Maybe I'd find the words after I dealt with the newest drama.

Craig's face paled, but he raised his chin, never one to admit defeat. "I'm doing what's best for Noah."

I shook my head. Incredibly, I thought he might believe his own bullshit. It would explain why he was so desperate to keep Micah away from me. Too little, far too late. "I'm fine, Craig. It sounds like Micah and I have a lot to talk about. Why don't you head back to your hotel, and I'll call you later."

He didn't like being dismissed, but faced with an unmoving wall of muscle, he gave in. "I'm at the Vaughn. You have my number." Craig stiffly circled Micah, who refused to move one inch out of his way, and didn't look back.

I eyed my friends, now posturing for my father. "Go inside. Please."

Mac broke the stare off. "We're not leaving you alone with this guy."

I rolled my eyes, both annoyed and warmed by their absolute refusal. Craig's anemic version of protecting me had nothing on these guys. Chloe had been right. My real family had nothing to do with Craig or Micah and everything to do with these assholes making the situation awkward.

26

Noah

"I'm bigger than all of you," I pointed out.

Mac jerked his chin at Micah. "Not bigger than him."

I sighed and made an appeal to the only one who'd ever been able to control Mac besides Eva. "D, get them out of here please. I'll explain everything after."

D nodded and clapped me on the back. "Nice work sending Chloe inside. She never listens to a damn thing I say. Okay, crew. Back inside. Mac, you can watch out the window."

At D's order, my friends all retreated into our apartment, but Mac pointed two fingers at his eyes then swung them toward Micah before he closed the door. I loved those idiots.

Finally alone, Micah jerked his head toward the pathway around the buildings. "Want to take a walk?"

Not particularly, but we were unlikely to finish a conversation if we stayed between the two apartments. "Sure."

For once, I didn't have to shorten my stride for the person next to me. Micah walked with his hands in his pockets, the same as me, until we passed the parking lot and the bench where I'd talked with D the night before. It seemed like an eternity had passed since I scolded him for being a shit to his sister.

I wanted to get back to her, but I wasn't sure where to begin with Micah. Volunteering information had never been one of my strengths.

As if he knew we'd circle the complex in silence with me in charge, Micah eyed me with trepidation. "You have questions."

My mouth went rogue before I could consider the best course of action. "Why come back now?"

"That answer was in the letter, but I'll tell you again. I served my time and got out. It took me a while to find you. I knew you were playing college ball thanks to something Craig let slip, but I didn't know where."

I stopped to stare at him. "You talked to Craig?"

Annoyance passed over his face. "Yeah. I'm guessing from his comments today my asshole brother didn't tell you."

"No."

"Craig was so embarrassed when I was convicted, but I couldn't bring myself to care. Your mom..." Micah took a deep breath, staring at the pine trees in the distance. "I'd already lost everything I loved besides you, and I wasn't in the right place to take care of you."

"Prison *does* seem like a poor choice for raising a child."

He gave me a half-smirk for my sarcasm. "You're not wrong, but I was broken before I went to jail."

"I spent a lot of time working on my demons, and by the time I came out of the darkness, you were long gone. Craig had moved you somewhere out of state. He was legally your guardian, and I'd lost all rights to you. In the end, I told myself you were better off. You wouldn't miss me."

"Are you kidding?" I scoffed. "I was six. Of course I missed you. I wrote you letters. I begged to go visit you. Craig told me you weren't interested. You never wrote back, so I believed him."

Micah's jaw tightened, but he didn't show any other signs of his anger, despite his history. "I never got any of your letters. Probably Craig's version of protecting you from his dangerous little brother."

Even angry and hurt, Micah's insults weren't really insults. Compared to Craig's constant belittling, I had trouble believing my father was the bad influence.

"I never meant to abandon you," he said gruffly. "I looked everywhere. But my resources were limited, and Craig's online presence was anemic."

I snorted, trying to keep myself from simply taking Micah's intentions at his word. He couldn't show up after fifteen years, apologize, say he didn't mean for my life to unwind the way it did, and then expect everything to be okay.

Still, he wasn't wrong about Craig. "He refuses to use social media, says it rots the brain. Aunt Melissa handles all the online stuff."

"He always did look down his nose at technology as entertainment. I imagine he only got worse after I went to jail."

We walked for a few more minutes, both of us comfortable in the silence, but I had one last question. My shoulders tensed, curling forward. Like I told Chloe at that first lunch, I wasn't sure I was ready to hear the answer.

"What happened?"

He didn't need me to explain what I was asking about. Micah turned back the direction we'd come and met my eyes. "How much do you remember about your mom?"

An image of a smiling woman with dark brown hair hanging past her shoulders flashed in my mind. She was singing off-key and dancing around with me in her arms. "Not much. I know she died not long before you beat someone almost to death."

Micah nodded. "She worked at this little bar and grill place. We didn't have much money, but we were getting by. One night, on the way home, she was killed by a drunk driver. I lost it. She—and you—were my entire world."

My chest ached for him. The thought of anything happening to Chloe made my throat close up.

"He was our age, young, but unlike us, he came from money. His lawyers got him off with a slap on the wrist claiming your mom was at fault. It was a load of bullshit. He went home, and I got drunk. You were having nightmares because mom was gone, and I couldn't sleep without her there. Craig came over to lecture me, and I sent you with him. '*Go play with Uncle Craig. Dad has to do something.*'" His gaze slid toward me.

"You still called me dad then. I drove over to his house, stone cold sober, and when he answered the door with a beer in his hand, I hit him. I didn't stop hitting him until three random joggers dragged me away."

"Was it worth it?"

"No. It didn't bring your mom back—didn't take the pain away—and I lost you too."

I wanted to hate him. For giving in to his rage. For making revenge more important than his son. For the years I spent believing I could grow up to be a monster like him.

Except I couldn't. I understood. Hadn't I threatened two idiots simply for touching Chloe? If someone took her from me? I shook my head. The monster lived in me rent-free.

The only difference is I would *never* abandon my child.

Micah let out a long breath. "I'm sorry. We were happy once. Love is a beautiful thing, but it can be as destructive as a wildfire. I hope you never have to live that lesson."

My landing came into view, still blessedly empty. I felt like I'd run sprints for two hours—or another 5K. I was emptied out, but it felt clean. Like starting fresh. Maybe we could build something new outside of Craig's toxic influence.

I cleared my throat. "I'm not making any promises, but thanks for talking to me."

He glanced at Chloe's door. "Good luck. I hope she's worth it."

"She is."

"Then I hope I'm around to see how it all shakes out." His eyes lingered on me for a beat, then he inclined his head and walked toward the parking lot with his hands in the pockets of his jeans.

Not one word about how having a kid ruined his life. The opposite, really. *We were happy once.* I wasn't even sure Craig had lied so much as pasted his own misbeliefs onto Micah's life.

The roar of a motorcycle starting up dragged a memory from the depths of my mind. Dad laying under a shiny chrome bike with tools scattered around him. Mom turning on music and dragging him up from the ground to dance with her.

I had no idea how old I was or what I'd been doing, but they were both smiling, completely lost in each other. Some of the happiness he'd been talking about.

Chloe was that happiness for me, and she was waiting.

———

Chloe

I sat in my bathroom, alone, trying to suck in enough air to keep my brain functioning. Eva had hovered and pestered me until I wanted to shove her head in the toilet, so I'd kicked her out. Anywhere else.

When the door creaked open, I grabbed the extra toilet paper roll and aimed for the face. My shot was good, but instead of bouncing off my tiny best friend's nose, I nailed Noah in the pec.

Being an elite athlete, he caught the toilet paper on the rebound and held it up. "Everything okay?"

A hysterical laugh bubbled out of me. "Yep. Totally fine. Just sitting here chugging water, waiting for my boyfriend to finish talking to his long-lost father so we can see if Prison Daddy should be Prison Granddaddy."

I dropped my head into my hands in an attempt to *stop talking.*

Noah chuckled and tossed the toilet paper into the sink. He slid his arms under me, lifted me with about the same amount of effort, and sat down with me in his lap. I curled my arms around his neck, already feeling the tension melt away from being in my favorite spot in the whole world.

He nuzzled my neck, breathing me in. "Can we please not call him Prison Daddy?"

"How about Daddy Micah?"

Noah let out a long-suffering sigh. "This wasn't

anywhere on the list of things I thought you'd torture me with, Trouble."

I perked up. "You have a list?"

He nipped the sensitive skin at the base of my neck, and I yipped. "How much longer do we have to wait?"

"I think I'm ready now." My stomach clenched, but with nerves instead of the urge to purge all the food I'd had in the last day.

Noah set me on the ground, then moved out of the way. The instructions were straightforward, but trying to pee on a tiny stick without getting my hand was impossible. At least Noah found the situation amusing.

He sat on the floor with his back to the cabinet and offered useless advice until I set the test on the counter and started my timer. After washing my hands several times, I joined him on the tile. He pulled me between his legs so I could lean against him, and we traded horrible nicknames for his dad until my phone went off.

I turned to meet Noah's brilliant green gaze, and all I saw there was confidence—in me, in us. Whatever the stick said, he'd be there. I cupped his rough cheek and kissed him. A quiet promise sealed with lips and breath.

I'd been afraid before, but nothing would stop me from loving this man who held my entire heart.

Without looking away from him, I reached up for the test. Noah squeezed my waist and gave me a full, dazzling smile, then we peeked together.

Not pregnant. Thank fuck. I wasn't having a baby—I was just dying from some unknown stomach bug. I should probably call my doctor about that just in case.

Noah engulfed me in his arms and lifted me off the floor, tucking his face against my neck. "I love you, Chloe."

"I love you too. No offense, but I'm glad your giant baby isn't going to wreck my vagina."

"Yet," he growled into my ear.

My breath caught when he pulled back and lifted his brow in challenge. Yep, giant babies were definitely in my future.

I grinned at him. "Yet. I'm finishing college first."

"Deal, as long as I get to wreck you in the meantime." He sat me on the counter, spreading my legs with his hips, and I couldn't hold back the needy moan.

"I don't know... you going to get on your knees for me?" I teased.

He chuckled as he knelt on the tile. "Whatever you need, Trouble."

EPILOGUE

Chloe

Four months later...

"Surprise! I'm back."

I blinked at the sight of Eva standing amid a cluster of luggage in the living room. I'd had the apartment to myself all summer, and I hadn't expected her back until next week. Well, mostly to myself. Noah was basically an extension of me at this point, so he didn't count.

"You're back *early*." I grinned and squeezed her into a hug.

Eva had left as soon as the semester ended, claiming she needed a summer away. Her parents continued to pay her half of the rent while she lounged at their beach house, terrorizing the local male population. I suspected she'd run away from the Mac aftermath.

He'd spent the summer moping in the weight room, and he didn't suggest a single party after Eva left. It got so bad RJ banned him from coming with her because he ruined the vibe. In the last two weeks, he'd started to return to the old

Mac, though a less manically happy one. At least he'd stopped quietly singing sad songs to himself.

Eva and I had talked regularly, but I'd made it a point to avoid the topic of Mac. Now I stood hugging her in one of Noah's shirts and my undies because she hadn't told me she was returning early.

I pulled back and touched the pink streaks in her blonde hair. "You were right. Purple would have been too much."

Eva shook her head to fluff the strands, then stopped with her gaze trained on the second bedroom. "What's going on with my door?"

I blinked, then realized what she was talking about. The door was a pale blue with a chalkboard sign listing my schedule for the week. "Oh, right. I sort of turned your room into an office. I needed more space after Noah insisted on getting a giant ass bed for over here too."

Eva darted over to peek into my room, but I jumped in front of her. When I'd heard the front door, I'd thrown on the closest shirt and left Noah sprawled face down, bare-assed naked on the bed. He was a beautiful specimen of man, but he was my beautiful specimen, and he wouldn't appreciate me sharing the sight. Not that I wanted to.

"Maybe start with the other room. We should probably end there too."

Eva raised a brow, but she let me steer her toward the other bedroom. "You know I've seen Noah naked before, right?"

"Don't care." My mind immediately called up all the ways she might have seen him naked. "Wait, I do care, so I expect the story of naked Noah later, but his butt is for my eyes only now."

She snickered. "Yours and the entire football team's."

I rolled my eyes. "Fine. Them too."

She gasped when I opened the door, and I stood back to let her get the full view. Harper had been working my ass off, so I collaborated with one of the design students I met in classes over the summer to redo the room with the goal of an efficient workspace.

"This place is gorgeous, Chloe. Did you do this?"

"I had help—a lot of help."

We'd settled on a modern boho look with white furniture, glass and metal accents, and rich textures sprinkled throughout. I had soft pillows and cushy blankets and a collection of succulents I hadn't killed yet. Every time I stepped into this room, I felt my future reaching out to me.

But now Eva was back.

When I glanced her way, she was watching me with tears glimmering in her eyes. "I'm so happy for you."

To my surprise, a full-sized duck sans diaper wandered into the room and quacked at Eva.

I stared at her with wide eyes. "I thought you were giving Henry back. You said it was temporary."

She threw her hands up. "It was. Henry was perfectly behaved here, but the second I left him in the pen he got destructive. Alexis was talking about having to get rid of him because they were about to get in some new babies."

I pressed my lips together to keep the laugh inside. "You adopted Henry, didn't you?"

Eva scowled at me. "It was basically blackmail. Someone had to take him."

"You kept him a secret from me *all summer*?"

She leveled me with a flat look. "Do I need to mention the office makeover I didn't know about? I keep secrets from everyone. The price I pay for knowing almost everything."

"I was going to convert it back before you got home," I muttered.

"No need. I can't live here anymore. It's too close."

She didn't need to say any more. I wouldn't forget the crazy weekend this last spring with the Eva/Mac revelation, Micah showing up, and the pregnancy scare. Things were strained after that for the last few weeks of the semester. Eva stopped having mandatory movie nights, and Mac started checking the landing before he left the apartment.

Her wanting to move didn't surprise me, but the panic I expected to feel never came. With the money Harper was paying me plus what my parents kicked in, I could afford the apartment on my own. I'd miss Eva, but I'd gotten used to a long-distance friendship. Anywhere in town was better than the beach house.

Eva let her gaze wander the room with a sad look in her eyes. "It's for the best anyway. Henry needs his own bathroom, and I'm not sure the apartment manager would be willing to overlook him living here permanently."

"Can't you just use your voodoo on him and make him do whatever you ask?"

She shrugged. "Even *my* powers have limits."

I huffed out a laugh. I doubted anyone could stand against the full force of Eva's manipulations.

"Where are you going to live?"

"I'm not sure yet, but I already had my mom's assistant looking into duck-friendly places. It shouldn't take us long to find somewhere."

I opened my mouth to offer her Noah's room as a temporary measure, but I managed to stop the words before I suggested she move in across the hall from Mac. "Noah and I can stay at his place until you find somewhere."

She patted my arm. "That's sweet, but you're doing good

things here and I'm not going to ruin that. I can stay with Blue for a few days."

Only Eva would be confident she could secure a duck-friendly place to live on a couple of days' notice right before the start of the fall semester. I loved this girl something fierce.

"What are you doing right now?"

"Henry and I are going to grab coffee and work my magic on potential landlords." She sent me a wicked smile. "Enjoy doing your good things, and you're welcome for setting up you and Noah at the alumni dinner."

I narrowed my eyes at her. "I hope you never use your powers for evil."

She bent to put on her shoes, then frowned down at one of them.

"Oh my god, Henry. You laid an egg!" Eva pulled a speckled brown egg, slightly bigger than a chicken egg, out of her sneaker.

I stared at the egg for a second, shocked into silence, then I glanced down at the duck, who'd grown into the distinctive pattern of his brown feathers—*her* brown feathers. "Unless I missed more than I thought in my biology classes, I think Henry is a Henrietta."

The damn duck quacked, looking extremely proud of herself. Eva laughed and set the egg on the kitchen counter.

"Alexis is going to love this," she said, sounding genuinely happy for the first time since Mac's ultimatum.

"Dinner tonight?" I asked. "Margs and tacos on me."

"You're on. I'll see if Blue is free." She checked both shoes carefully before sliding her feet inside them. "I'll send someone to grab my luggage later this afternoon."

I hugged her tight. "I hate that this feels like goodbye."

She rubbed my back. "It's never goodbye. You can't get rid of me that easily."

Eva grabbed her duck and left with a cheeky wave, but the sadness crept from my heart to my head. Luckily, I knew a guaranteed way to cheer myself up.

I flipped the lock, useless since the people most likely to walk in had keys, and returned to the bedroom with a smile. Noah hadn't moved despite all the ruckus.

A stream of light crossed the phoenix spread across his back, and I smiled like I always did at the new addition. The word *trouble* scrawled in messy handwriting along the edges of the feathers. It wasn't my name on his ass, but we were getting there.

I tossed his shirt back on the floor where I'd found it and cuddled next to him on top of the covers. We went to bed under the blankets every night, but Noah was a furnace. By morning, most of the bedding was on the floor.

"Morning, Trouble," he rumbled, peering at me from under his pillow. "What's wrong?"

"Eva's moving out."

He yawned and wrapped an arm around my waist to pull me underneath him. "You knew this was coming."

"Yeah, but that doesn't make it any easier. She's pulling away from the group." I hated it for me, but I loved Eva stepping out of her comfort zone.

Noah kissed my shoulder and trailed his lips down the valley between my breasts. "Eva knows what's best for her. She's been intertwined with Mac for a long time. It's going to be hard standing on her own, but she'll crush it."

"Is Mac okay? Really?"

"No, but he's dealing with the Eva thing in his own way."

I hesitated a beat to ask my next question, but I'd been

thinking about it on and off all summer. "If Eva's not coming back, how would you feel about moving in? Officially."

He smiled as his tongue curled around my nipple then flicked the tight bud in an agonizing tease. "You mean I don't already live here? What kind of a situationship have I gotten involved in?"

I pinched his side as liquid heat pooled between my legs. "A serious one."

"I love you, Chloe. I want to be wherever you are—I was only waiting for you to ask. Seemed like the polite thing to do."

I traced the phoenix wing flexing on his shoulder as he scooted lower. "What about the guys? Will they be okay without you? I don't want Mac to feel lonely."

"Mac has never met a person he didn't immediately befriend, and we live across the landing. Do you really want to talk about him right now?" he asked, working his way down my stomach.

"Nope. All done talking."

He kissed each of the tattoos on my inner thighs, and I shivered at the prickly feel of his stubble on my skin. The heat of his breath against my core made me wiggle trying to get closer. Noah chuckled and laid two big hands on my hips.

"So impatient," he murmured.

I sank my fingers into his hair and dropped my head back with a sigh. Noah insisted on taking his sweet time. Tormenting me with his tongue and fingers before finally letting me come. I didn't have time to stop shaking before he grabbed a condom and slid home, exactly where I wanted him.

He groaned as he drove into me with a frantic pace that matched my wild need. My nails sunk into his shoulder, and he wrapped my hair around his fist, pulling just enough to make me crazy.

"Say it," he demanded with a wicked gleam, driving me right to the edge.

"I love you. *IloveyouIloveyouIloveyou*," I chanted as my body shattered in white hot pleasure.

Noah growled into my neck and followed me right after. "Never letting you go," he whispered into my hair.

I stroked down his back, letting my fingers ride the ridges of his muscles tight from holding his weight off me even when the rest of him was utterly spent. "You better not. Who knows what kind of trouble I'd get into."

He rolled to his side, pulling me with him and kissing my temple. "Wouldn't matter. I'd still be the one you called... and I'd still come running."

Maybe we'd been stupid for waiting so long to admit our feelings, or maybe we needed the time to get to a place where we could accept the other person. Either way, he was right. I couldn't imagine my life without him in it, and I didn't want to.

Old Chloe, the closed-off party girl only looking for a good time, was dead. New Chloe couldn't wait to see what challenges the future brought. I wouldn't be facing them alone.

———

Want more Hard Hitter?

Who doesn't? Get a glimpse of Noah and Chloe's happy ever after when they show up for Friendsgiving with Micah tagging along.

Click here for your free bonus epilogue!

**If you're having trouble clicking, go to <u>http://www.</u>
<u>nikkihallbooks.com/hard-hitter</u> **

———

Want more of the Teagan University Wildcats?

Turn the page to see what happens with Mac and Blue in
<u>Play Maker</u>, the next book in the Wild Card series.

PLAY MAKER

Mac

Something was wrong with me. Not physically—these abs didn't quit—but something in my brain. I stood in the sun-splashed backyard of a sorority house, surrounded by beautiful women frolicking in bikinis, and I didn't give a shit.

The summer before my senior year should have been spent honing my skills to a razor-sharp point and enjoying the notoriety that came with a national football championship. Instead, I'd fucked up and gotten involved with my best friend, Eva. Former best friend?

I sighed and grabbed a beer from the cooler on the patio, trying to blend in as I meandered my way across the yard.

She was avoiding me by spending the summer at her family's beach house, and I was trying to give her the space she clearly needed from all the feelings I'd tossed at her. Stupid, I know. The worst part was that I couldn't stop wondering what if I'd left things the way they were. What if I hadn't jumped at her offer to complicate things.

Our relationship was one big question mark at the

moment, kind of like my plans for the next few months. I usually spent the summer training with the cheerleaders when I wasn't busy with football stuff or classes, but I didn't need to be told that Eva's squad was off-limits now. The gaping hole in my schedule was nothing compared to the Eva-sized chunk missing from the rest of me. She had her ways of coping, and so did I. Except my usual strategy wasn't working.

I frowned down at my junk—immobile under my lucky pink cargo shorts—and pointed out the abundance of opportunity, but no amount of pep talking got Big Mac to pay attention. Honestly, I didn't even think he was listening.

Fuck, this summer was going to suck.

"This game makes no sense." The familiar husky voice stopped me in my tracks.

Eva's friend, Blue, was somewhere at this low-key back-yard party, and I desperately hoped she was alone. Not for any sexy reasons—my dick was officially on hiatus—but because I needed a break from Eva.

From all of them, really.

I'd picked a Chi Omega party specifically because this sorority didn't pander to athletes. They went for the high-powered business type, which should have guaranteed me obscurity among the crowd.

None of my crew knew I was back at TU, and I wanted to keep it that way for a few more hours. I didn't need the sad looks and the pity. Bad enough my mom had gone on and on about how unfortunate it was Eva couldn't make it home with me.

My family had always been careful not to put pressure on our relationship, but everyone knew Mom had been planning our wedding from the day Eva had gotten suspended in first grade for punching the asshole kid who stole my lunch.

No one knew, but that day was the beginning of my love affair with Wonder Woman. Eva had worn her star-spangled dress and lasso of truth when she defended me. As much as I loved Gal Gadot, my first Wonder Woman was tiny and blonde.

And now, she's gone.

I took a long pull of my beer, raising the bottle to my mouth as I scanned the people milling around on the grass, enjoying the sunshine. It took me two passes, but I finally spotted Blue standing with her hands on her hips next to a cornhole set-up.

My hand stilled with the cool glass pressed against my lips. The sun brought out a pink flush on her bare shoulders, and her black tank top clung to her curves. Curves I hadn't noticed before, but I was sure as hell noticing now.

Rainbow streaks peeked between strands of her dark hair as she tilted her head to glare at the little beanbags littering the area around the boards. Shorts rode high on her thighs, and my gaze traveled down the long length of her legs to her pink-tipped toes.

Blue was a smokeshow... when had that happened? Every time I saw her, she looked like a different person. Overalls, a slinky dress, yoga pants—she'd worn it all. Usually lurking on the fringes when she showed up. I knew Chloe invited her out a few times after Eva left, but I hadn't considered Blue having a social life outside our crew.

Today's outfit fit right in with the sorority, relaxed and uncomplicated. For some reason, the kaleidoscope of Blue drew me. I wanted to peel back her chameleon layers until I found the real person beneath.

Belatedly, I checked the faces around her and relaxed

when I didn't see a tiny blonde cheerleader holding court. If Eva were here, she'd be with Blue and surrounded by her adoring fans. Her absence meant I could have the afternoon to myself if I wanted it.

Suddenly, the idea of being alone in a crowd wasn't nearly as interesting as finding out what Blue was doing at a sorority party. Preferably somewhere away from the half-drunk co-eds. I chuckled as I finished off my beer. The guys would definitely give me shit if they knew I came to a party and planned to hide from the ladies.

Almost as much as if they realized I still had my shirt on when there was a bright yellow slip and slide stretched across the large backyard. I trained hard, and I liked the effect my efforts had on the female population. No shame in my game.

Two girls wearing almost nothing shrieked as they launched themselves over the slick surface, but my gaze landed back on Blue. Unlike most of the women I knew, Blue had never shown any appreciation for my body. As a matter of fact, I wasn't sure she'd said more than two words to me in the months since she'd started coming around with Eva.

Another mystery I wanted to solve. Some part of me insisted I was focusing on Blue as a distraction from my splintered insides, but my interest in her was real. It was nice to feel something other than misery and exhaustion.

I bided my time, watching like a creeper until Blue shook her head in disgust and abandoned the game to head for the big house. She slipped through the sliding glass doors, and I took the opportunity offered to me.

The entrance from the patio led to a large white kitchen, empty except for the girl I was suddenly obsessed with digging through the refrigerator and mumbling to herself.

She didn't stop when I pulled the door shut behind me, and I grinned at the frustration in her voice.

I leaned on the island and peeked around the door to see her collecting cheese cubes from a tray. "Do the Chi Omegas know you're raiding their fancy snacks?"

Blue gave a tiny shriek and slammed the fridge closed hard enough to rattle the glass bottles. Her blue green eyes landed on me—the color of water in paradise, another thing I hadn't noticed about her—and somehow got bigger.

"It's you," she spit out.

My smile widened. "It's me. You want to share some of your pilfered cheese?"

She blinked, then looked down at her handful of food with a frown. "It's not stolen. Courtney said I could help myself to the snacks."

I chuckled. "She probably meant the ones covering the tables outside, but what do I know?"

Blue held out her hand, and I plucked an orange cube from her palm. "No, you're probably right. I just wanted something cold."

"I won't tell if you won't." I popped the cheese in my mouth, and she followed my lead.

We shared her snack while she peered at me with growing suspicion. "Did you follow me here?"

Busted. "To the party? No. Into the kitchen? Yes."

"Why?"

I didn't want to admit she'd been the only thing to capture my attention in weeks—or how much she intrigued me. Sharing my feelings had gotten me into this mess in the first place. To buy myself some time, I came around the island to grab two plastic water bottles from the pack on the counter next to her, handing her one.

She twitched toward the door like she wanted to run. "I'm not having sex with you."

My brows shot up. "Was that an option?"

Blue cleared her throat and took a swig of water. "I don't know, but it felt relevant."

Her eyes caught mine, and the kitchen narrowed to the two of us. I could make a joke and laugh off her knee-jerk response, but the lingering need to burrow under her ever-changing exterior knocked me off guard.

"It's not. Relevant. I don't actually try to get every woman I meet into bed. I mean, the interested ones, yeah, but not for a while. And the whole thing with Eva kind of knocked me out of the game. I couldn't handle a hookup even if I wanted to." My words tumbled over themselves in an awkward tangle, threatening to strangle me if I didn't get a grip on my tongue. I sucked at keeping things to myself.

Blue looked like she'd gladly strangle me too if it would stop this awkward conversation. "I'm sorry your penis isn't working, but that doesn't explain why you followed me."

"My junk works, sunshine. I just don't have any interest in using it."

She tilted her head, confused. "Then why are you here?"

"I don't know." The truth slipped from me without permission from my brain. "I noticed you outside, and it was like seeing you for the first time—like you'd finally come out from behind your cloud. Despite your scowl. I thought I might be looking at the real you for once."

So much for not spilling my guts all over the kitchen. I waited for her to run screaming from the room, but her uneasy expression smoothed away.

"I'm always the real me. Hardcore, unfiltered truth. Whether you want it or not." She didn't sound particularly pleased with the observation, but it was exactly what I hadn't realized I needed until now.

Unfiltered truth. Someone get this girl a lasso.

"The real you sounds perfect. I'm tired of the bullshit."

She took a step closer, examining my face. "I can see why you'd feel that way with the others tiptoeing around you. Why come to a party then?"

I laughed low, without humor. "I don't know. Loneliness. Stupidity. Hope."

"At least the last one is a good reason. Though I doubt it will do you much good if you're hoping for a reunion with Eva."

Blue knew more than I'd anticipated. Had Eva been talking about me? Hurt tried to slice me open before I squashed it flat. Eva and I were done. She'd made it perfectly clear she had no interest in a romantic relationship beyond a good dicking when she felt the urge.

As if she could read my mind, Blue frowned again. "Sorry. I'm not good with sensitive subjects."

Instead of sinking into the defeat and anger and hurt, I found myself coming up with ways to erase the frustration from Blue's face. I hadn't seen her smile yet, and I desperately wanted to make it happen. I wanted to see her full lips curl just for me.

My dick twitched at the thought, and despite the little voice yelling *hallelujah!*, I tried not to stare at her mouth.

Tried and failed. A faint blush lit Blue's cheeks, and she caught her bottom lip with her teeth. The tension ratcheted up, and I went from twitching to rock hard in seconds.

"If you're looking for sympathy, you're better off spending time with anyone outside." Even her voice had gone soft and breathy.

I stepped closer to her, narrowing the distance between

us to mere inches, unable to stop myself from testing the reaction. "I don't want to spend time with them—I want to spend time with you."

Her lips parted on an indrawn breath, quick and surprised, and her tropical eyes darkened with hunger. My pulse rocketed to match. Huh. My attraction to Blue wasn't exactly a surprise—smokeshow—but she felt it too.

The slow-spreading heat, the subtle buzz of electricity, the urge to do something supremely stupid.

Blue hauled in a deep breath, and in true form, blurted out the truth. "Friends with benefits seems like a bad idea with Eva between us."

Fuck. Yes, it did. I ordered Big Mac to stand down and scrubbed a hand down my face. She didn't move, as if she hadn't convinced herself either. I could simply turn and walk away. Go back to my sad existence where everyone was afraid to whisper Eva's name in my vicinity.

A vivid memory of Blue's legs peeking out from under a short black dress at one of my Sunday karaoke deals flashed across my mind, followed by the image of her glaring down at the beanbags like they'd personally offended her.

To hell with walking away. It wasn't about Eva or my miserable ass. I'd gotten a taste of the real Blue, and I wanted more.

"How about friends without benefits? Keep me company this summer. I need to expand my inner circle, and I'm choosing you." I tried not to let the plea sneak into my words, but when her eyes narrowed, I was pretty sure I'd failed.

"If this is a ploy, I want you to know I have no problem using my pepper spray to make a point."

And just like that, my life became interesting again. I

smiled at her threat, though I was one hundred percent certain she was serious. Hardcore, unfiltered truth.

"No need for your pepper spray, sunshine, only your refreshing company." I shoved the benefits to the back of my mind. Blue hit every box for me, but I'd learned my lesson about mixing friendship with pleasure.

She blew out a breath. "Fine. Friends without benefits. At least until Eva comes back."

The major victory I'd just won felt strangely hollow, but I wasn't going to miss my chance to feel like myself for a few months.

"Fair warning, I'm a cuddler." With a wicked grin, I pulled her close for a hug. A platonic hug. Purely to see how she'd react. Touching was my love language, after all.

Blue stiffened for a split second, then relaxed in my arms. We were immediately treading dangerous territory, but my girl came up with the save once again.

She looked up at me and patted my bicep. "Fair warning, when startled, I punch first and ask questions later."

I laughed, a long, loud, unrestrained belly laugh, but I didn't let her go. She was mine for the summer, and I wasn't wasting a second.

Did you enjoy your first chapter? Snag your copy of Play Maker today!

A NOTE FROM NIKKI

Thank you so much for reading Hard Hitter! Noah was a tough one to crack, but once he opened up, man, did he have a lot to say. Chloe lives up to the hype. Sunshine party girl meets real-world consequences, what else would you expect from someone living in D's shadow all her life.

This book was a quiet moment compared to what's coming next. Mac is going to finish this series with a bang. Blue seems like an unlikely friend, but she's exactly what Mac needs in his lowest moment. Especially when she starts off by emphatically stating she will absolutely *not* be having sex with him. Mac failed at his last female friendship by getting his dick involved, so he's up for the challenge. Friends without benefits. For now.

I know many of you were hoping for Eva to be Mac's heroine, but she has her own story to live in Ice Cold Player, the first book in my spin-off hockey series where she's stuck with the man she loves to hate—her enemy at Wildcat Coffee and right winger for the TU hockey team.

If you have a second, please consider leaving a review.

Even better, tag me with the review so we can be besties. You can find me on Facebook or TikTok. Finally, if you want updates on future books and other fun stuff, join my newsletter. I promise not to bite.

ACKNOWLEDGMENTS

I'd like to thank (in no particular order):

- Nicole Schneider, Liz Gallegos, and Megan Clements, they make me sound good
- Jolene Perry, you deserve a break after holding on for so long
- Angela Haddon, cover wizardry extraordinaire
- Holly Roberds, the ducks are your fault
- The Hubs, still no private jet, maybe next book
- Crumbl Cookies, so delicious and willing to deliver while I'm on a deadline
- All of you, I'm nothing without my readers, and here you are—reading. Thank you.

ALSO BY NIKKI HALL

ABOUT THE AUTHOR

Nikki Hall is a smart-ass with a Ph.D. and a potty mouth. She writes stories that have spice and sass because she doesn't know any other way. Coffee makes her happy, messes make her stabby, and she'd sell one of her children for a second season of Firefly. She also writes paranormal romance under the name Nicole Hall.

Want to find out when the newest Nikki Hall book hits the shelves? Sign up for her newsletter at www.nikkihall books.com/signup.

facebook.com/nikkihallbooks

instagram.com/nicolehallbooks

tiktok.com/@nikkihallbooks

HARD HITTER

Copyright © 2023 Nikki Hall

All rights reserved.

This is a work of fiction. Any similarity between the characters and situations within its pages and places or persons, living or dead, is unintentional and co-incidental.

Cover designed by Angela Haddon

Edited by Megan Clements, Waypoint Author Academy

Printed in Great Britain
by Amazon